Good Grief

SCEPTRE

Good Grief

KEITH WATERHOUSE

SCEPTRE

Copyright © 1997 by Keith Waterhouse

First published in 1997 by Hodder and Stoughton
A division of Hodder Headline PLC
A Sceptre Book

10 9 8 7 6 5 4 3 2 1

British Library Cataloguing in Publication Data

Waterhouse, Keith, 1929–
  Good grief
  1. English fiction – 20th century
  I. Title
  823.9'14 [F]

ISBN 0 340 65986 6

Typeset by Palimpsest Book Production Limited,
Polmont, Stirlingshire
Printed and bound in Great Britain by
Mackays of Chatham Plc, Chatham, Kent

Hodder and Stoughton
A division of Hodder Headline PLC
338 Euston Road
London NW1 3BH

∫

Dear Diary. Got up. Grieved.

That what you had in mind, pet?

And when to start? You didn't say. As soon as I got back from the hospital? When? Straight after the funeral?

I could never have managed that, I can tell you that for nothing, it was a busy time for me. You wouldn't know, you've never had to organise anything like that. Your mam's funeral, even, you left all the arrangements to me.

I can hear you now: Look, June, do it. Get it bloody done. Don't come running to me over details – I wouldn't know fumed bloody oak from stripped pine. Just get it fixed, girl, for preference any day except the Tuesday, that's the chairman's monthly conference.

He wasn't there, you know. He was represented. I mean today. The memorial service. I should say the service to celebrate the life of Samuel Herbert Pepper. No, he sent Pennydew, didn't he? His new deputy.

Of course, you won't know any of that. Well, you'd know some of it. Bob Carp becomes editor as expected, and Eric Grant takes over from Bob as deputy. Stop groaning. Somebody did tell me who the new night editor is but it's gone right out of my head. But surprise surprise, who comes in over Bob's head as editorial director? They've only brought Charlie Whittington back from the grave, haven't they? Whoops, shouldn't have said that, Back from early retirement. So Pennydew's kicked even further upstairs than he was already. Deputy chairman. Non-job, according to what you've always said.

He can't sing, I can tell you that much. You should have heard him murdering 'Now The Day Is Over', and why we had to have that out of all the hymns ancient and modern you could have picked I shall never know. You knew it always makes me cry. Ever since I was in hospital with my throat ulcers as a little girl, and that flaming choir from St John the Evangelist next door would come in and sing it at us on Sunday evenings, and I'd think that's it, then, that means I'll be dead tomorrow morning. But nothing would do but that you wanted 'Now The Day Is Over'. And it was you that was dead next morning, wasn't it, Sam?

Anyway, you'll be glad to hear we did it your way. Regrets I've had a few, including going along with you on Frank Sinatra. How many memorial services have we been to where they had 'I Did It My Way'?

Not to mention Death is nothing at all, I have only slipped away into the next room. Still, originality never was your middle name, was it, love? You didn't get where you were before you started coughing up blood by being original, did you? The number of times I've heard you say, The thought that hasn't already been thunk isn't worth thinking. And even that wasn't original, you got it out of a fortune cookie. Still.

Do you know what I miss? The office car. I shall have to learn to drive, after all these years. It'll give me something to do. You did say I should find something to do.

You'd think they'd have sent one round, though, on this day of all days, wouldn't you? If only out of respect for you. I don't suppose it crossed anyone's mind. Or if it did, I bet Bob Carp's already on the same cloud nine you were on. He'll believe he only has to think a thing and he doesn't have to put it into words, it gets done. Fleet Street. Thank God none of you's running the government.

I did think of asking Eric Grant for a lift in, being as he's the only one who lives nearby, but then I thought in the circumstances better not, if he'd caught a whiff that you were trying your level best to ease him off the night desk on to special projects before you were carted off to hospital, it might have seemed a bit of a cheek. Special projects, he'd have loved that, I don't think. Elephant's graveyard. Why couldn't you just sack people if they weren't up to it? You were only making tension for yourself. They'd have sacked you if that circulation had dropped much further, and you know it.

At the death, or in the end as I'd better say, sorry, I was just on the verge of booking a mini-cab when your Pauline rings up to ask if I'd like picking up, so long as I don't mind the pair of us cadging a lift back because Jack's got to drive straight on to Birmingham after the service, some sales conference I believe. Very nice of them considering it must have taken them I don't know how far out of their way when they could have gone straight up the M23 is it? Don't ask me, navigating was never my strongest point.

As you never failed to point out: You don't know your bloody east from your bloody west, woman! We turn right! Look at that thing up in the sky — it's called the sun! Now where is it rising from?

But of course the upshot is that we have to beg a lift back from Eric, so I might just as well have asked him to take me to St Bride's in the first place. Except your daughter could very easily have taken it the wrong way if I'd said, Oh, now that's very kind of you, Pauline, but I've already made my arrangements.

You know what she's like. Well, you don't know what she's like, when did you ever have time for her, but I do.

As it happens, Jack never made the service, because what

with Blackfriars Bridge being one lane with the repairs going on, we only just got there in time, and as he said, by the time he'd found a car park in all that traffic it'd be half over, and with not knowing exactly how long it was going to be he was already anxious about getting out of London in good time for his sales conference, so in the end he dropped us and vroomed off. I told him I was sure you wouldn't mind. I could have said you wouldn't have given a toss.

It was a very good turnout. Better than some we've been to. Two-thirds full, I'd say – more than half, anyway. Lots of old faces. I'll tell you who was there, Sam – Wilf Blackett from the old *Chronicle* days. He'd come down specially – well, not specially, he'd some business in London, but he made it coincide. He's a consultant now, as you know. As who isn't. The church was crawling with consultants – I don't know how they get the work. Editorial consultants, in-house journal consultants, publicity consultants, lecturers in journalism. The same as you should have been if you'd had any sense. If you'd eased off a bit you might be here now.

Tricia was there, obviously. Your Derek was ever so funny – he was a sidesman or usher or whatever they call themselves, as you'd expect. Apparently Tricia trolls into the church, makes a beeline for him and says, Which side am I supposed to sit, Derek?

He says, It's not a wedding, Tricia, you sit where you like.

She goes, But which side is our family and which is hers?

Hers is me, of course. But I mean to say, Sam. Twenty-five years you've been divorced and she still calls herself your family. In the end, she sits next to Pauline across the aisle from me, in the row behind some of those who were going to speak.

It went very smoothly, considering. Tommy Little was half-cut, it goes without saying, but you would have him read the lesson, so there we were. I don't think any of the relatives noticed – they don't, outsiders, do they, they just think he's got a naturally thick voice.

Then the readings – I'm afraid your Derek made a complete cock-up of not being dead but only in the next room. Honestly, you'd have thought he was dyslexic. Turns out he's forgotten his reading glasses – typical.

Still, never mind: we made up for it with 'To Be A Pilgrim'. You've got some very good voices on that staff of yours, Sam, barring Robert Pennydew. Eric Grant's a lovely baritone, did you know? No, you were never on singalong terms, were you, the pair of you?

The address. I was afraid that was going to go down like a lead balloon as well, but he just got away with it. Charlie Whittington, that is. I know you wanted Bob Carp but he wouldn't do it, says he gets terrible stage fright and the only thing he's dreading about the job is having to speak in public. Soppy haporth. Wait till he's spoken at the editorial Christmas lunch and had a few bread rolls thrown at him, that's if he lasts that long – how can you get to be editor and not be able to make a speech? You would have done it on your head, you know you would. It's a pity you couldn't, after all it was your funeral. Memorial service, I should say.

So anyway, Charlie Whittington. He got off completely on the wrong foot, in my opinion. Said how delighted he was to be back on the paper – I mean who cares about that, at somebody else's memorial service? – and how his only regret was that you're not there with him to work as a team. He seems to forget he wouldn't be editorial director at all if you'd still been alive – you'd be sitting where he's sitting now, sooner or later. If there was any justice.

Then after saying that you didn't suffer fools gladly but that you'd helped many a lame dog over the stile – kicked would have been a better word – he gets going down Back

Memory Lane and launches into that tale about you and him in that hotel in Nottingham when you were both on the road.

Yes, that one. Where one of you was peeing in the sink – you always said it was him, but he says it was you – when you lost your balance and brought the fitting down from the wall and flooded the place. Now if he had to tell that story at all in a place of worship he should have left it at that but no, being Charlie, he has to drag it out to the night manager coming up and all the rest of it and honestly, he just went on and on and on, you would have thought he'd rented that lectern for the morning.

As you can imagine, by now everyone's murmuring and smirking at one another until even Charlie must have realised he was outstaying his welcome so he comes down at last. Then it was 'And Did Those Feet In Ancient Time', and bugger me as you would have put it, Sam, if the organist wasn't playing the wrong tune. Nobody knew it. I was that cross with myself, it was the one thing I hadn't thought of, to check that we had the traditional hymn tunes and none of these new-fangled arrangements. You'd have been livid, it's a good job you weren't there.

Still, we struggled through it, then it was the blessing, and then out we all troop to the strains of Vera Lynn singing 'We'll Meet Again'. At least she got the tune right. So barring accidents, it was all done just as you wanted, pet.

I had to stand out in the porch shaking hands so Tricia couldn't help but stop for a word whether she wanted to or not. Actually, she was quite pleasant, if on the condescending side – I'm sure she still sees me as the scheming little newsroom secretary who bedded the assistant news editor, knowing he was destined for higher things. If only she knew. If only I did either, come to that. If I'd known you were going to finish up editor, I think I'd have run a mile.

She wouldn't join the gang at El Vino's, thank goodness.

Charlie Whittington went on ahead to organise the case of champagne you'd told me to order – we should have ordered two – so the Bollinger was already flowing by the time I got there with Pauline, who'd very kindly waited back for me.

We didn't stay long. Everybody was telling stories, none of them anything to do with you at all, and Eric Grant was anxious to get away because it was his day off and he wanted to get some golf in, so we just sneaked off. I'm saying sneaked off: there were most of your mates crowding round and kissing me on the cheek and saying keep in touch, we'll all have a pissy lunch.

We won't, of course. We never did before, aside from the odd office shindig when it was all on the house and wives were invited, so why should we now? We'll exchange Christmas cards, most of us, and that'll be about it. And they'll have the same problem I've had to ponder before now: if she was widowed in February, will it be late enough to decently wish her a merry Christmas?

Then I started thinking about this diary you want me to keep. I asked Eric if he could stop off for a minute at that stationery shop on the corner of Chancery Lane so I could buy one of those big desk diaries that they've probably got on remainder by now, but he was chuntering on about double yellow lines and how he had to keep in lane for Waterloo Bridge, and then suddenly I thought, Hang on a sec, June, he never said anything about writing it all down.

Because you didn't, did you? I can remember word for word what you said in between your bouts of coughing and spluttering, even though I wasn't taking much notice at the time, partly because I thought you were just rambling on for the sake of something to say, and partly because I didn't think you were going and I didn't think you really thought you were going either. Not at that stage.

And what you said was, Now listen here, girl, once I'm gone I want you to start keeping a diary. Just let it all pour out, what you're thinking day by day, how you're coping, what it's like to be left on your own, the bloody lot. Because I know you, you said – otherwise you'll just bottle it all up and you'll finish up having a bloody nervous breakdown or going into a depression, and we don't want that. Get it all out, and by the way, this isn't my idea.

No, pet, I didn't think for a minute it was.

You said, No, it was a piece I read in the *Guardian*, how that bloody women's writer, what's her name, complete pain in the arse, coped with losing her husband. She kept a diary. For a whole year. And that's what I want you to do. Unless—

And you said this with one of your winks.

—Unless you meet someone else in the meantime.

I says, Chance'd be a fine thing.

But even as I took your hand, part of me was thinking, I wonder if I will?

Funny thing to wonder, while you were lying there on your deathbed. That's it, you see: you think thoughts you don't want to think, they just float through your head like clouds. It's going to be very difficult, Sam. Very difficult indeed.

But you never said to write it down. I'd be hard put to at this moment in time, anyway. Apart from the message pads by the telephones, there's barely a scrap of paper in the house. Good to tell I was wed to a journalist.

So I'll keep it in my head, if you don't mind. It's better this way, I'm sure of it. Because instead of talking to a blank sheet of paper and getting all self-conscious – you know how I've always hated having to write anything, I've always said one writer in the family's enough, not that you were all that fond of putting pen to paper yourself – I'll be talking to you.

And yes I will keep a diary, and yes I will keep it up for a year, but what good it'll do either me or you, God only knows. In fact although I can see what you're driving at,

Sam, in some ways it's a bloody silly idea, because all you're doing is encouraging me to be what's the word, introspective, to brood about it. And I'd be doing that even if I'd bought that desk diary and was writing it down all neat and tidy, in fact more so, because I'd have to think out everything I was going to say before I put it down.

I'll tell you when I will give it up, though, and that's if people start noticing my lips moving. I don't want them thinking poor June Pepper's gone round the twist.

So I promised, and off I went, and home I came, and as I walked into the house the phone was ringing, and I picked it up, and you'd gone too. Twenty minutes after I'd left.

And do you know what I thought, Sam? I'm going to tell you, but you won't like it. I thought, You silly bugger. Fifty-three years old, sixty a day, bottle of Bell's a day, and that's only counting what you admitted to, three stone overweight, no exercise. And you were told and told, but you wouldn't be told, would you?

I Did It My Way. Thank you very much. I was that cross.

And then of course it hit me, that there was nobody there to be cross *with*, that I'd ticked you off for the very last time, and I wouldn't even have the satisfaction of saying, See, I was right.

Didn't suffer fools. You were a fool to yourself, Sam. I wish I'd been up at that lectern instead of Charlie. I could have said a thing or two.

So where was I? El Vino's. Pauline came back home with me, did I say? And she was like a clucking little hen, you know how she can be. Would I be all right, would I like her to stay over while Jack was in Birmingham, shouldn't I have a lie down, was there anything she could get?

I says, Pauline, will you stop being such a tower of strength and get me a drink?

She says, Another drink?

Meaning by the tone of her voice, Yet another? I wouldn't mind, but I'd only had half an inch of champagne.

She says, You sure you wouldn't like some tea?

I says, No, vodka.

So of course, she goes out to the fridge, and there's no vodka.

I says, No, I don't keep it in the fridge.

She says, But you've always kept it in the fridge.

I says, No, your father kept it in the fridge, I prefer my vodka at room temperature.

That earns me a funny look as you can imagine, and she goes over to the drinks trolley. No vodka.

I says, No, it's in the bedroom.

Now that really did get me a funny look. Up she goes, and I can hear her moving about upstairs. I'll swear I could hear her opening the wardrobe. She'd found the vodka, no problem there, it was on my bedside table, but I reckon she was looking for the brandy, because she would have noticed that it had gone missing from the drinks trolley too. If she'd asked, I could have told her I finished the bottle the night you passed away.

So she gets me this small weak vodka, flavoured tonic more like, and after a bit more fussing around she picks up her handbag, thank the Lord, and says, Now are you all right, June?

I says, No, of course I'm not all right, you silly cat. Not snappy like – what you'd call good-humoured exasperation.

She says, But will you *be* all right?

I says, Well, we won't know that till tomorrow morning, will we, Pauline? And we left it at that.

Then just as she's about to ring for a mini-cab, the doorbell rings and it's Eric Grant. She'd left her order of service in his car and he thought it might be mine. As if it could have been. That order of service never left my hands, and

I was careful to keep it pristine, no folds or creases and no wine-glass stains. It goes with the obituaries I clipped out – the *Telegraph* did you proud, ten column inches: He was a larger-than-life figure, perhaps the last of the Fleet Street buccaneers . . .

I wonder who wrote it. Charlie, most likely. Larger-than-life, what does it mean? Shouting a lot and getting pissed every night. Anyway, I shall put them all in a scrapbook when I find time. Find time – I shan't have far to look. *The Times* had a photo I'd never seen before, ages old it was, you looked like you did when we first started bedding one another and how long's that ago? It's twenty-seven years ago, that's how long.

I'll have to find a special drawer for that scrapbook. The obituaries, the death notice, my letters of condolence, the order of service, and then there'll be a list of those present at St Bride's in tomorrow's *Times* and *Telegraph*, won't there? Among my souvenirs, eh? And what comes next?

Having got his feet over the threshold, Eric goes through Pauline's routine all over again. Am I sure I'll be all right? Is there anything I want, anything I need, anything he can do, I've only got to say the word.

I'll shock you now, Sam.

I'd this almost overwhelming urge to blurt out: I suppose a fuck's out of the question?

There, I've said it. To you, not to him, but if Pauline had made that vodka and tonic with vodka I could have come near it. Not that I felt in the least like anything of that sort, although I've heard that some women do go completely off the rails the moment their husbands pop their clogs, it's a form of hysteria, must be, cry for help style of thing. But I just wanted to stop Eric and Pauline fussing, fussing, fussing, fidgeting around me as if I were a cushion that needed to be plumped. I wanted to stop them buzzing at me, they were like flaming wasps.

He is a gloompot, though, that Eric, isn't he?

He was worse than the blooming undertaker, and he was bad enough – did I tell you, he said if I was thinking of selling the house and moving, he'd advise me to hang on, because according to his brother who's an estate agent you've died at the worst possible time for the property market. That's what comes of giving people cups of tea. I suppose I was glad of five minutes' company.

What Eric says, looking round all gloomy, was: It's going to be a bit big for you now, this place, isn't it, June? A bit empty?

I says, It's no bigger now than it was with just the two of us here, and as for empty, Sam was more often out of the house than in it, as you'd know more than most, being as you were supposed to be his night editor.

He said something funny then, Sam.

He says with a huffy little laugh, Supposed to be?

Well, I asked for that, it just slipped out. But then he goes on:

—Oh, I wouldn't say that, June. Compared with some editors I've known, Sam usually got himself off in very short order. He didn't hang about, he trusted us night owls to get on with it.

Now why did he want to say a thing like that? Because I knew very well you did hang about – that once you had plonked yourself down at that desk it was like prising a barnacle off a boat's bottom, trying to get you out of your swivel chair again. But for some unknown reason, and dressing it up as a compliment – how you trusted your night staff to run the paper as you wanted it run – he was trying to plant the seed in my mind that you were in the habit of leaving earlier of a night than I was aware of. Or so it sounded. Maybe paranoia's one of the side effects of grieving.

I knew what he was saying was rubbish, because where

would you have gone? But I wanted you to tell me it was rubbish – not for reassurance, just to get it out of the way at once. And of course, you weren't there to ask.

What would you have said? I think I could quote you as verbatim as my shorthand used to be:

—Didn't hang about? I didn't hang about in Eric Grant's bloody company, that's for sure. I kept out of his way and he kept out of mine.

Which is what you told me many and many a time. How you ran the paper and he was just the bloody night-watchman. How your office was like King's Cross while his was like the Tomb of the Unknown Soldier. We've heard it. But why did I want you to tell me what I already knew?

I'm sure I couldn't say, Sam, but I did know that this had to be the first of many questions on these lines I'd want to ask, and answers would come there none. There we go.

And there they went at last, after Pauline had asked for the umpteenth time if I'd like her to make some tea. What she meant of course was no more vodka. Try as she may she couldn't keep her eyes off the bottle, she would have taken it away with her if she'd had the nerve.

I says, Pauline, when I want some tea I'm quite capable of making it myself, it's a bereavement I've suffered, not a stroke thank you very much.

Eric offered to give her a lift, which she took up – if it wasn't taking him out of his way, she says.

But of course it was taking him out of his way, it was taking him what, five or six miles out of his way. As she very well knew.

No mention now, despite all the fussing, of was I sure I wouldn't like her to stay over while Jack was in Birmingham. Not with Eric in tow. What I did wonder, though, you know how things cross your mind, was why was Jack staying up in Birmingham anyway? I mean to say it's only a couple of hours up the motorway, if that.

And I'll tell you something else that's funny. By which I mean odd. If he'd wanted to give her a lift, why couldn't he have made a little detour on the way back from Fleet Street and dropped her off first? And then that order of service – he must have known very well it wasn't mine, because it must have been on the dashboard where Pauline was sitting next to him, and I was sitting in the back. If you ask me, Sam, the reason she left it there like a dropped glove and the reason he brought it back was to give them an excuse for his giving her a lift home, though why he couldn't have said, Shall I wait for you, Pauline, it's no trouble when he dropped me off, we shall never know.

It'll give me something to ponder over. I shall welcome things to ponder over, it'll pass the time.

I see them off, making sure they're gone, then I make a beeline for that vodka bottle. I tell you, it went down like lemonade, I'd finished the bottle in no time at all. Reaction, I expect, after the memorial service. I hadn't realised how tensed up I'd been, wanting it all to go off all right, thinking what kind of fools we should both look if hardly anybody turned up, hoping it would be just as you'd planned it. What a thing to do, though, sitting up in bed with a bulldog clipboard, planning your own memorial service. You really enjoyed that, pet, didn't you? How you kept chuckling and chortling. If only you'd had all your right-hand men round that bedside, I should have thought you were bringing out a rival memorial service to the *Sun*'s or the *Daily Mirror*'s.

Here's a thing, and it's nothing I'm proud of. As I threw out the empty bottle I found myself thinking, I must get another bottle when I do my bit of shopping in the morning but I won't go to Oddbins this time, I'll get it from that little wine shop further along, because they don't know me there. And that prompted me to work out how many bottles of vodka I've bought from Oddbins since the day you died, I won't tell you how many but it's terrifying when you look at it that way. Although I'm certainly not drinking anywhere near what you ever did, in Scotch alone, never mind the triple vodkas you put away at weekends. It's not eating, that's the problem. It's a wonder Pauline didn't notice, when she was looking for the vodka in the fridge where you used to keep it, that there was hardly a scrap of food in there. Perhaps she did and she's keeping it for another day. But why should bereavement take the appetite away? You'd think it would be the other way round, that you'd go in for an orgy of comfort eating, Jaffa cakes and that. Maybe some do. Not me, though, and it's not until now, this very minute when I'm draining my glass and beginning to see double of the rubbish that's on telly, that I realise not a morsel of food has passed my lips this day since the bran flakes I had for breakfast.

It's got to stop, Sam, it's got to stop. It'll have to, I'd be wanting to throw up if I wasn't so near the loo where I know I can get to if I have to.

And so to bed.

Night-time holds no terrors for me so far, touch wood.

That's one thing about having been married to a newspaper all these years, it puts you in training for widowhood. It's a good many years since I reached out in bed and expected to find anyone there, no matter what time it was.

First it was the old Press Club days when it was that poker school every night, which according to you your career depended upon. And you must have played your cards wrong enough times because next thing you're night editor and I only ever got to see you at weekends, sober at any rate. You used to wake up pissed, do you realise that? Big breakfast, then off.

And I'd say, You're not on till six, lad, what's the rush?

And you'd say, Time and tide wait for no man in that bloody Street, chuck, and I'm the bastard that's going to get the bastard who'd get me if I spent my afternoons playing golf.

And off you'd go. And the next thing we know, Allinson has his stroke and you're acting editor because Charlie's off ill himself with an impacted wisdom tooth, so by this time you're practically sleeping at the office.

And this is one of the times when I do miss you, Sam, when I want to ask you something just out of simple curiosity. Because I never did ask this. When it came to it, when the Board reckoned Allinson had better call it a day and it was between you and Charlie for the editorship, would you really have handed in your resignation if you hadn't got it? I mean really really? I mean we know Charlie Whittington did, but then he was of an age for early retirement where you weren't. And look at him now. Alive and well and editorial director. What would you have done, Sam? If you had resigned? Not mooned about the house, that's for sure. I like to think you'd have slowed down, become one of those consultants, started a little freesheet.

But you wouldn't, would you? You'd be working on the bloody *Sun* by now. That's if you were still with us. You might have been, who knows?

Who am I fooling? You don't get the Big C as you called it from overwork. But the Big C followed by a massive heart attack, that's asking for trouble. Whereas all Charlie ever got was toothache, so you showed them what you could do and they made you editor.

And you still didn't get home at nights. Three and four in the morning sometimes. Unwinding, as you'd say. Waiting for just one more edition to come up. And once in a blue moon you'd call me and say, Why don't you come over to the slave factory, I'll send a car round, we'll go have a bite to eat while I wait for the last editions, I want to see what the *Sun* have managed to cobble together on that cracking exclusive of ours.

But I rarely did. You were among your cronies, and that's what you wanted, wasn't it? I didn't mind. It never bothered me, and it doesn't bother me now, whatever Eric Grant might have been getting at, silky sod that he is. You wouldn't have been out with another woman, I knew that much. You were never a womaniser, were you? Too fat, too pissed, too bone idle. I know that from when I was the other woman. You never chased me, I had to do the chasing, and if I'd known how much weight you were going to put on maybe I'd never have bothered.

So no, whereas a lot of women in my position would get all upset at the thought of going up to an empty bed, it's what I've been used to. And what with the vodka and the brandy, I have been sleeping. What has bothered me once or twice is when I've woken up at some unearthly hour and I've thought, Where the thump is he till this time? And then I've remembered. And then before I could let myself get depressed I'd say to myself, Now look here, June, all right, so he's not here, but if he was alive he still wouldn't be here, so what's the difference? As often as not I'd be asleep when you fell into bed, and as often as not I'd still be asleep when you got up in the morning, until you woke me up with your shouting and bawling down the phone, but then by the time I'd thrown on my dressing gown and gone down you were gulping back a cup of coffee, the car would be here and you'd be off.

Apart from weekends. Sunday dinner I miss cooking, but I never thought I'd miss bringing you up your breakfast in bed of a Saturday morning. I used to think, The lazy swine, why can't he come down for breakfast, if he doesn't get enough sleep whose fault is that?

And any rows that we were going to have, they'd always be on Saturday morning, did you notice? I suppose I used to save them up. When are you going to do something about that lawn, did you have to bring Tommy Little back with you last night, this isn't the Press Club you know, and think on, I'm not going over to Pauline and Jack's on my own next Friday, so if we're going there for dinner you come home first, never mind your Start without me, we've got a little mini-crisis on, chuck.

I say rows, they weren't really rows, they were too one-sided for that, just me chuntering. I miss them, all that trying to pin you down, to get you to go to the theatre or to a party or whatever, it was all about making plans. There's no plans to make now.

That's a worry. Up to today there's been all the arrangements. Always something to do. First the funeral, and then replying to all those letters of condolence – you'd be amazed who took the trouble to write, Sam, I mean besides who you'd expect to write. The Prime Minister, would you believe?

Oh, I can see you sitting there with your big fat grin and saying, Get away with you, woman, it's a standard letter, he'll just say to someone, That editor who's just died, what's-his-name, just draft something to his widow, would you? But it wasn't like that, Sam, it was a personal letter, you could tell it was a personal letter. My dear June, we both send you our heartfelt sympathy at Sam's untimely demise. He will be badly missed. He . . . now how the hell did it go on?

He will be hard to replace . . . hard to replace . . . Trenchant . . . always vigorous point of view . . . never fearful . . . fools gladly . . .

G'night, Sam.

And this is something else that's got to stop – slummocking about in a candlewick robe till all hours of the day. Talk about Woman in a Dressing Gown. I didn't do it before and I won't do it now.

I've got to get a routine, Sam. Especially now, now that

the memorial service is over and done with. The parade's
gone by, eh? Until today I'd had that to look forward to. Yes,
look forward to. I suppose some folk dread it but not me, I'd
the same kind of feeling as when I was a little girl and I was
looking forward to the pantomime. Well, perhaps not quite
like that, because there were the anxieties of course – would
all the bigwigs show up, would Tricia try and upstage me,
would Charlie be too rat-arsed pissed to remember his lines,
would I break down, would Pauline start snivelling? Not she!
Not that one! She was too busy crossing and uncrossing her
legs for the benefit of Eric Grant, wasn't she?

But all that aside I was looking forward to it. It was
how can I put this without sounding . . . it was my due,
Sam. Look at it this way, it isn't everyone gets a memorial
service, not even in Fleet Street where there's some would
turn out to bury the office cat so long as there was a drink in
it afterwards. But you have to judge these things. You have
to ask yourself, did he really merit the Fleet Street send-off?
And the answer's yes, and they did you proud.

I was going to say I wish you'd been there but of course
you were there, all through the service, still making the
arrangements, still stage-managing. Because when they put
on 'My Way' I wasn't hearing Sinatra, I was hearing you
saying, Of course the bloody Rector won't mind, why should
he, bloody hell, woman, they had the Teddy Bears' Picnic
down there when we saw off Ted Rawcliffe from the *Express*!
Because when Charlie overstayed his welcome at the lectern
I could hear you growling, Get him off, for Gawd's sake!
Because all through the service and in all the days leading
up to it I could hear your voice dictating how it was going
to go and what had to be done, and that kept you alive for
me, Sam, do you know what I mean?

And you didn't die in that hospital and you didn't die at
the funeral, you didn't die until right at the end of your
memorial service when the Rector gave the blessing and they

all waited for me to walk up the aisle like some raddled old bride before filing out of the church and up to the pub. The Grace of our Lord Jesus Christ be with us all evermore, and then you were gone. Funny, that.

I bought a new toothbrush today. A green one, the first green one I've had for years and years and years. It was always blue for me, red for you. We were colour-coded. No need to bother now.

It's the first thing of yours I've thrown out, your tooth-brush. I just couldn't bear facing it in the tooth-mug each morning and night, but I couldn't bring myself to toss it into the bin. In the end I slung our old toothbrushes out together, as a pair. And now I'm on green.

You've got to start somewhere, rebuilding your life. If that's what I'm supposed to be doing.

Comfort eating. No sooner do I tell you it's not for me than I take it up, don't I? Though not with Jaffa cakes I'm glad to say, because start me on them and I could get through a whole packet at one go, like those bulimic girls you read about. But this is yet another thing that's got to stop.

Do you know that Baskin-Robbins across from W. H. Smith's? Next to the health food shop. No, of course you don't, you wouldn't be seen dead in a place like that, although you did have a sweet tooth, didn't you, eh? All the ginger puddings I've made for you. And half of them gone to waste because they were boiled dry by the time you turned up. What's for afters? you'd shout, and if it wasn't a ginger pudding your lower lip would go out like a little lad who's been told he's had enough crisps for one day. I'm trying something new, it's a bombe glacée, I'd call back from the kitchen, just to tease you. But of course you knew it was a ginger pudding. Bombe glacée? You'd have thrown it on the fireback, like the miners used to when their Sunday dinner wasn't to their liking.

Anyway, what with calling in at the health food shop for the muesli you'd never eat – because it's nice to know I can have the odd bowlful of it now without you mocking me and calling it middle-class chicken fodder – I've taken to dropping in at Baskin-Robbins. Funny places to have next door to one another, you've got to agree, but it's somewhere to rest your feet and I've grown quite partial to the Very Berry Strawberry that they do. That and their Banana Royale, £3.25.

No, but Sam, there is some method in my madness. I make it a reward. I tell myself, All right, June, eat either a proper breakfast or a proper lunch, brunch, call it what you like, and I'll let you go to Baskin-Robbins later. And I do. Today I had mushroom soup, out of a packet, true, but soup nevertheless, with some of those salty biscuits that you like, used to like, and yesterday morning I had a boiled egg. And as I say, muesli and a chopped banana again, which I have for my supper. So that's one hurdle jumped. I'm eating, after a fashion.

But it still won't do, Sam. I've gained four pounds since you left us, do you know that? I thought one thing to be said for widowhood was that it made you thinner, you were supposed to pine away style of thing. Not me. I'll be as fat as you were, at this rate.

Go on, say it. It's the booze. I wish you were here to read the Riot Act, lad. But if you were, you'd have no need of doing it.

And it's not only the booze and the Baskin-Robbins, it's the chocolate, though not Jaffa cakes. Have I mentioned the chocolate? I'm on mint Aero at the moment, one bar a day. I was determined to switch from Rolos, to which I was getting too partial for my own good, and I thought the bubbles in Aero have got to mean it's less fattening. As to why I chose mint Aero, well you know I'm not all that fond of peppermint so I thought that would help me cut down. But it hasn't. It's the same with smoking. I switched to Disque Bleu in the belief that as they're so strong they'd affect my throat so I'd have to give up whether I wanted to or no. But now I'm hooked on Disque Bleu.

Disque Bleu, mint Aero and Very Berry Strawberry. They never said death was addictive.

Well, the days go by and the weeks go by. I don't know how they manage it with time stood still, but they do. But I'd ever such a shock this morning.

I was just coming out of that little Minimart or whatever it calls itself, on The Parade – yes, Sam, I know Sainsbury's is cheaper despite what they say about Mr Patel's corner shops, and I know that series of yours proved it, but you see I've given up bulk buying, my big Friday morning shop-in, so I now spread my shopping all through the week, it gives me something to do, all right? Not that I've any less to do than when you were here – the same chores have got to be done. It's just that the days seem longer.

So there I was, coming out of the Minimart, when who should I see across the street but you.

No, I know it wasn't you, you silly article, but at first glance, from the back, he looked like you – although thinner, which doesn't take a lot of doing. So much so that I galloped along the opposite pavement parallel with him to see his face, and of course then he looked nothing like you. But he was wearing one of your suits. It didn't fit him, but then it didn't fit you either. Not after you put on all that weight.

I'd baled up most of your things and given them to Oxfam – did I say? Suits. Blazers. Casual stuff. No, well I decided to take the plunge. It was getting rid of the toothbrush that started me off – I thought right, June, let's take that as a landmark, shall we?

I was afraid it would take some doing, which is why I kept on putting it off and putting it off, but when I got down to it, it was just – well, it was just sorting stuff out for Oxfam, the same as I've done a million times. No pressing lapels to my lips, none of that, not with them all over dandruff. And they stank of nicotine. Funny, I never noticed the smell when you were here, smoking like a chimney, but now it hit me in the face, even though I must pong of tobacco myself. It was ever so stale. Like death. If it'd been the smell of pipe tobacco that was clinging to your suits and pullies, I might have got a bit weepy. But you don't get sentimental over a packet of Silk Cut, do you?

Even so, it could have been a bit of an ordeal, I'm sure it must be for some. Pauline wanted to come over and do it for me but I wouldn't have it. I didn't want her prying and poking through your belongings – you never know what she might have found, for one thing.

Now that side of it was a teeny bit nerve-racking, because I didn't know what I might find either. I held my breath, I can tell you. Bookmatches, restaurant receipts, business cards from people I've never heard of and I don't suppose you could remember them either, five minutes later; cheque book, diary – I very sensibly didn't peek into that because if I'd found an appointment for that self-same day I should have got very maudlin, I can tell you. What else was there? Wallet, credit cards – I'll have them to cut in half when I can bring myself to do it. Keys. Lighters, none of which work – why did you make me buy you disposable lighters if you wouldn't dispose of them? Coins. Oh, yes, and a twenty-pound note you'd got tucked into the top pocket of your dinner jacket and forgotten about, thank you very much – my goodness, couldn't that dinner jacket tell a tale or two? And then scraps of paper in every pocket, all your bits of scribble on the backs of cigarette packets, and scrawled telephone numbers with no names to them. But nothing incriminating, thank God, although if I rang my way through some of those numbers I'd like to know who answers.

It must happen, though, with some widows. Love letters. Porn. Photographs. Something nasty in the woodshed, eh?

I know very well there will be something, something I don't want to see, even if it's not in that line, there's got to be, bound to be, but at least it was nothing in the wardrobe, I've got that cleared. But ooh, Sam, the sound of those clanking wire coat hangers when I closed the wardrobe doors, they were like Jacob Marley's chains, I had to get 'em out and chuck them in a black sack with all your socks and underthings. They've gone to the Crypt, by the way – I don't think Oxfam welcomes Y-fronts.

I got round to seeing Mr Trimble at last – something else I've been putting off. I've never liked solicitors at the best of times, I've always associated them with libel actions, when despite your saying, We've got them on toast, kid, I'll have their brains for breakfast, your blood pressure always used to go up, you know it did, the doctor told me.

Mind, if I'd had any worries about money I'd have gone sooner, but I knew everything would be just as you'd explained it. You were very good at that sort of thing – will, trust fund, pension arrangements et cetera et cetera, completely out of character some would say but I knew better. You gave the impression of living hand to mouth and day to day but you were always looking to the future. Not far enough, as it now turns out, but there we go.

Pauline came with me. She should be well satisfied, she can't say you've not looked after her. I think all's not well between her and Jack, by the way. Nothing she said – well, it *was* something she said, in point of actual fact. We were having a glass of champagne after the meeting – you won't mind, Sam, I'm sure, but there was this very nice wine bar next door to the solicitor's, and after all it's not every day we both come into a legacy, and we did drink your health –

and I happened to pass a remark on something Mr Trimble had said.

What he'd said, just as he was showing us out, was, Well, I won't ask if you've yet come to terms with your great loss, Mrs Pepper, I do know how long these things take, but if you should ever need any practical advice blah blah blah blah.

And as I said to Pauline, What in God's name does that expression mean, come to terms? People are always coming out with it. Come to terms, he sounds like one of those flaming stress counsellors. Of course I've not come to terms, why should I? Your father's dead, full stop, we know that, I've got a certificate to prove it. But why have I got to come to terms with it?

I was that mad. Only in passing, but I was. I was working myself up.

Until Pauline says, Keep your voice down, June, we know you've not come to terms with it, it'll be a long time yet. You must miss him, bound to. But at least, she says, you know where he is at night.

What you used to call coming out of left field, that one. I never bothered to ask what it meant and I didn't ask Pauline what she meant either – she might have told me, and I didn't want to know. But as I say, there's something brewing between her and Jack, mark my words.

I was surprised at how much you'd left to Tricia, by the way, but Mr Trimble said it was – how did he put it? – par for the course. As he said, she won't have her alimony to fall back on any more. Would you believe, it'd completely gone out of my mind that you were still paying it? All those years. That's what you get for screwing your secretary. Was it worth it, Sam? Or has it been a lesson?

I got to wondering, after Pauline and I'd had a couple: if women had to pay the alimony instead of men, would I have been content to shell out one-third of my earnings for life for the pleasure of having it off over a desk and all that followed? And answer came there none as they say.

I've started dreaming about you.

I say started – of course I've been having dreams about you since Day One. Nightmares, some of them – we won't go into that. Mostly they've been anxiety dreams. Like I get to the hospital and I know you're in there dying, but nobody seems to know where you are. Or I'm in a car on the way to the funeral, on my own for some strange reason, no cortège or anything, and that thick office driver you had at one time, Joe was it, can't find the way.

Anxiety, did I say? Now what have I got to be anxious about?

But this dream is different altogether. It's, what's the word, recurrent, and I kid you not, it's so ordinary as to be downright boring. Do you remember years ago, when you had a spell at features editing, and you ran that series, Your Dreams Explained? By a Harley Street psychiatrist? Yes you do, you wrote it all yourself, with the aid of some cheap little dream booklet you picked up in a corner newsagent's somewhere. Anyway, you wouldn't have given this one house-room.

You're still alive, that's the whole point and purpose of it. And it's either a weekday evening, when I'm waiting and waiting for you to get home, then I think bugger him and I'm on my way up to bed when I hear the office car drawing up and you calling, 'Night, Ted as you slam the door; or it's Saturday morning, and I've twisted your arm and twisted your arm and at long last got you to do something about that loose pane of glass in the landing skylight where the rain seeps in, and I'm putting an old bedsheet down to take the bits of putty you'll be chipping away at when you get back from that DIY shop I've made you go to, what's it called, Do It All; or it's Sunday, with the roast on, and I'm looking

at the kitchen clock and wondering whether to pick a row
with you when you get back late from the pub or just let it
slide as of course at the death I always did.

At the death. I must stop using that phrase. Death. Dying.
Dead. Cancer. Heart attack. Funeral. They make me jump,
those words.

There's other variations, just as boring. But every time
I have this dream it finishes with me hearing your key
in the lock, and then I wake up, and of course you're
not here, and it takes me a full quarter of a minute to
realise it.

That's how I know how condemned prisoners must feel
when they dream, as I'm sure they do, that they've just been
released or reprieved and there they go blinking out into the
sunlight with all the buses roaring by and then they wake
up, and they can see the sun all right, but it's streaming in
through the little barred window, and that hammering is
the scaffold going up.

Is there any cure for dreaming, anything to stop it? Or
if not a cure for the dream, which is quite pleasant even
though you never actually appear in it, then a cure for
waking up?

I tell you, Sam, it's like being led out and bloody executed
some mornings. Each dawn I die, eh? Worst thing that's
happened so far.

I keep bumping into The Suit as I've started calling him.
Your suit. Did I mention, it's the light grey check that you
had to buy after that pissed MP knocked a bottle of red wine
over your jacket at the Tory Party Conference? Considering
you bought it in Blackpool it's a very good suit – he shows
good taste.

When I say bumping into him, of course I haven't spoken
to him, but I do seem to come across him a lot. He goes into
that newsagent's on The Parade, where as I say I do a lot of

my bits and pieces of shopping these days, and that's where I keep seeing him.

In his early forties he must be, younger than the pair of us anyway, brownish hair, not much grey in it yet, stockily built, burly I'd say, about your height which is why I keep getting that little lurch in my stomach when I catch his back view. White-collar worker obviously, Marks and Sparks shirts, flashy ties, always the same suede shoes with the heels worn down, I don't think he can be all that well paid whatever he does, well he wouldn't be if he buys his suits from Oxfam, would he? And it's always around lunchtime when I see him on The Parade, so I reckon he must work thereabouts. Estate agent's, insurance office, something of that kind.

He looks quite nice, actually. I mean nothing to write home about, but he doesn't exactly have hair growing out of his ears or a squint or any obvious blemish. Ordinary, you'd call him. Married? I shouldn't think so. You don't let your husband buy his clothes from Oxfam, or if you do, you give the sleeves and trousers a good pressing before he wears them.

I've seen him four or five times now. He once held the Minimart door open for me and smiled, even. Crooked teeth, discoloured from smoking, like yours. But I wouldn't say he's ever what you'd call noticed me, why should he, even though he must have sensed himself being looked up and down?

I've been on the verge of speaking to him once or twice. I've felt like saying, Excuse me, but that's my husband's suit you're wearing, do you like it? But who wants to be reminded he's wearing charity clothes? He'd have thought I was barmy, anyway.

Maybe I am, pet, rambling away like this, talking to someone who's just a jar of ashes. Now that's something I've thought about from time to time, talking of night terrors

– how long it takes to get cremated. I always thought you were gone in a flash, but no, it's the same as being a longlife candle, seemingly. You were still burning merrily away long after we'd left the crematorium and were tucking into the ham sandwiches. Brr. It's the cemetery for me when my turn comes round.

By the way, I hope you're not expecting me to keep this up on a day-to-day basis, because having made a start with getting all that stuff off to Oxfam I've quite got the taste for it, so I'll have enough on my plate without chuntering to you every ten minutes.

Your fishing tackle, that's gone. Your Derek dropped in the other day on his way back from Brighton where he'd been for some reason, just to see how I was, very kind of him I'm sure, and he said he could find a good home for it although he's not an angler himself. Neither were you come to that – at least you've never been fishing in all the years I've known you, those rods and lines and waders and paraphernalia have been cluttering up that garage since Adam was a lad. I don't believe you ever went fishing, or if you did it was no more than the once. Some of the lads will have got you enthused about going on an angling trip one weekend, big piss-up, get you away from Tricia, and you'll have bought all the gear and then found it bored you rigid. You, sitting on a river bank for hours on end? I can't see it.

There's still a lot of clearing out to be done, though, and at the back of my mind I'm still wondering what's going to turn up that I don't want to see. I'll be glad when it's finished.

There was a conversation I thought I'd had with you, it was that vivid. In fact I'm still not one hundred per cent certain I was dreaming. Sometimes when I came to see you in the hospital, towards the end, I'd had so little sleep and was so stuffed up with tranquillisers I was practically in a trance, and with the drugs you were on, so were you. So this conversation might have taken place or it might not, who's to say for certain?

You kept on saying, I've got to get home, girl, I've got things to do.

And for a second it was like what you were when you were well. Only then it was always, It's no good, I've got to get back to the office.

And I said, What have you got to do at home, pet, that's so urgent?

And you said, Nothing. Nothing at all. Just some stuff to get rid of.

And I said, Stuff, what stuff, Sam?

And you said, Don't think about it, just stuff for the compost heap.

And that was all you'd say – if you did say it. Did you say it, Sam, or did I dream it? Whichever, it shows it's on my mind. It's a worry.

Meanwhile the clear-out continues. I've got all those files and papers and cuttings to go through, next. All those invitations that we've kept – 10 Downing Street, Queen's garden party, Lord Mayor's banquet, all those daft promotion do's that we had to go to. I don't know what you want me to do with them all, put them in an album or what. They don't do a lot for me, I have to say. I mean they don't stir up memories, not specifically. They all jumble together into one blurred evening – me still struggling into my frock while the office car's at the door, because he was always ten minutes early, was Ted, while that other driver, the dozy one, Joe, was always ten minutes late, and I don't know which of them was worse for my nerves when it came to trying not to be flustered because I was meeting some bigwig.

And then I'd go up into the office and there you'd be in your dinner jacket knocking back a large Bell's with the chaps, and I'd say, You'll be pissed before we even get there, you will, and you saying, I've never been to Buckingham Palace sober, woman, and I'm not going to start now.

Now that I do miss. That jolly half-hour in that fuggy office before we set off, all the joshing and joking and you telling somebody to give somebody a bollocking, and off we'd blow in a cloud of cigar smoke. Got your invite, I'd say, and you'd say, Give over, woman, I'm the editor of a one and a half bloody million circulation national newspaper, and you don't turn that number of bloody readers away, I don't care who you are – it's not me, you'd say, it's the title, I could get through the eye of a bloody needle without an invite. Some needle.

That dinner jacket's seen better days, I can tell you. I've a confession to make, Sam. It didn't go to Oxfam with the rest of the wardrobe. I've kept it. Just the jacket, not the trousers – funny, the trousers do nothing for me at all. But the jacket. Oh, I can see you in it, and I can see me flicking dandruff and cigarette ash off the shoulders. And yes, I did press the lapel to my face, just once, I'll come clean, and I could hear you saying, If you get all face powder over this jacket you'll know about it, it's only just come back from the cleaners.

And I wondered whether to have a little weep, whether it'd do me good. But I didn't. I put the DJ in one of those zip-up airline bags that you had, and it's in the spare bedroom, because I didn't want it staring at me every time I open that wardrobe, but then I couldn't bring myself to throw it out either.

I had to go to the medical practice this morning. The health centre, whatever it calls itself. Dr Colefield's gone, not that you ever met her, or in fact any of them, because you'd never see a doctor, would you, until it was too late? It was a Dr Shilhom who saw me, silly cat that she was.

She says, Yes, I know all about you, Mrs Pepper, I'm putting you on Prozac.

I says, You're what, Doctor?

She says, I'm prescribing Prozac, I'm surprised you're not on it already although I'm sure Dr Colefield had her reasons, do you have a heart condition that I wouldn't know about?

I says, No, I don't, Doctor, and what do I want with Prozac, that's the so-called happy pill, isn't it?

She says, Well, that's what the sensationalist press call it, but it's to handle depression, really.

I says, Yes, I know all about it, My late husband ran a big series about it in his newspaper. But I says, I'm very sorry, I'm not suffering from depression.

She says, You'll excuse me, Mrs Pepper, but you don't know what you might be suffering from. Dr Colefield had you on tranquillisers, didn't she?

I says, Yes, against my better judgment, while my husband was in hospital. I says, I couldn't sleep, but that's hardly surprising when you're waiting for the phone to ring twenty-four hours a day. They finished up down the loo, I says. Which is true, Sam, I didn't need them after you were gone, nothing to stay awake for, nothing to stay calm about.

She says, And did Dr Colefield ever discuss grief counselling?

I says, No, she didn't, and that's something else my late husband ran a big piece about. But I says, Before you tell me not to believe everything I read in the tabloids, it didn't come down either on one side or the other.

She says, No one's going to force you into grief counselling, because that's the one sure way of not getting a result. But she says, I'm going to give you a leaflet, with a twenty-four-hour helpline number that you can ring, it's up to you. And she says, I'm going to give you a prescription, and I want you to make an appointment outside and come back to me in four weeks.

I says, Well, Doctor, I knew Prozac was the latest miracle drug but I'd be surprised if it does very much for my ingrowing toenail.

I felt better after that.

I met him today. Spoke to him. Had a drink with him.

Start as you mean to go on: I'll tell you the whole truth, pet, I followed him. Hope you don't mind, I was sure you wouldn't. The Suit, as I call him – I'd just got to find out that bit more about him.

It was lunchtime as usual and I was just on my way into the Minimart for a few bits and bobs when I saw him going into that pub across from The Parade. The Duke of Clarence, it's called – I don't think you ever used it, Tapster's house, and I know you always used to say Tapster's tasted like cat-piss. So I did my bit of shopping and then I came out and looked across at the pub, and I thought, Well, it seems a respectable sort of place and they think nothing of unaccompanied women going into pubs in this day and age, so go on, June, be a devil.

There was quite a lunchtime crush in but I spotted him straight away, perched on a stool at a little table near the cigarette machine. I got myself a half of Guinness, not vodka you'll be relieved to hear, no, not before six these days, and then I went across to the ciggy machine for twenty Silk Cut. Your brand. I could have got what's become my usual Disque Bleu across the street but I'm trying to wean myself off them. And after that I'm hoping to wean myself off Silk Cut. I blame you for this, Sam. You were the one who told me which undertaker to go to, and that cortège was four minutes late. All those weeks ago now. I says to your Pauline, Oh, for God's sake, Pauline, give me a cigarette. It was only the day before I'd thrown out most of a whole carton from the drinks trolley – I thought, I could give them away I suppose but considering what carried him off it'd be like handing out coffin nails. So that's what started me off again, after what, six years? And before you know it I'm back on fifteen, no, be honest June, twenty-five a day. And after all the nagging I've put in trying to persuade you to at least cut down. How many times have I said to you, If I can do it, Sam Pepper, so can you? Where's your willpower, I've said. And look at me. It's been thirty some days.

So the cigarette machine being over by where he was sitting, and there being a vacant stool at his table and all the other tables being occupied, it was only natural I should say, Excuse me, is there anybody sitting there?

And he snatches up the newspaper that he'd put down on the stool and he says, Not unless it's the Invisible Man.

You laugh, don't you, even when you've heard the joke a thousand times before. Nice voice he has – not what you'd call really educated but pleasant style of thing. No rough edges. Actually, he could have passed for one of your features staff, they always sounded a cut above everybody else on the paper for some strange reason, including you. I mean socially. I suppose because they were expected to use longer words. Or thought they were, according to you: you always had it in for the features lot, didn't you?

Anyway, we got chatting, as you do. There was a used National Lottery scratch card in the ashtray and when he saw me lighting up one of my Silk Cut he very kindly tipped it out for me, saying, Do you ever have any luck with these things because I'm sure I don't, complete waste of money so far.

Now there he is, Sam, sitting in your suit that he's bought from Oxfam, and there he is nursing half a pint when everybody around him's on pints, and there he is with an empty packet of ten in front of him but no dog ends in the ashtray, and there he is moaning because he's just lost a pound. I didn't have to be one of your crack reporters to work out that he had to count the pennies.

So by the time we'd talked about the Lottery for a bit and then I'd had a bit of a go at the Minimart for only serving their cinnamon crumpets that I'm getting such a taste for in packets of eight – how we got on to that I do not know, but before you say Oh, yes? in that smirky way that you had, I don't want you thinking I was trying to give him the hint that I'm all alone in the world nowadays, it just happened to fall into the conversation – I'd finished my Guinness and bold as brass as I got to my feet I heard myself saying, Can I get you one while I'm up?

He says in a shuffling, unconvincing sort of way, Oh no, he says, thank you very much, I'm not halfway through this one yet.

I says, Go on, by the time I've fought my way through to the bar and got served you'll have finished it.

He says, Well, that's very kind of you, I'll consider my arm twisted.

Of course, he could have said, No, sit down, let me, I'll get them. But he didn't. He probably didn't have two halfpennies left to scratch his bum with, as we used to say.

So after that we really did get chatting.

He says, Apropos what you were saying about crumpets, it's the same with their individual bananas now, they have them all done up in plastic bags of half a dozen.

So then I knew he was on his own too. Individual bananas, cinnamon crumpets, blueberry muffins – we got on to that subject as well – they're all comfort food too. Turns out he's divorced, has been for two years, his wife ran off with his best friend, or who he thought was his best friend until that fateful moment.

Douglas it seems his name is – Duggie he said I had to call him, but Duggie what I didn't quite catch. It doesn't matter, I shall always think of him as The Suit. Lives in that little block of flats over The Parade, which is why I've kept seeing him round there. And the only other thing I know is he worked for a building society, something managerial although he was nowhere near being top dog, more bottom dog I should imagine, and he was made redundant when they merged with some other building society, I forget which.

And that was that, Sam. We had our drink, we had our chat, and because I thought he might be embarrassed wriggling out of getting another round if he hadn't the wherewithal, I got up and says, Well, it's been very nice talking to you but it's high time I wasn't here, I've got a lot to get through today. Which I had: getting those piles of books you had stacked all over the house sorted out. All those review copies you'd fetch home and never read but wouldn't let me give away.

And he gets up as well and says, I should be making tracks too.

Where he should be making them to he didn't say. Nowhere in particular, I shouldn't wonder. He looked lost.

As we went out I couldn't resist saying, If you don't mind my saying so, that's a very nice suit you're wearing, it's a very good piece of cloth, could I ask you where you got it?

He says, Oh, that Oxfam shop on the corner of Chapel Street, you can get some very good stuff there, real bargains.

Now if he'd said Oh, Marks and Sparks, or Oh, Burton's, I should have left it at that. But as he came right out with Oxfam I could see no harm in saying, Yes, I thought so, it used to belong to my late husband.

He coloured. He did. He went red. Then he gave what I suppose you'd call a nervous laugh. More of a snigger.

He says, I wish you hadn't told me that.

I says, Why, it's nothing to be ashamed of, people do die, and their clothes have got to go somewhere, I'm glad you bought it, it suits you.

He says, Well, I did need something for everyday wear, and I've often fancied a check but I can never find anything approaching my size round here, let alone anything I really want, so of course when I noticed this suit in the window—

He was just burbling, while he screwed up courage to say what he'd got to say. At long last he comes out with it:

—If you don't mind my asking, what did he die of?

I couldn't help giggling. I says, Nothing contagious, if that's what's worrying you, if you must know it's what he always used to call the Big C. Or the dreaded lurgy. Plus, the treatment he was getting brought on a heart attack, or that's my opinion. But I says, So it was nothing catching.

He says, Thank you, I hope you didn't mind my asking. Only I must say, and don't take this the wrong way, I do wish you hadn't told me.

I says, What do you mean? You just asked me.

He says, No, I mean that he was dead. Your late husband. It feels – how shall I put this? – a bit spooky. Dead men's shoes.

I didn't know whether to take offence or not. I could have done, easily. But he meant no harm. As I say, he was just rattling on.

I says, glancing down at his beer-stained Hush Puppies, You should have treated yourself to a pair of dead men's shoes while you were about it, I sent six pairs down there. I says, And he kept good care of his shoes, my Sam, you'd think he was a Grenadier Guard to see him polishing them of a weekend. He wouldn't let me do it, willing though I was, he'd say, Get out of the way, woman, spit and polish is a man's job.

He says, does The Suit, I did try on one or two pairs but I couldn't find anything in my size.

I says, He was a size nine, broad fitting.

He says, I'm an eight and a half.

And that more or less brought the conversation to a stop. And I was just wondering whether to say, Well, I hope we bump into one another again some time, when across the street I saw your Pauline, staring round at us while she pretended to look in an estate agent's window.

I thought, She'll be round before the day's out.

Sure enough, just as I'm settling down with a vodka and tonic – my afternoon treat – to watch Gina Lollobrigida in *Go Naked in the World* as a good way of not getting round to sorting those books out for a while longer, the doorbell rings. I'm trying not to make a habit of watching telly in the afternoon, but I do like an old film as you know, and I just can't get the hang of setting that video.

I knew it'd be Pauline, so I glugged back the vodka and tipped the ice back in the bucket. One lecture from her in a day would be quite enough, thank you very much, and I knew very well what she'd come about.

So after the usual how are you keeping and are you looking after yourself and what have you had for lunch today, are you sure you're not neglecting yourself, she gets down to the nitty-gritty:

—So come on then, June, who is he, what does he do, and where did you find him?

I thought – well, I won't tell you what I thought, Sam, but the expression Little Miss Nosey Parker comes into it. I tell you, her nostrils were fair quivering with excitement. If I'd given her anything of a tale she'd have had it all over the neighbourhood by teatime, so of course, I played it cool, or tried to.

I says, Who's who?

She says, You know very well who, him that you were chatting up outside that pub. I just happened to be across the street when you came out.

I says, Yes, we know you did, Pauline, and I saw you just

happening to watch us and wishing you could lip-read. If it's any of your business, I says, he's a gentleman I *just happened* to get into conversation with in the Duke of Clarence when I *just happened* to call in for half a Guinness.

She says, It's not like you to go into public houses of a lunchtime, June. At least I'm sure you never did when Dad was here, are you sure it was Guinness?

I was livid. I was. But at the same time I was glad I'd got shot of that vodka and tonic.

I says, Excuse me, Pauline, but it's none of your business whether it was Guinness, rum, lager, brandy or what it was, and another thing, I says, it's none of your business where I go or when I go or who I'm with, I don't want to sound rude, Pauline, but can we just be clear about that and leave it?

She says, I'm sorry, June, I didn't mean to intrude, but can you tell me one thing? How does he come to be wearing Dad's suit?

I says, Who says he was wearing your father's suit?

She says, Well if he wasn't, it was one very much like it.

I'd a good mind to let her keep on guessing but instead I thought I'd better come clean and tell her how he came by it.

I see – quite a coincidence, she says when I'd finished.

There was no coincidence about it, I says sharply. If you'd seen your father's suit going into a pub, maybe you'd have gone in after it too.

Oh, so you're saying you followed him! she says.

I said, I'm saying nothing more, Pauline, now can we just drop it, once and for all?

And we did, but honestly, Sam! Is this what it's all about, then, being in mourning? If I can be said to be in mourning, that is. I mean, they used to make such a rigmarole of it, didn't they? You wore black for months on end, your widow's weeds, you didn't receive visitors, you never went out, and you certainly didn't go picking up strange men in public houses. It must have been very oppressive, very morbid. We have a healthier attitude these days, the motto seems to be carry on as normal as far as you can.

That's if other folk will let you. The corners they push you into! Having to be careful who you're seen with, having to hide your vodka glass, having to justify your behaviour. I mean to say here you are, Sam, not yet cold in your grave – well, you're not in a grave, you're in an urn, but you know what I mean – and already I'm having to put up with these sly innuendoes from your own daughter. She gets a kick out of it, that's obvious enough. Perks her up. In the midst of death we are in life, eh? Did you hear that? In the midst of death we are in life. Just my little joke, pet.

But she hadn't finished yet.

I reckoned I'd better make some tea, although it was the last thing I wanted I can tell you, and after the usual palaver over who was going to put the kettle on and Pauline saying, Sit you down now, I know where everything is – this is in my own house, mind! – I got *her* sat down with a cup of tea and a Garibaldi biscuit, and she starts again:

—Anyway, June, I'm sorry if I got you all upset but none of that was what I came round about.

I thought, You could have fooled me. But I didn't say anything.

She goes on, breaking her biscuits into little bits just as you yourself used to do when you'd something to say that needed saying but you didn't like to say it, such as you were very very sorry but you wouldn't be able to make it to the theatre tonight, there was a knife-edge division on the single currency or Ireland or whatever it might be. Like father, like daughter. Funny how she can be like you in so many of the little ways but none of the big ones.

So she goes, You might as well hear it from me before you hear it from everybody else, June, I'm thinking of leaving Jack.

Like father in some of the big ways too, eh?

I murmured something. Oh dear, I hope not, Pauline, or Don't do anything hasty, Pauline, these things often work themselves out. Something of the sort.

To tell you the truth, pet, and I'm ashamed of myself when I tell you this, I was furious. I've lost my husband, my whole way of life's been shattered, I'm trying to pick up the pieces and make of things what they've got to be made of – it's not easy, believe you me! And in she trolls saying, Oh, I'm thinking of leaving my husband. Shall I tell you the first thing I thought? That's your problem, sweetheart, I thought, I've got problems of my own. And at least you've got a husband to leave.

I must have asked her what it was all about, in a polite sort of way – because I'm sorry to say I wasn't very much interested – and of course that triggers her off. The whole saga. Mind you, she was aching to spill it out whether I'd asked her or not:

—The usual story. Bit of spare at the office.

I was on automatic. I says, Oh, I am sorry, how long has this been going on, then?

What did I care? A month, a year, two years? I can tell you this, Sam, if it was all a mistake with you, if it turned out you hadn't coughed your guts out after all but on the other hand you'd been having it away rotten with a bit of spare at the office for the last ten years – if that had to be a condition, I'd cheer for joy and sign on the dotted line.

—He says just a few weeks, I think it's been going on for a long time.

—How did you find out, did somebody tell you?

Why do we ask these questions? Women's questions. What does it matter how she found out? She found out.

—The usual way, these days, so I'm told, June. Itemised phone bill. He's been ringing her every chance he got, four or five times a day sometimes, every time I was out of the house.

Silly sod. They never learn. I mean he works with the woman, and anyway if he does have to ring her up what does he think phone boxes are for? You'd think he wanted to be found out. Maybe he did. It's been known.

But instead of paying any attention to Pauline's little problem I was thinking, itemised phone bill, yes, there must have been many and many a divorce brought on through somebody going through an itemised phone bill. And I was thinking, that's something I won't have to do any more, checking and checking every number, just on the off-chance. Not that I didn't trust you, Sam, and complete waste of time anyway, because you'd never have done anything that stupid. You'd have called her from your mobile, for which the bill went to the office, wouldn't you? Crafty bugger that you are. Were.

But talking of wanting to be found out, I suppose at the back of my mind I wanted, or half-wanted, to find you out, to catch you up to no good with some floozy I'd never heard of. Why? I can tell why – excitement. Something to get me going. It could be very dull, could marriage. Or so I used to think. You do, when you imagine it's all going to last for ever.

It goes without saying, if I ever had found anything out on those lines, I should have gone through the roof. And so would you, Sam Pepper, feet first.

But if it isn't a woman, what is it? It keeps on nagging away at me, that there's got to be something, some guilty secret. I know very well that's why I keep on turning cup-boards out and emptying drawers of your old pill bottles and God knows what else, as if death ought to be the occasion for a spot of spring cleaning. I'm looking for something, aren't I?

I let Pauline witter on about her itemised phone bill for

a while and then I says, not really interested, because I'm very sorry, Sam, I really do have problems of my own and it's not as if your daughter and I have ever been big buddies, I says:

—So what are you going to do then, love, is it the big showdown, the big ultimatum, or what?

She says, Oh no, June, we've been through that stage, ten times over – I would have told you before but you'd enough on your plate. It's a case of him wanting his cake and eating it, he swears blind he's going to stop seeing her but then he says he's got to take her out for one more lunch so he can tell her properly, I mean would you stand for that, June? She says, And you know what he's like, he's weak, and anyway how can he stop seeing her when they work in the same office?

She's turning the waterworks on by now and the thought crossed my mind, I wonder if I could tempt her to a vodka. But I knew that really would get her going, we would have been there all day and all night if I'd got that bottle out.

Even on tea, there was no stopping her. She snivels, Do you know what I can't get over, June? Do you remember the day of Dad's memorial service?

I said, quite sharpish to make her pull herself together, No, Pauline, it's gone clean out of my mind.

She says, I'm sorry, June, you know what I mean. Well, you remember he had to go to Birmingham, and he stayed over? He was with her. I found the hotel bill, Mr and Mrs.

He really was asking for trouble, that one. Mind you, I do remember having my suspicions at the time. So did Pauline, evidently, which is why she must have gone through his pockets.

She goes, having another little sniffle, How could he, June, on that day of all days? And then pretending he was coming to the service when he knew very well he wasn't, when all the time, as soon as he'd made his excuses about the heavy traffic, he was meeting her wherever he was meeting her, I mean imagine, June, the planning that must have gone into that, while you were organising the memorial service, the scheming bastard, doesn't it just make you feel sick?

It didn't make me feel anything, tell the truth. I never liked Jack and you never liked Jack. I could hear you saying, It doesn't matter a pig's fart to me. But I could see where this little episode had put the tin lid on it.

So I just says, At least he turned up for the funeral.

She says, staring at me, How can you be so forgiving, June? Because I know I'll never forgive him, never.

I says, So how have you left it, then?

But she wasn't coming round to that yet. She says, I nearly went to see her.

I thought, Yes, we know you did, dear, and if I'd poured out that vodka you would have told me everything you were going to say to her but didn't.

But all I said was, Why – to see what she looks like, or to scratch her eyes out, or what?

She says, To tell her to leave my husband alone, June. Because if she doesn't, she can have him, and I mean that.

I hoped she wasn't looking to me for advice, Sam, because I'd none to offer. I mean to say we know she's your daughter but I was keeping right out of it. I did think, thank God there's no kiddies, that's one small mercy.

But then I had another thought. I said, Does that mean you'd leave him, or tell him to pack his bags and go, which would it be?

She says, Oh, I should be the one to leave, June, make a clean break. Definitely. Because, she says, if I stayed in that flat I know what would happen, he'd be round after a fortnight begging me to take him back, and then it'd all start again, and I'm not having that, June. No, it'll be me that packs my suitcases, I've never gone much on that flat anyway, and we can work all the finances out later.

And of course that's when I knew what she was leading up to. She wants to move in with me. Oh, my godfathers.

Now I know what you're going to say, Sam, she's got a moral entitlement. She gets the house when I'm gone, or if I want to sell up and move somewhere more manageable, whatever's left in the kitty goes into a trust fund and I can draw the interest but it all goes to her in the end, Mr Trimble explained it all over again. We agreed to it, Sam, I know we did, you'll agree to anything when death's a far-off thing. And it did seem to make sense at the time. You bought the blessed house after all, and if it didn't go to your own daughter, who would it go to? My cousin Mary in York's the next of kin as far as I know and I haven't set eyes on her since my mother's funeral, she might even be dead herself. Of course, the idea that I might marry again never crossed your mind, now did it, be honest? Or mine either. And still doesn't. And won't. Or will it, come to think of it? There's such a thing as company.

Yes, and there's company and there's company. The idea of Pauline moving in sends shivers up my spine, I'm very sorry, Sam, but there it is. But short of telling her point blank I don't want her here, what can I do?

Ah well, it'll be something to worry about. Like that damp patch in the spare bedroom. I know I should have had it done – let's face it, lad, you should have had it done – but I haven't, and shall I tell you why? So that I have it gnawing away at me – and while that's gnawing at me, the other thing isn't, or anyway not so much.

On the other hand, if I got the damp specialists and then the decorators into the spare room, that'd keep your Pauline out of it. I shall have to think.

Comfort eating, comfort reading.

Do you know what I found when I started sorting out all those books? A stack of those old green-backed Penguins you used to read, years ago when you were night editing. Agatha Christie. Raymond Chandler. Margery Allingham. I started dipping into them, you know how you do when you're sitting in the middle of a pile of books, and before I knew it I was actually reading one of them, took it back into the living room with a bar of mint Aero and really got stuck in. *The Murder of Roger Ackroyd.* I never used to care for detective stories as you know, Jilly Cooper was more in my line, but I've read three of them so far, all of them Agatha Christies.

Sheer escapism, it goes without saying. Still, that's what they're for, isn't it? They're a security blanket – is that why you used to devour them at the rate of two or three a week? Country houses, quiet little villages, vicars, mousy Miss Marple, all so peaceful and secure and the worst thing that's going to happen is another body in the library. They're a cocoon. I don't suppose I'll be the first to have said that.

The rubbish I've thrown out, though. Michael Dukakis, *The Man Who Would Be President.* What were you hanging on to that for – did you think he might make a comeback? Willie Whitelaw's memoirs – never been opened, so far as I can judge. And all those other political books, none of which you've read a word of, I'll be bound. Politics was never your scene unless there was a big scandal brewing but you had to keep in touch with what they were up to, you've got to when you're a newspaper editor, and I think you believed that if you had a lot of political books in close proximity you'd be able to absorb what was in them, the same way that by ordering a side salad at lunch but never touching it you thought you were getting your proper intake of vitamins, just by looking at it.

I was going to throw all those out too, but then I thought hold your horses, June, they're not yours to throw. They belong to the office, those books do, and the political staff might be glad of some of them. Or if they don't want them,

I know that whatever that books editor is called, although what the dickens a paper like yours wants with a books editor we shall never know, he has an arrangement with a dealer to sell his review copies at half price, and the money goes towards the office Christmas party.

So I gave young Sheila a ring, thinking I wouldn't bother anyone more senior. Turns out she's been promoted to editor's secretary, did you know, Jo having been poached by Charlie Whittington, apparently. Anyway, she was very nice, asked how I was keeping, and she said if I'd put them in a box or a plastic bag she'd get one of the drivers to pick them up when he was round this way. My good deed for the day. Bet it doesn't get me an invite to the office party, though.

My aching back, doing all this bending and stooping! Shall I tell you something, Sam? Clearing up after the dead is worse than clearing up after a party.

Is this what you meant by keeping a diary, then? Am I doing it right, just rambling away like this? I don't know how therapeutic it is but I will say this: I'm glad of a chance to have someone to talk to. Because otherwise, apart from shopkeepers and your Pauline when she drops in, I can go for days and days without speaking to a soul. I'm beginning to wish I hadn't let the bridge afternoons slide, but then again, they used to irritate me that much with all the petty gossip and the spiteful little digs at all and sundry, that's why I gave them up.

They never call me, none of them. They did, but they don't. I think people don't know what to say, once the novelty of your being a widow wears off on them. I've got the definite impression that some of them are quite irritated at the idea that I will go on and on being widowed, that I persist in it, that I haven't snapped out of it. And then guilt comes into it. They feel guilty because they've all got husbands and I haven't. Even if their husbands are mean and shitty and ten kinds of bastard and playing away like your Pauline's Jack, yet they've still got husbands, and I haven't. Very remiss of me, I know.

And the divorced ones are as bad, if not worse. They talk as if you'd waltzed off on purpose. As if I ought to close ranks with them. Without putting it in so many words, they have a general air of Men, we're better off without them.

Speak for yourself, I should tell them.

It's at times like this you know who your friends are, I was going to say. But who are my friends? I've never really had any, not what you'd call close friends, only The Girls as you used to call them in sarcastic capital letters, chums to go shopping with and have coffee mornings with.

I expect that's what comes of starting my married life or what was to be my married life as a mistress: you put everything into waiting for him to ring, waiting for him to come round, waiting for him to find time for you, and while you're waiting and waiting and waiting, everybody else gets put on the back burner, sorry to sound like one of your Saturday magazine confession stories but it happens to be true, and by the time it's all blown up in your face and he's moved in with you and you've settled down into a marriage that's going to be as humdrum as anybody else's once the glitter's worn off, you've just got out of the habit of having proper friends.

So there's The Girls, but I don't relish the idea of inviting myself into their company and even less do I like the suspicion that when they invite me it's out of guilt or duty or feeling sorry for poor little June, poor big June as she's becoming. Maybe I should start going to Weight Watchers, meet some new people.

But I don't really crave company, tell the truth. I always was self-sufficient, Sam, wasn't I? So why do I feel lonely?

You don't have to tell me. Because it's one thing not to speak to a soul all day when you know that sooner or later you're going to hear the sound of a key in the lock, and quite another when the key that used to turn in the lock is now in a desk drawer.

And why are the days longer? It's not as if I've any less to do now that I've only myself to look after, in fact with all the clearing out that I'm doing I'm a damned sight busier than I ever was. But why does so much of what I'm doing now seem pointless, when it was obviously pointless in the first place?

Tidying the house before Mrs Rington comes in on a Tuesday and Friday morning – as you always said, Where's the sense in paying a bloody cleaning woman when you're doing the bloody cleaning for her? But I did it, and I do it. But now I don't know why I'm doing it, or rather I don't want to know. Pride, it used to be. Now it's shame. I don't want her to think I'm letting myself go.

Opening and reading junk mail. That used to drive you bonkers. Throw it in the bloody bin, woman, you'd rant on, you've no more chance of winning twenty-five grand than you have of flying, so why are you wasting your bloody time?

To waste my bloody time, that's why I do it now. Before, it was nothing but a reflex action, you get an envelope in the post and you open it. Part of life's routine. It never seemed pointless then.

There's still a steady trickle of letters coming in for you, I mean besides bills and circulars that still have your name on them – and that's another thing that makes me jump when I see it. Letters from people who don't know you've gone, like the Inland Revenue to name but one, I send those on to Mr Trimble unopened. There was a letter from one of these university media courses last week, they must have got your address from *Who's Who*, they want you to give them a talk on When Sensationalism Is Justified. Media studies, and they don't know one of the top dogs in the media is dead. As you would put it, Sam, Don't these bloody cretins read the bloody papers?

That's something else: reading the bloody papers. I never had your addiction to newsprint as you know, not that it ever bothered you, but I did try to keep up with what was going on in the world so as not to let you down at any of those swanky dinners that we went to. And I still take half a dozen papers a day. Why, seeing that I no longer even look at them beyond the front pages? It can only be so I can see you in my mind's eye, cackling with glee as you throw down the *Mirror* and the *Sun* and the *Express* and saying, Look at this, June – now would you honestly call that a page one story in ten million years?

Death is nothing at all, I have only slipped away into the next room. But there's no one in the next room, that's the trouble.

Ah well, back to your books. *The Rough Guide to Paris*, now what did you want with *The Rough Guide to Paris*? The only times we ever went to Paris we were met by a limo at the airport, we stayed at the George V and ate at the Tour d'Argent, we got pissed with the correspondents in the Crillon Bar and frankly I'd rather have had a quiet dirty weekend in Brighton.

That's another one for the bin-liner. At least there's no mucky books squat away. But what do I think I'm doing, Sam? I didn't get rid of all this stuff while you were here so why am I doing it now? Am I trying to exorcise you or what? Or just giving myself something to do?

And life goes on – at least mine does. And you come to realise, quite to your own surprise, that death doesn't wipe everything out like a blackboard duster. The rain still comes through the skylight. The damp patch in the spare room still needs looking at. The fridge door still bangs against the kitchen wall when I open it. And I think to myself, quite indignant, now why couldn't he have taken these problems with him? He might have never done anything about them, true, but while he was here they were never my problems. And a little voice says, They are now, ducky.

And another thing, Sam Pepper: you really are a sod, you know. I thought we'd agreed on a late holiday, first two weeks in December before all the Christmas knees-ups, to make up for that fortnight in Positano we didn't have, when we had to cancel because of you having to suck up to the chairman at some newsprint jamboree in Canada. New York you were going to take me to, so that I could do some Christmas shopping on Fifth Avenue while you got pissed with the chaps in that Irish bar behind the *Daily News* Building. So I open your diary, which I've avoided looking in so far, and what do I find but nothing. And not only nothing, not only are those first two weeks of December not marked in, but even though it's months and months away, you've already made three appointments during that fortnight — one to go to the Nottingham Press Ball, thank you very much for telling me, one to judge some student journalism awards, and one to speak at the Police Federation annual dinner. Well I hope young Sheila has cancelled all these engagements because I've certainly no intention of doing so, so bubbles to you.

Not that it matters a toss any more. I would have liked to have been in New York in December, to have seen all the lights along Fifth Avenue and the ice skaters at Rockefeller Plaza is it? But I don't suppose we should ever have gone anyway.

And life goes on as I say – and as everyone else keeps on saying, along with Time heals all wounds, Count your blessings, and Life is for the living. At least they don't say you had a good innings, because you didn't.

Dentist tomorrow. Chiropodist Friday, oh yes, it's come to that – that new doctor put me on to him with my ingrowing toenail, it makes me feel like a flaming pensioner.

Which brings to mind another well-known phrase or saying – You're still young enough to find a new partner. No one's said that to me, either.

You'll never guess who dropped in this morning. Eric Grant. Deputy editor now, did I mention? Last person I'd expect to see, because he was never your firmest of favourites, was he?

No, because it transpires he just chanced to be in the office when I was ringing young Sheila about those books of yours, and having got the gist he'd said to her, I don't mind picking them up one day on my way in, Sheila, save you making other arrangements, it doesn't take me far off my route and anyway there's something I've been wanting to have a word with June about.

I said when he'd told me this, Oh yes, and what would that be, Eric?

He says, Oh, something and nothing, June, it'll keep, just let me get this lot in the boot.

I was quite mystified. I says, Shall I give you a hand or shall I be putting the coffee on, I know you've time for a cup because it's not even half past nine yet?

He says, That's right, you get the coffee on, and don't look so worried, as I say, it's something and nothing.

He's a bit like that, Eric Grant, isn't he, Sam? Always one for building a story up, even when there's no story to build up. You always said it was because he'd no confidence in his own news sense, I don't know about that but I didn't see why he had to be so flaming mysterious.

Anyway, he gets staggering out to his car with these heavy bin-liners full of books while I make some coffee, and eventually he flops down in your armchair red in the face, because they really were heavy, you would have thought they were tons of bricks he was humping out to that boot.

I says, Well done, Eric, I'll be glad to see the back of that lot, now if you're sure you've not ruptured yourself do you take it black or white?

So he gets his coffee and I wait for him to say whatever it is he's come to say, but he doesn't, he just sits there huffing and puffing. If you ask me that's another one that's looking for a heart attack if he's not careful, talk about out of condition.

So I says, So what's this something or nothing you wanted to have a word about?

He says, Just a minute, June, let me get my breath back, I'm not used to all this exertion.

I could have shook him. But I thought, Bubbles to him, I've asked him twice and I'm not going to ask him again, much as he'd like me to, he can say what he's come to say in his own good time.

Very nice coffee, he says, what blend is it?

I says, St Michael Medium Roast, decaffeinated, Sam always liked it, he wouldn't have any other kind. But, I said, in all those years I never told him it was decaff, because he wouldn't have drunk it.

And you wouldn't, would you, stubborn pig that you are?

He says, Do you miss him?

I says, Yes, of course I miss him.

Very sharpish I was, as you can imagine.

He says, a bit awkward, But you'll have got over the worst of it by now?

I says, How do you mean, got over it? It's not like measles, Eric, I says, it's something you have to live with. And I said, It's worse some days than others.

And he says, Yes, I can imagine.

Then after nodding dolefully like an undertaker, silly fool that he is, he goes, He's much missed at the paper, you know.

I wondered where all this was going, whether it was just clumsy sympathetic chitchat or was he leading up to what he'd come for? If he was going to go all round the houses it was up to him, I wasn't going to help him, Sam.

I says, and I know you would have backed me up on this one, You surprise me, Eric, because in my experience of the newspaper world such as it is, once you're gone you're gone, and no one thinks twice about you any more except in their cups.

He says, No, I can't agree with you there, June, he really is missed, he's often talked about.

I says, Oh, yes, who talks about him for instance?

He says, Everyone who worked with him, or should I say everyone outside the editor's office. Now don't quote me on this, June, he says, or you'll get me shot, but there's quite a bit of dissatisfaction at the way Bob Carp's running the paper.

I was quite stiff with him. I said, Well Bob would have been Sam's choice as you know, Eric, because he'd nothing but praise for him.

And I thought, Which is more than he had for you, chum.

He says, Oh, yes, he's a good newspaperman, he thinks on his feet, but he doesn't plan ahead, he doesn't think about next week, never mind next year, as Sam used to.

This was jealousy talking, of course.

I says, catty as they come, Maybe it needs an Editor in charge of Forward Thinking to do that.

He flushed. And he bit his lip. I wasn't too sure until that minute that he knew you'd meant to sidetrack him to Forward Thinking or Special Projects or whatever name of the moment you gave to the non-job you were dreaming up for him. But he does know. Oh, he knows.

I took pity on him. I poured him some more coffee and offered him a biscuit.

He nibbles away for a bit, and then he says, I wish I could have got closer to Sam, you know, June.

I says, Well, he was always approachable, Eric.

He says, Yes – to some.

I thought, I can't believe this, what I'm hearing. He comes barging into my house, he won't tell me what it is he wants to see me about, and within ten minutes he's on the verge of slagging off my dead husband. I mean, is he just insensitive, or what?

I said, Excuse me, Eric, just hold it right there. Whatever you're about to say, don't, because you're talking about your old boss and my late husband, so let's have that little bit of respect.

He throws his arms up in this jokey surrender gesture, and he goes, June, June, June, please hear me out, no one had more respect for Sam than me.

That was a lie for a start. I bet he used to talk about you the way he now obviously talks about Bob Carp.

He says, But if you know anything about how he used to run the paper, it can't be denied that he did have his little coterie, and unfortunately I wasn't one of their number.

I says, That I wouldn't know, because Sam didn't bring his work home with him, but if you weren't one of his close circle I'm sure he had his reasons.

He says, I'm sure he did, June, I'm sure he did.

Do you know, Sam, if it wasn't yet ten in the morning I'd swear he'd been drinking.

He goes on: Bob Carp was deputy editor, right, and I was night editor, right, and one of us when Sam went upstairs, excuse me, June, I don't mean upstairs in the sense of being dead, I mean upstairs as editorial director, which is what he would have become if he'd been spared, whereupon one or other of us would have been made editor. Which Bob duly was.

I'd had enough of this. I said, What is it you're driving at, Eric?

He says, Only that Sam was playing favourites, he was blind to Bob's faults and blind to my virtues.

I could have said, Oh, yes, and what were they, may I ask? But I didn't. I just wanted him out. He's a seething mass of resentment, that man, you were right about him all along, Sam, he's a prat as you very rightly said. It's obviously been festering away with him all this time, but why does he want to come and get it off his chest to me? Has he any idea what effect it has? Of course he hasn't.

I was beginning to tremble. I said, Now I can see what's been upsetting you, Eric, but I'm not having you coming here and upsetting me, because I'm not up to dealing with it. And now I'd be glad, I said, if you'd please go.

He gets up at once. I'm sorry, June, he says, I'm afraid I'm out of order.

You are out of order, I said.

He begins to say, It's just that—

I cut in quickly:

—It's just nothing, Eric, now leave it. And yourself, I want *you* to leave. Thank you for picking up the books.

Then I remembered:

—You said you'd been wanting to have a word with me. And that was it, was it?

He slapped his forehead, and then said, as if I hadn't already asked him three times:

—Thank goodness you reminded me, June, it had gone clean out of my head, the letters, I'd completely forgotten about the letters.

My heart jumped, Sam. It did.

I said, Letters, what letters, what are you talking about, letters?

He says, and I could have strangled him where he stood: First can we get one thing straight, June, I didn't come here

to slag off Sam as you put it, that was just something I've
wanted to get off my chest but obviously this was not the
right time, I can see that now and I'm sorry.

I said, What letters, what are these letters?

He says, Well, I don't know whether you remember,
there's no reason why you should, but way back when Sam
worked out in the newsroom he had a locker, we all do.

I said, Yes, he used to keep an old raincoat hanging up in
there, when he was on the news desk.

He says, chortling: It's still there, June, after all these
years! He says, No, because we've just taken on a new chief
sub, Tim Stanton from the *Sun*, good bloke, I shouldn't
think you know him, and he was looking for somewhere
to put his things. And someone said, There's a locker over
there, Tim, I've never seen anyone use it for as long as I've
been here, see if it's vacant. So of course, someone else
remembered it was Sam's, from all that time ago. But it
was locked.

Can we get on with it, Eric? I says. You'll be late for work
at the rate you're spinning it out.

He says, Well, we get security to open it, and there's Sam's
old raincoat looking very much the worse for wear, I should
say it's ready for the skip unless you want to hang on to it
for sentiment's sake, June.

I says, Never mind his raincoat, what else was in that
locker?

I was shaking. And Eric Grant could see I was shaking,
he was dragging it out and dragging it out on purpose, the
crafty little so-and-so that he is.

He says, Nothing much, few bits and pieces. Couple of
paperbacks, empty Bell's bottle, three or four packets of
Silk Cut, gone dry by now I should think. And this bundle
of letters.

—Oh, yes?

—Tied up with blue ribbon.

So this was it, then, was it? The skeleton in the cupboard. What we've been waiting for. The Big One, by the
sound of it.

I could have gone one of two ways. I could have swooned
at his feet or I could have become calm. I became calm. Very,
very calm. I surprised myself.

—Do you think you should be telling me this, Eric?

He looks at me blank-faced for a minute, or pretending to
look blank-faced. Then he makes a great show of the penny
dropping.

—Oh, there's nothing to get yourself het up about, June,
nothing at all. I can see the way your mind's working, but
I can promise you they're not what you might be thinking.
Not that anybody's read them, of course.

I thought, No, no, of course not, it's never even crossed
their minds, Bundle of letters tied up with ribbon, newsroom
full of slavering tabloid hacks, and nobody thinks to open
them? Perish the thought.

He says, But going by the childish writing on the envelopes, I'd say they were from a little girl, and going by the
dates on the postmarks I'd say that little girl was Pauline,
when she was about what – seven? eight? nine?

Or at least we hope they're from Pauline. If not, Sammy
lad, you're in trouble.

Only joking, pet. I was that relieved I could have kissed the
little snake. But then at once I was angry again. Fuming.

I says, And couldn't you have told me that straight away,
instead of coming round here and playing cat and mouse
games?

He says, I don't know what you mean, June.

I says, You know very well what I mean. So where is this
bundle of letters, then?

He says, They're locked in my desk at the office just at
present, I wasn't at all sure whether you'd want to see them,
some things can bring back painful memories.

I says, For once you've got something right, Eric, I do not want to see them, they're not mine to see, but I'm sure Pauline would like to have them.

He says, very cryptic: Well, we don't know that for sure, June.

He *has* read those letters, I know he has. And there's something in those letters to open old wounds.

But what old wounds? There's no old wounds to open. If he means the divorce, if that's what the sly little bugger was driving at, he wasn't around at the time and he can't know that it passed off without too much rancour as these things go. It isn't as if we ran off together – Tricia found out and threw you out and that was that. She didn't keep you but she kept her pride. Plus the nice house in London you moved her into before moving out yourself. As for Pauline, she must have been seven at the time and you always said she took it reasonably well.

But she never wanted to meet me. Well, that was her privilege. Didn't get to meet me until she was what, sixteen she must have been, when she was thrown out of that boarding school she was at in Hove, and Tricia thought she'd better come and stay with you for a while seeing that at that awkward age there was nothing she could do with her.

Nothing I could do with her, either. She didn't take to me and quite frankly I didn't take to her, little sulkpot that she was. And of course you were never there except weekends, so it didn't work out, did it? It was a worrying time for me, those few weeks, sitting up night after night waiting for her to roll back from whichever club or rave-up or wherever she was with that bunch she got mixed up with, and worrying about who'd get the blame if she came home doped to the eyeballs or didn't come home at all or if the police came round or she got herself pregnant or the thousand things that other people's teenagers can get up to and I'd no experience of coping with.

Nor had you, come to that. It was a bloody stupid idea, sending her to that tinpot la-di-da school full of the delinquent daughters of TV stars and rock singers – from what I heard of it, I'm only surprised she didn't finish up on the game in Brighton. Lucky for us all that Tricia had a late late flash of common sense and got her enrolled on that beauty aids and waxing course, which I will say she really took to and having sown enough wild oats for someone twice her age she began to settle down and develop into the Pauline we know and love today. Although considering how she's turned out, I'm not sure I didn't prefer the madcap version, so long as I didn't have to look after her.

But getting back to those letters. Of course when she was away at school she used to write to you here, about once a month on average, not that you ever showed me her letters but you'd read out the odd snippet and then you'd put them in your desk which is where they are to this day, untouched. I keep meaning to ask Pauline what she wants me to do with them. But these other letters, the ones in Eric's possession – I'm saying in Eric's possession, that makes him sound like a blackmailer, I wouldn't put it past him – they must have been written as he said when she was a little girl, and she must have sent them to the office. Funny that, but maybe Tricia didn't like her writing to you at home with me under the same roof. Yet her Christmas cards and birthday cards and Father's Day cards always came here. It's a puzzle. And what would she have had to write to you about, when you were seeing her nearly every Saturday afternoon to troll her off to the Zoo or Madame Tussaud's or the Planetarium? You never said.

Although he hadn't asked me a question, Eric seemed to be waiting for an answer.

I says, They're a little girl's letters to her Daddy, Eric, why shouldn't she want them back?

And he goes, It's not for me to say.

This with just a wisp of a sneer. He's read them and for some warped reason of his own he wants me to read them too.

Then he says, So shall I bring them round one evening then or what, June, I don't know Pauline well enough to go knocking on her door?

I didn't want him coming round again. I said, I'd like you to post them if you wouldn't mind, Eric, I'm often out in the evenings these days.

Complete fabrication, as you know, but I'll swear he licked his lips. He went, Oh, yes? as if to say, Got ourself a fancy man already, have we?

I says, resisting the impulse to clock him one, Recorded delivery.

And we left it at that. Ooh, he's a nasty bugger, Sam, and that's swearing.

That was over a week ago. Those letters still haven't arrived so I thought I'd better ring the office. I was beginning to wonder, has he just not got round to it or does he want me to sweat for a bit? I thought I knew which. I decided to put a spoke in his wheel by saying, Oh, about those letters, Eric, if you haven't already posted them why don't you send them direct to Pauline, I'll give you her postal code, I think you already know her address, don't you?

I got young Sheila. She said, Eric Grant? He's left, June, didn't you know?

I says, He's what?

She says, Yes, it was ever so sudden, it was on Monday, I don't know the details because nobody tells me anything around here, but apparently he was duty editor on Sunday and there's been a difference of opinion about us being the only paper not to front-page the royal story, but you didn't hear that from me, all right?

I didn't give a toss whether he'd led the paper on the royal story or the prize crossword. I said, Sheila, would you happen to know if there's still a bundle of my stepdaughter's letters to Sam in his desk?

She says, His desk was cleared by security while he was up seeing Mr Whittington about his pay-off, June. Everything went into a black bin-liner and I suppose it will have been waiting for him at the transport office when he went down to hand over his car keys.

—Could you possibly give me his address, Sheila?

—I can, June, but you won't find him there, from what I gather he's whizzed straight off to Miami, he's got friends there, he's hoping to get work on one of those supermarket tabloids.

Best place for him, I thought. I fully intended to write to him – somebody's bound to be forwarding his mail – but then I thought he's not going to be traipsing your Pauline's letters to Florida and anyway why not let sleeping dogs lie? If they are sleeping dogs, that is.

Tell the truth, I was far more interested in young Sheila's little bit of office gossip. Although I've never counted myself a newspaperwoman I've always got a kick out of these Fleet Street dramas – a sudden firing, an unexpected job switch, a big exclusive, a sensational libel action, a title folding. All human life is there, eh? Or all the human life we were interested in. I always made a point of staying up for you when there was something going on. And you'd finally roll in roaring on all cylinders and get the bottle out and go over the whole story, every detail, every morsel, blow by blow.

And I can just imagine you on Eric Grant's well-deserved come-uppance. The stupid prat, you would have said, if that's a page one story, my prick's a bloater. And we'd sit here chewing over the bones until four in the morning.

As it is now, getting on for. And I've never felt so lonely, not since you went.

He turns out to be a big DIY man. The Suit, that is. Douglas. Duggie, as he'd have me call him. Nothing he cannot do with a Black and Decker. Which is just as well, because he saved my life today. And then your Pauline saved me from what we used to call a fate worse than death. It's been an interesting day all round.

I've started going into the Duke of Clarence of a Sunday morning, did I tell you? No, I know I didn't, and when I say started, I went last Sunday and I've been this, I know I should have mentioned it earlier. Well, they do you a nice Sunday snack-type lunch – Yorkshire pudding with savoury fillings style of thing, not up to my standard, but I have been missing my Yorkshire pudding fix. Because I've given up making a Sunday lunch, I've stopped bothering, there's no satisfaction in cooking for one, not on that scale. I did think of inviting Pauline and Jack over for a Sunday lunch, before they had their bust-up, but I never got round to it.

He wasn't there last Sunday, so don't get the idea into your head I went in looking for him because I didn't, but he was there today, sitting at what I suppose must be his usual little table, sipping half a pint and reading the Sunday you-know-what would you believe. And wearing your suit.

If he hadn't been, I don't suppose I should have recognised him, but I thought it was funny, who wears a suit on Sunday? I mean all the other chaps in the pub were in jeans and T-shirts or jeans and pullies but there he was, looking as if he'd just stepped out of the office. Only he didn't have an office to go to.

He didn't see me come in but I couldn't resist going over after I'd got my half of Guinness and ordered my Yorkshire and rabbit gravy. I had to find a place to sit for one thing and besides, I'm just telling you this as it happened, Sam, he looked so – there's only one word for it, chuck – vulnerable. In fact I'll tell you how I thought he looked: he looked somehow as if he'd just come back from putting flowers on his wife's grave. So that gave us a bond style of thing. Even though his wife was far from dead and buried, much as he'd like her to be. And even though you don't have a grave to put flowers on.

He goes, Well well well, you're the last person I'd expect to see here on a Sunday.

I says, Oh, yes, why's that?

He says, I pictured you round at your married daughter's. (I must have mentioned Pauline to him, although without saying whose daughter she exactly was.)

I felt a bit flustered, he sounded so bold and familiar, though I'm sure without meaning to be anything but friendly. I said, It's news to me that you pictured me doing anything.

He says, and give him credit it was the right thing to say, Don't get me wrong, I only meant that all the widowed people I know, and I know one or two by now, seem to spend their weekends with their families. Because they reckon that's the worst time.

It is and it isn't, I said, though what I meant by that I've no more idea than you, Sam. To change the subject I says, I see you read a particular Sunday paper.

He says, What's particular about it?

I says, It's particular to some people, all newspapers are, do you take it every week?

He says, No, only when I can't get a *Mail on Sunday*.

I says, What do you think of it as a paper then, and before you answer I should mention that my late husband used to do what are called Saturday shifts on it, in his younger days up in Manchester. But ever since coming down south, I told him, he's always worked on the Daily.

Oh yes, he says, and what did he do then? Printer?

I says, Goodness me, no, they don't have printers in this day and age, you're out of touch. No, I says—

And then I told him you were the editor. And do you know, Sam, I still get a thrill of pride when I hear myself saying that. My husband the Editor. And there's less than twenty women in what we used to call Fleet Street can say that.

He says, Well, I suppose someone's got to edit these things.

At least he was honest, and at least he didn't push it. Neither did I. I suppose I could have said something on the lines of, Oh, yes, and what do you mean by that? But then he might have told me, and I didn't want an argument because they'd just called out my number from the kitchen serving hatch and I was ready to murder that Yorkshire pudding and rabbit gravy. I wasn't disloyal, was I, Sam? The rows we've had with civilians, as you called them, who didn't understand tabloid newspapers. I can hear you ranting away now. The gutter, you'd say, performs a vital function, my friend, and never forget it. You'd crucify them. But I can't do it on my own, Sam, for all that together we were like Bonnie and Clyde when anybody started knocking the paper.

That Duke of Clarence Yorkshire pud with rabbit gravy wasn't half bad, I'd recommend it.

But how the thump did we get on the subject of fridges? Oh, I know: I was asking if he cooked for himself, because he'd ordered some lunch for himself as well, shepherd's pie. And he says, Oh, I can boil the usual egg but I don't stray too far from Sainsbury's microwave bags culinary-wise, I don't bother, nothing adventurous anyway. And he says, Anyway, talk about room to swing a cat round, I've got a kitchenette about the size of this table, so even if I did want to cook I wouldn't have the room to do it.

So I says, Well, I haven't seen your kitchenette, but in

nine cases out of ten it's not the size, it's the design. I says, Take mine, for instance, it stretches from one end of the house to the other, yet every time I open my fridge I graze my knuckles against the wall, because of the awkward position it's in.

He says, So why don't you move it, then?

I says, That's easier said than done, we can't move it (funny how I still say we) because it's all built in, it's part of a fitted unit, I'm stuck with it.

He says, Yes, I can see that, if you've got one of these fitted kitchen units, though it sounds to me as if they should have put a bit more care into the design, you ought to write to them. But he says, Why don't you reverse your fridge door?

I says, Reverse the fridge door, how do you mean?

He says, Reverse your fridge door, so instead of opening this way it opens that way.

And he demonstrates with his hands.

I says, thick as they come, But it doesn't open that way, it opens this way.

Same difference, he says.

I says, But in any case, it's not just like changing round an ordinary door, it's a flipping refrigerator.

He says, It doesn't matter what it is, whether it's a fridge or a front door or a back door or a rabbit hutch, a door is a door, take my word for it. He says, Are you the proud possessor of a screwdriver?

I says, Yes of course I've got a screwdriver, don't take me for one of those women who can't use their hands. I says, I've had to, because my husband never could.

Couldn't or wouldn't. You were that shagged out of a weekend that I never had the heart to ask you to put up shelves or anything in that line. Especially because if I did you'd always say, Shelves, shelves, do you think we're living in a bloody strip cartoon, woman? And then if it was anything else you'd say, Look in the bloody Yellow Pages for God's sake, there's people make a living out of that sort of thing, why do you want to do them out of a job, how would you like it if they came round and started editing my newspaper?

Whether you were capable of doing anything handy about the house except in that recurring dream of mine I never really learned, and I've never asked Pauline how she and her mother got on when you lived with them. You once fused all the lights after you'd put a plug on that little fan heater we bought for the spare room, I know that much.

He says, Well this is what you do, after you've taken all your food items out and allowed it to defrost. He says, What model is it?

I told him.

He says, Right, that's the make, but what's the model?

I says, I've absolutely no idea.

He says, Well has it got a door-fitted egg rack?

I says, Yes, it has, as a matter of fact.

He says, Right, now we're getting somewhere, now with that particular model, it's simplicity itself. You should find two screws on top of your door, one on either side, right, and what you do, you unscrew these and put them somewhere safe, say in a saucepan lid.

I says, A saucepan lid, why a saucepan lid?

He says, Or a cup, or a saucer, or an ashtray, anything that's handy, I'm just assuming your fridge is in easy access to a saucepan, like mine. So then what you do, you unscrew your level adjuster assembly.

I says, My what?

He says, What they call your level adjuster assembly, I only know this because I've had occasion to read the instructions, it's what you and I would call the handle.

I says, Right, I've unscrewed the handle and put it in the saucepan lid, now what do I do?

He says, Then there's two more screws to remove, there might be more on your model, in fact just remove all the screws in sight.

—And put them in the saucepan lid.

—Then very carefully lift the fridge door away from the cabinet with a downward motion to disengage it from the middle hinge pin.

I says, Middle hinge pin, I'm sorry, you've lost me.

He says, It's simple really, I'm making it sound more complicated than it is.

I says, No, I'm sorry, I can't take it in, it's not you, Douglas, it's me.

—Duggie. You've to call me Duggie.

—Duggie, then. It's the same with anything technical, my mind blanks off. It's the same with the instructions for the video recorder, I says – they might as well be in Japanese.

He says, They usually are. Then he says, Well, it's up to you, if you don't mind grazing your knuckles every time you open the fridge door. Of course, you could always wear an oven glove.

He has quite a sense of humour.

I says, Well, they must have a maintenance service, I suppose they're quite capable of coming over and changing a door round.

He says, Cost you an arm and a leg, love, besides, how old is it? Because they'll probably try and sell you a new fridge, don't forget they're all on commission, this day and age. He says, I'll tell you what, though, if you'd like me to come over and do it for you one of these days, I'd be only too happy. He says, Do you live locally, it's only a ten-minute job, no problem at all.

I says, Oh, I couldn't put you to the trouble.

He says, Are you going home after this? I'll walk back with you, honestly there's nothing I like to do more after my lunchtime shepherd's pie than take a fridge door off its hinges. Mark you, he says with a wink, knocking back his half pint, there's no guarantee I can get it back on again.

So that was that. Talked me into it. And why did I encourage him, or put it this way, Sam, fair's fair, why did I not discourage him? Company. I wanted a bit of company. I mean at home. I wanted to hear another human voice in that house, because apart from Pauline coming round at all hours and the telly blaring away and the odd telephone call, and that ratbag Eric Grant barging in, the only voice I've heard for many a week now is mine, talking to myself.

We get back to my place, as I shall have to get used to calling it, and I could see he was impressed. Very nice, he kept on saying as he took it all in, very nice indeed. As of course it is very nice, mainly thanks to you, my love, who made it all possible, and I could tell it was on the tip of his tongue to say, You've done very well for yourself, which I'm very glad he didn't and I don't think would have done, for fear of being taken the wrong way. But do you know, Sam, I wouldn't have minded. I *have* done well for myself, no question, and I was pleased and proud for him to see what you've made for me and done for me and left for me. So there. And if I have one regret it's that my mother never lived to see it too, after chuntering on as she did about what a big mistake I was making running away with a married man. I'd make her look round at all my bits and pieces, my thimble collection, my Staffordshire dogs and shepherdesses that you've bought me over the years, my commemorative plates, and I'd say, Well, Mam, who's the flibbertigibbet now?

I show him into the kitchen and he throws open the fridge door, meaning only to see how far it swings back, but of course it's like a greyhound out of a trap is that door as you well know, and before he knows it, it's got his hand trapped against the wall.

Yes, he says, I see what you mean. And he sets to with the

idea of helping me empty the freezer compartment, which is what has to be done first, apparently.

Now except for diving into it for the ice cube tray I don't think I've had that freezer open since you went, Sam, in fact I know I haven't, what little I do eat comes out of the fridge itself, usually bought that same day. There was a vegetable flan in there that I was going to give you for your supper on that last Friday you went off to work, if you came home in time – or as things worked out if you'd ever made it back for supper at all instead of being carted off in the ambulance.

The last supper: a Waitrose's mixed vegetable flan. Oh, Sam, Sam.

Now stop it, June, you're getting maudlin.

As I did when I set eyes on that vegetable flan after all that time. My eyes prickled, I can tell you.

Maybe he sensed I was becoming upset, because he says, all brisk, Well, I don't know whether it's your thermostat playing up or what, but I don't reckon this unit needs defrosting at all.

I says, Probably not, it wasn't done all that very long ago, come to think of it.

And come to think of it, that set me thinking back too.

He starts going on about, Only you can't be too careful, keeping frozen goods at too low a temperature, because there is such a thing as salmonella, or do I mean listeria?

But I wasn't listening. As I say, I was thinking back.

It was the last time we went to bed together, Sam, about two weeks before you were taken to hospital. Or it could have been three. God knows we were never at it like knives, apart from the few months before we started living together, when if you recall you had permanently grazed knees from us doing it on the carpet in your little office that you had at that time, after everybody else'd gone – because of course I was still living at my mother's and couldn't give her any good reason why I should want to move out. But after we got together, we settled down rather quickly, didn't we, eh? Perhaps too quickly.

It was understandable. You were moving up the ladder and climbing those rungs had more to offer you than any staircase. The job kept you occupied long after any sane person's bedtime. So it got to be weekends, then every second weekend, then every third weekend, if that – you were always so tensed up and shagged out after five days at the coalface as you called it, all you wanted to do on your days off was relax. I didn't mind, honest to God. I'd plenty to be going on with in my life and it got to be that when it did happen, it was a bonus. And I enjoyed it. As a general rule.

So where were we? The fridge. This particular night I didn't know when to expect you, you hadn't rung up as you usually do – did – at some point in the evening when you had a moment, and you know me, I never liked to disturb you at the office unless I had to. So I thought I'd wait up at least until you phoned, and then I thought, if I am waiting up, I might as well defrost the fridge, it'll save me a job tomorrow.

And I'd got everything out and all the frozen stuff wrapped in three layers of newspaper on the kitchen table, and I was just reaching down for a couple of baking trays out of the cupboard to catch the drips when you came rolling in. I hadn't even heard the car. Naturally, you were half cut – been celebrating what's-his-name-again, ginger-haired chap, getting made up to chief sub-editor. A fat lot of chief subbing he must have done that evening.

You were that good-humoured, I thought you'd brought someone home with you. You were practically singing. I said something about had you had any supper and you roared, Supper! Supper! I'll tell you what I want for my supper!

And with that you threw your arms around me and you

– well, you know very well what you did. I'm only surprised we didn't christen the kitchen table.

I says, What's got into you tonight, then?

And you went, It's not what's got into me, lass, it's what's going into thee!

You always lapsed into broad Lancashire when you'd anything vulgar to say. Not that I minded. It saved me heating up a frozen pizza.

So you poured us a drink apiece and we went upstairs. And I'll say this: considering the state you were in, it was very good. I won't say the earth moved, but that bed did. And that was the very last time, and I'm glad to have the memory of it.

Of course, what did wipe the smile off my face was when I came down to lock up and switch off, for you were spark out by then, only to find the kitchen floor swimming in water, because of course there was the fridge merrily defrosting itself and I'd never got round to putting in the baking trays to catch the drips, had I?

A funny thing to be remembering of a Sunday afternoon with a strange man taking off his jacket, your jacket I should say, in my kitchen. I took the liberty of pouring him one of your beers – there's still a six-pack in the fridge doing nothing – and got him the screwdriver he wanted, then left him to it, though not before I'd plonked the saucepan lid he'd been going on about on the kitchen table by way of my little joke, for him to put the screws into. He has such a nice smile, Sam. Warm. You don't mind my saying this? You will when you hear what's coming.

I busied myself in the living room doing nothing very much, straightening cushions and that, and trying to keep what I can only describe as certain thoughts out of my head. Not what you'd call lustful thoughts, I mean nothing graphic, or even pornographic come to that, nothing to be ashamed of – only how, to put it plainly, I could do just for once with going to bed with somebody again. I believe it's common enough in early widowhood. Late widowhood too, for all I know.

In no time at all he comes to the doorway in his shirt sleeves and he says, Right, now would you like to come through and test your latest-model left-handed fridge?

I says, You've never done it already?

I was that flustered, as if he'd caught me half-undressed. All I was doing was straightening a few newspapers. My heart was pounding. I can't explain it, Sam, any more than I've done already. He's not the greatest catch in the world – I should never have looked at him twice if he hadn't been wearing your suit. But all alone with a man in my own house on a Sunday afternoon – and him in his shirtsleeves, too. It set my blood racing.

We go through and true to his word he's got that fridge door opening smooth as you like in the opposite direction to what it was, away from the wall instead of towards it. With not a scratch and no sign that it's ever been touched.

So it's goodbye scraped knuckles, he says, as I swung the door open once or twice, just to test it.

I says, Well, I can't thank you enough, Duggie, will you let me give you a drink for your trouble?

He says, If by a drink you do mean a drink, June, fair enough, but offer me anything else and I shall be mortally offended.

I nearly blurted it out there and then, but I didn't, I held it back. Credit yourself with just that little bit of dignity, June, I said to myself.

Help yourself, I says, my voice shaking a bit, and he pours himself another beer. I could have done with one myself, my throat was dry.

Cheers, he says, holding up his glass. Then taking a look around the kitchen he says, Now is there anything else I can do for you while I'm here, any other little task, you've only got to say the word, leaking taps our speciality.

And I said it. I'm sorry, Sam, but I did:

—I suppose a fuck's out of the question?

Why I had to put it like that I shall never know. Either it was a compulsion, like that swearing disorder I've read about, somebody's syndrome, I can't remember what it's called, same reason I had to hold myself back from blurting it out to Eric Grant that time, when I'd rather start an affair with a monkey on a stick than have it off with him; or I wanted to shock The Suit into doing something about it and getting it over with without a lot of gooey preliminaries; or I wanted to shock myself – maybe out of a deep sleep. Anyway, I did say it, for the first and last time ever.

He wasn't exactly spluttering his beer but I could see him having trouble gulping it back. He puts his beer can down on the kitchen table and his hand's shaking. No more than mine, I can tell you.

He says, Would you mind saying that again, June?

I says, I don't chew my cabbages twice.

He says, Are you serious?

I says, Never more so.

He says, But are you sure?

I says, No, I'm not sure at all so don't push your luck, lad, I'm not exactly begging for it, do you want to come upstairs or not?

All words that came out wrong. They must have made me sound like a bit of Manchester Piccadilly brass.

He says, Yes, of course I do, it's been a long time for me too, you know.

I says, How do you know it's been a long time for me?

He says, Because I do know it, you're not that kind of – Then he breaks off.

I says, That kind of girl? No, you're right there, I says, and

I don't usually come out with what I've just come out with, so don't think I do.

And during all this we hadn't touched one another. He says, awkwardly, Shall we take a drink up?

Now I didn't like that at all, Sam. It would have reminded me of that time we had together. This sounds daft, I know, but it would have made me feel unfaithful. Funny how you can adjust your moral standards to suit your own needs. Reminds me of that girl you told me about who wouldn't let her boyfriends touch her left boob because that was the one she was keeping for her fiancé in the navy.

So I said, quite coldly, No, I don't want a drink, let's just go up before I change my mind.

He takes hold of my elbows and he says, very earnestly, Which you can do at any time you like, June, now you do know that, don't you?

Whether he was genuinely concerned for my welfare or just covering himself in case I turned round and accused him of rape I couldn't say. The former, I hope. I nodded, and he follows me upstairs.

But there's a happy ending, Sam – for you at any rate. We'd just got to the turn in the landing when there's a sharp ring on the doorbell. Talk about being on cue.

He says, Don't answer it.

I says, I'd better do, it could be one of my nosey neighbours with a parcel or something, and they would have seen us coming in.

So we troll downstairs again. I open the front door and it's your Pauline, clutching a pair of suitcases.

Saved by the bell, eh?

But who knows, pet, I might not have fancied him once he had taken your suit off.

She didn't believe for a second he was only there to fix the fridge door, of course. No reason why she should, considering what we'd been about to get up to. And she'd probably caught our outlines on the stairs through the coloured glass in the front door. Still: none of her business.

I made a joke of it. I says, Now, Pauline, you've already met your father's suit – well, this is my friend Douglas, wearing it.

But I was in far from a joking mood. I was not best pleased, I can tell you. It wasn't so much that she'd prevented The Suit – or The Trousers as he was at that moment in time, seeing as he was in his shirtsleeves, and to my guilty mind looking next door to naked – from having his evil way with me, or to be more honest me having my evil way with him. I didn't care about that, the moment had passed, gone with the wind, and it was a relief if you want to know, Sam, I was glad not to have made a fool of myself. No, it was her barging in with her luggage like that, as if this was a bed and breakfast place I'm running. Even if I was, I should have expected her to book. What does she think telephones are for? I could have been having a coffee morning, I could have gone away for the weekend, I could have been in the bath, I could have been doing what she knows very well I was just about to do. What got my goat was her assumption, or do I mean presumption, that I'd nothing better to occupy myself with than sitting around waiting for her to leave her husband and holding myself ready to rush upstairs and make her bed up.

I says, trying to be civil, So the balloon's gone up, has it?

She says, with a look at The Suit as if he's something she's found in her salad, We'll talk about it later.

He's not slow to take a hint, you can say that for him. He says, Don't worry about me, Pauline, it is Pauline isn't it, I was just on my merry way.

I wasn't having your daughter coming in and turning my guests out on to the street, I'm very sorry but I wasn't.

I says, There's no hurry, Duggie, you've a can of beer in the kitchen you haven't finished.

He says, I'll just knock it back while I'm getting my jacket and putting your screwdriver away, then I'll be making tracks, I'm sure you two have got a lot to talk about.

He goes into the kitchen. I says to Pauline in a low voice, Couldn't you have rung?

She says with a catty smile, as if I'd just made a little joke, I can see I should have done.

The Suit comes back with his jacket over his arm. He says from the doorway, speaking loudly and slowly as if the pair of us had just been struck stone deaf, Well, June, I think you'll find that fridge door's no trouble now, but if it does start playing up you know where to find me, I'm in the Duke of Clarence most lunchtimes, in fact I should be in there tomorrow if you have any problems.

I could have shaken the daft beggar. He might just as well have said in so many words, Meet me tomorrow, same time, same place, and we'll start again where we left off.

Which I had no intention of doing. Not this week, and not next week either. But you never say never, do you? That's what you always told me, anyway. It was another of your fortune cookie sayings.

He takes himself off, and to stop Pauline rolling her eyes and looking as if she were entitled to an explanation, as soon as I've shut the front door on him I remove myself to the kitchen to put the kettle on. And it's a good job I did, because otherwise she'd have taken it upon herself to start making the tea while I put my feet up, as she likes to say. She's got this thing about how I should always be putting my feet up, has your daughter. And if she had gone into the kitchen she would have found the note he left on the kitchen table, the silly article, scribbled on the back of one of those trade cards they shove through the door and that always finish up in the fruit bowl for some reason. BETTER LUCK NEXT TIME. RING ME. And there's his phone number.

Talk about pushing it.

I expected her to follow me into the kitchen so as not to waste any yakkity-yakking time, but instead, when I get back into the living room with the tea things, she's only lugging the second of her suitcases up the stairs, the first one as it turns out already being up there.

I thought, Make yourself at home, Pauline, do.

Now I don't want you to think I've got it in for your daughter, Sam, but there is such a thing as waiting for an invitation before moving into somebody's second bedroom. All right, so I don't expect I could have turned her away, but it is nice to be asked.

You know, it's a funny thing, Sam, but when you've lost somebody, there's a class of people who seem to think they can walk all over you – that they can come in and just take over, pouring drinks, making cups of cocoa, boiling soup up, or in her case simply moving in. They mean well, I'm sure, although I'm prepared to make an exception in Pauline's case, but why do they imagine they've got the run of the household? You feel like saying, Look, it's my husband I've lost, not the use of my flipping limbs. Or my wits, come to that.

I said, You take a lot on yourself, Pauline, don't you?

She says, Oh, I thought this would be the one place where I'd be made welcome, June, but if you want me to go I'll go.

I says, No one's asking you to go, Pauline.

And that was a flat lie for a start.

But I says, I could have done with a bit of warning, I'm not used to people dropping in out of the blue and as you must have gathered it wasn't the most convenient of times.

I thought, Get your twopennorth in first, June, put her on the defensive. And I was right.

She said, No, I'm sorry about that, June.

And that was the last we heard about The Suit. For this day, anyway.

But she says, It all happened so quickly and so unexpectedly, just let me get this case up into my room then I'll come down and tell you the whole story.

Did you hear that, Sam? My room, she says. Did you ever tell her it was her room? If so, it wasn't in my hearing. And it must be sixteen years since she last stayed here overnight, so how does it come to be her room?

I said, How do you know I want to be told the whole story? But I said it to myself. And truth to tell, I did quite want to hear it, so long as she kept it short. I know I could hardly have cared less the last time she was moaning and groaning about her troubles with Jack, but just now, after that narrow escape with The Suit as I'd already forced myself to think of it, I was of a mood for keeping my mind off myself.

You're not going to believe what she had to tell me, Sam. Or maybe you are – she's your only daughter, you know her better than I do. But I'm not at all sure I ought to be passing it on. If it doesn't suit, lad, blame yourself. This was your idea, not mine.

I says to her, after she's had me up and down those stairs like a yo-yo wanting padded coat hangers and God knows what all, Right, Pauline, and now if you've made yourself quite at home, you can get down to the nitty-gritty, you've walked out on him, we can all see that, but let's have the blow-by-blow account, did you catch him red-handed with his fancy woman or what?

She says, No, I'm sorry to say it was the other way round, June, I don't want to shock you I'm sure but I'm afraid he caught me red-handed with my fancy man, more or less anyway.

I was that surprised, but I didn't show it, or I hope I didn't.

I says, looking very woman of the world, Oh, yes, it was a case of two can play at that game, was it, well between these four walls I can't say I blame you.

She says, Something like that, June, but to be quite frank with you it wasn't tit for tat or anything you can do I can do better or anything of that sort, it was just somebody I happened to flip for, the hair conditioner rep who comes into the nail clinic now we've expanded into trichology. Whether it would have happened if Jack hadn't been putting himself about I couldn't say, probably not, maybe he was just the right guy in the right place at the right time but that we'll never know, will we?

It wasn't for me to make judgments one way or the other, but the thought did stray into my mind, was this the first time Pauline's wandered off the straight and narrow? Just asking. But somehow, looking at her in a new light and being wise after the event and all that, I begged leave to doubt it.

I says, And how did your Jack find out, or did you tell him?

Meaning did she tell him out of spite, but I didn't say that.

She says, No, somebody saw us in a steak bar in Shaftesbury Avenue while Jack was either in Birmingham or pretending to be, and as luck would have it whoever it was seems to have known Len, that's the bloke I've been seeing, as well as me, so when Jack hears about it the balloon goes up as you quite rightly say, unknown to me when I start trying to talk my way out of it he's already been round to see Len and got the full confession, silly berk that he is, Len I mean, so of course I didn't have a leg to stand on.

I says, This Len, is he married?

She says, I don't think I need answer that, June, if he wasn't married I'd be round at his place instead of sitting here with you, now wouldn't I?

Nice to be second choice, I thought. And how I wish she could have had her first choice. I said, And has he any plans for leaving his wife?

—No, they've got two kiddies.

Of course they have.

—And are you going on seeing him?

—No, Jack seems to have put the fear of God in him, his wife's not very well, she's subject to severe depressions apparently, and he's frightened of upsetting her in any way.

God, I thought that line had gone out with *My Weekly*.

I says, So how have you left things with Jack, then, is it all over or are you both cooling off?

She says, No, it's all over, June, and not even bar the shouting, after some of the things he said to me I wouldn't go back even if he begged me on his bended, which I know he wouldn't, she says, because those suitcases I've brought with me, she says, I didn't pack them, he did, and I haven't walked out as you put it, he threw me out.

So there we are. Her husband won't have her back and her fancy man doesn't want her. What am I supposed to do, Sam? Put an advert in the *Private Eye* personals – Fun-loving Thirty-something Seeks Live-in Partner, Must Have Own Flat? Because she's not staying here for ever and a day, I can tell you that much. Jack's not the only one who can pack her suitcases for her.

She's a deep one, though, your Pauline. There's been others before this Len, I'd swear to it, and I'd like to hear the full story of how her Jack came to go off the rails, although I don't suppose I ever shall.

I had one of my panic attacks last night. I'm saying last night, it was more like three in the morning. Night has no terrors, did I once say? I spoke too soon. I should have told you about it there and then but what could I have said?

I'm frightened, Sam, I'm frightened? And what could you have said, if you could have said anything? Get yourself up, lass, pour yourself a big slug of brandy and watch whatever rubbish you can find on the box at that hour. I should have done just that, but I couldn't trust my legs to get me downstairs.

I'm having them every two or three weeks, usually after something's happened to upset me, in this case your Pauline's arrival. And always when I'm in bed and I've woken up and can't get off again, which is just as well because if I had one in the middle of Marks and Spencer or Sainsbury's and I started shaking as I do, I wouldn't know where to put myself.

It's the kind of lurch in the stomach feeling you get when you wake up convinced there's a burglar in the house. And I lie there all of a tremble, thinking, What am I going to do? What am I going to do?

I'll tell you what these spells remind me of, Sam. When I was a little girl and I'd lie awake far into the night worrying about who'd look after me if my mother died, or what if I came home from school and she'd vanished, or the house itself wasn't there any more for some strange reason. And then I'd start wondering how I'd get on when I was grown up. Who'd take care of me? What if I couldn't earn enough to pay the rent? What if I was ill, who'd fetch the doctor? What if nobody would marry me?

Except now there's no what if about it. It's here, and I'm here. What am I going to do?

It can't go on yet it will go on. I can't take any more of it yet I have to. It's got to have all been a big mistake and perhaps it is but there's no rubbing out and starting again. Onwards and downwards. And then comes the panic. It's like being buried alive.

I get out of it by taking big deep breaths while at the same time thinking how much worse it could be. I could have murdered you and have you buried in the garden. Or you could have lingered on helpless and speechless for years and years. Is that worse? At least it'd give me something to do, somewhere to go. And if I did have you in bin-liners under the compost heap at least I could pass the time building a rockery.

What am I going to do? What am I to do about the compost heap, it just keeps on mouldering, am I supposed to turn it over with the garden fork or what? And the grass keeps on growing and I haven't the first idea how to start that mower. And the house insurance, when is it due, do they send you a reminder or what? And how do I claim if the house catches fire? They should have a school for widows. Maybe I should start it myself. What am I going to do?

What am I to do about the damp in the spare bedroom? Your Pauline's already complained about it and she's only been here five minutes. Do you know what she had the cheek to suggest this morning? Only that she moves into our bedroom with me until I get it seen to.

I put my foot down. I said, I'm very sorry, Pauline, I value my privacy.

She says, Oh, I thought I'd be company for you, because I know what it can be like, being all alone in the long night hours.

Thanks a bundle, Pauline, I'd rather have the panic attacks.

So then she says, So what are you doing about that damp, June, because you know it'll only get worse if you leave it, don't you?

I says, Pauline, I've got more to worry about than damp patches in spare bedrooms, if you don't like it here you know what you can do.

She says, Well don't blame me if I pass on a streaming cold.

What if I'm found dead and eaten by maggots? It's almost worth having your Pauline here not to have to face that prospect. But she's not staying here for ever, you know, so she needn't think she is.

Thank God she's got a job to go to. Ten past nine and she's off to that nail clinic where she works and I shan't see her again till after five. And in future, I shan't have to see her at breakfast even, because I've no intention of coming down until she's gone. But what am I going to do? This isn't what I want, Sam. I want a husband, I want you. Now I've got a lodger that I don't even like. What am I going to do?

I drift off back to sleep at last by thinking of dafter and dafter things to worry about, like supposing I took myself off on holiday, because God knows I could do with one, and I can't find my passport, would I be able to get a refund? And where *is* my passport come to that, Sam Pepper, you had it last?

You did, you know, when it was due for renewal. Because Give it to me, woman, you said, let the foreign desk look after it, they've got bugger all else to do. Did you ever get it back? And where's your own passport, anyway, much use that it is now? They'll be together, wherever they are, in your desk probably, I hope so anyway because if they're not, one of us is in trouble . . .

I wake up feeling headachy and not so much depressed as washed-out, with so little energy that if I see a scrap of paper on the floor or a spot of milk on the kitchen table, I can't put myself to the bother of clearing it up, I'll just stare at it and think to myself I ought to get a J-cloth and what on earth is wrong with me, am I going down with something or what? Then I remind myself, You already *are* down with something, June, it's called bereavement, for God's sake get some clothes on and take yourself out, the tea's cold, the toast's cold, and you've done nothing but stare at that crack in the kitchen wall for an hour.

The fridge door has started creaking, and whether it's my imagination or not I think it might be beginning to sag. So that's something else to worry about. But I shan't ring him, Sam, so don't go thinking I will. And should I chance to bump into him in the Duke of Clarence, I wouldn't dream of mentioning it. If the bloody door looks as if it's coming off its hinges, I'll turn to the Yellow Pages.

I dragged myself out at last to do a bit of shopping, and while I did go past the Duke of Clarence I didn't go in, I wouldn't have known what to say to him, and anyway if it turned out he thought we were having a fling it would have to be the end of a beautiful friendship. So I thought I'd allow a cooling-off period as it's called in those life assurance documents I've been having to browse through.

I've been saying it's a good thing I don't have these panic attacks in the middle of Sainsbury's or wherever, but I nearly did, in Grisby's, that department store. What I was doing in there we shall never know, because there was nothing I needed, I'd just drifted in killing time I suppose, and the next thing I know I'm on the escalator waltzing up to Men's Clothing. I must have been in a daze. So then I'm wandering about among all this casual wear and racks of suits and blazers and I become aware that every which way I look there's middle-aged husbands trying things on in front of full-length mirrors while middle-aged wives hold their jackets and tug and pull at their lapels and sleeves to see if they're about to try and buy something that doesn't fit. And I wanted to cry, What about me? What about me? There was a nice lemon pullover that you would have liked, Sam. I would have bought it for your birthday, and that's coming up soon, don't even let me think about it. You always liked a yellow pullie.

I had to get out. They don't seem to have a downward escalator so I found a flight of stairs, but I went down them that fast in my eagerness to escape from Men's Clothing that I missed my footing and wrenched my ankle, so that by the time I was through the revolving doors and out on the street

I was hobbling. Nothing to write home about, a bit swollen by now but I'll live; but as I reached the Duke of Clarence again it was throbbing that much I was beginning to think I'd broken something.

You're ahead of me now, aren't you? Yes, I did go in. I badly wanted a sit-down and I was ready to murder a Guinness and a sandwich. But if you're thinking I set out with that intention, that I lured myself into the Duke of Clarence so to speak, you're quite mistaken.

The Suit was there all right – he would be, wouldn't he? – and ever so solicitous he was about the ankle. He says, Put an old-fashioned poultice on it, you won't take it the wrong way if I say you're old enough to know what a bread poultice is, and if it's still painful tomorrow morning get yourself round to the doctor's, because although you can walk on it you could have broken a small bone.

I said, The only bread poultice I want is a ham bap with a glass of Guinness, let me give you the money so I can have a sit-down, and have one yourself, Douglas.

He comes back from the bar and sees that I'm resting my leg up on the stool he's been sitting on. Well, he says, pulling up another one, that gets us off on the right foot!

I did tell you he has a sense of humour.

I'd wondered and wondered, about when I saw him next, whether to take the bull by the horns and say something on the lines of, Well, talk about life's embarrassing moments, eh, I'm sorry Pauline had to burst in like that but who knows, maybe it was all for the best.

Or whether I should have left it to him to raise the subject and then said, Douglas, Duggie, before you go any further I think this is one of those cases where the least said's soonest mended, let's leave it at that, shall we, now then, what have you been doing with yourself?

It didn't go like that at all.

He says, Now June, before you take the froth off that

Guinness, will you just let me say one thing and one thing only and get it over with?

I says, It depends what the one thing is.

—That note that I left for you on your kitchen table, I was definitely out of order there, June, I can only say it was in the heat of the moment kind of thing, I only hope your daughter didn't see it.

I said, She isn't my daughter, she's my stepdaughter as luck would have it and no, she didn't, thank goodness, or I should never have heard the last of it. But I said, Think no more about it, it was quite understandable in the circumstances, no harm done, we were neither of us ourselves, now can we just put it behind us and forget the whole episode.

He says, You've taken the words out of my mouth, June, whatever could have happened didn't happen and that's that, there's no going back on these things, take my word for it. Then he goes on, all sprightly, So she's your stepdaughter, is she? I conclude from the suitcases she must be moving in with you for a while.

I was that relieved at having turned that awkward corner I blathered out the whole Pauline saga from start to finish.

After I'd finished he drains his glass and says, Well, she's still a young woman and quite easy on the eye, so I don't suppose she'll be under your feet for very long.

I says, It's to be hoped not.

But I was glad he'd got the message that Pauline had moved in, just in case he was contemplating trying his luck with your not so merry widow again, Sam. Not that I think he would because he's turned out to be a real gentleman I'm happy to say.

I was taking it for granted we'd be having another round but instead he stands up with a glance at his watch and says, Well, wish me luck, June, job interview, complete waste of time at my age but they expect you to go through the motions, in fact they insist on it. And he says, And don't think any more about what we were talking about, put it right out of your mind, no problem.

And off he blows.

I felt that desolate after he'd gone, I could have cried. Nothing to do with The Suit, you understand – I wanted someone to talk to, that's all. It's just the way I've been feeling, after this latest bout of the panics.

I'm afraid it's become one of those days when I get to thinking how pointless it all is. Take no notice, pet, it's only my mood. Next thing you know I'll be asking, What's it all about, June?

Do you think I should get a cat?

It's been going through my mind, off and on. Something to tickle under the chin. Something to stroke, that purrs back at you. A mouth to feed. Something to look after.

I wouldn't mind a cat, Sam. I don't see myself going so far as to take myself down to the cats' home and asking for one, but if I found a little tabby miaowing on the doorstep I'd take it in, I know I would.

But then what if it vanished – because they do, cats. Or got itself run over, poor thing. I couldn't cope with that, not on top of you going. And there's no way I'm ever going to get you back with a notice on a tree, is there?

Yes, yes, I do know what a cat really is – substitute child, same as a dog is supposed to be a substitute slave. Or so we were assured by one of your bright sparks interviewing some non-existent leading psychiatrist when you'd nothing better to fill one of your feature pages. Honestly, some of the rubbish you printed.

Should we have had kiddies?

What a question. You didn't want them, I didn't want them, so where's the point in an inquest now? All right, maybe I didn't want them because you didn't want them, but we'd be here for ever if we got started on that, and I haven't got for ever, yet, even if you have.

They could be in their early twenties or late teens by now. Probably on drugs – I must say that was one of the fears I had. That and them being run over, like the cat. Would they have been a comfort? They would have been someone to fuss over, anyway, and let's hope they would have fussed over me. Would we have had any grandchildren? I should like to have grandchildren, now, more than I ever wanted children, then.

Who knows these things? What might have been? Ah well, it'll all be the same in a hundred years as you used to say. A hundred years? If I only live to be as old as my mother when she went, it'll all be the same in twenty years. Talk about brief lives. How short they are, and it's only through family we can make them longer. Yes, I do wish we'd had one, Sam, so now you know.

I didn't bother to have another glass of Guinness. I hobbled home and bathed my foot, still feeling sorry for myself, and for once I was almost looking forward to your Pauline coming back from work.

Did I say, I'm toying with the notion of taking a job? Oxfam shop, Samaritans, that sort of thing. Well, perhaps not the Samaritans, even if they'd have me, which they probably wouldn't considering I believe doing away with yourself is about the most selfish act a person can commit, which is why I've never contemplated it even in my blackest moments, not that there's anyone who gives two shakes of a pig's bottom whether I'm alive or dead. I'd get angry with them, that'd be my trouble. I should say, Self, self, self, is that all you ever think about, what about those that love you, who'd have to cope after you've gone? I don't know, though – it could just be the right approach, maybe I'd make a good Samaritan after all. Good Samaritan, Sam. One of my jokes.

But the Oxfam shop I shouldn't mind. That or the Sue Ryder Foundation or similar, three or four afternoons a week, say. There's not much else I could do. I did think of asking the paper if they needed any casual secretarial help, I wouldn't have minded a whiff of the newsroom again after all these years, but then I thought, Don't be so daft, June, all those girls have been on one computer course after another in this day and age, you couldn't handle a VDU to save your life. Untrained, you see. Unequipped to be a widow, except full-time. Because you were dead set against my ever going back to work, weren't you, Sam? Yes you were. You don't need to, girl, you'd say, I'm earning for both of us now, and besides, I don't want you tired when we've got to go out of an evening to all these functions.

What you meant was you didn't want your wife working as a lowly secretary while you were shinning up the ladder to become the great I Am, it's true, isn't it, go on, admit it.

Voluntary work you would probably have stood for but for some reason the thought never crossed my mind. Too busy doing nothing, I suppose. Frittering the years away as if there was an endless supply where they came from.

I should be glad of something to occupy myself, though. Only how do you go about getting yourself taken on? Do you just walk in and ask if they could do with another pair of hands, or do you write, or what? I should be quite put out if after I'd got all braced up to put myself forward they said they didn't need anybody just at present, thank you very much.

I mentioned it to your Pauline but she was as much help as a fart in a barrel, as you so elegantly used to put it. Which reminds me, Sam – the first time you ever took me to No. 10 Downing Street, and I was terrified. But you said, you said, All you've got to remember, lass, is that no matter how grand they are, under their dress suits and evening frocks they're all silently farting, the same as you and me.

And I said, going pink I'm sure, Speak for yourself, Sam Pepper. And you said, I'm speaking for both of us. I was that mortified. But it did the trick.

But your Pauline. Oh, she says, well if it's a part-time job you're after, June, I might just be able to help, I mean I know the Nail Boutique's not looking for anyone in the receptionist line at present but bear in mind we've got six branches this side of the river and there's always someone wanting holiday reliefs or as it might be a stand-in for someone who's on maternity leave, would you like me to put in a word with Gerry next time he comes in, he's the area general manager?

I says, No, you miss the point, Pauline, it's voluntary work I'm looking for, just something to take me out of myself. Because it'll do me good, I says, to know I'm helping some of those more fortunate than myself.

She says, without a glimmer, You mean less fortunate, don't you, June?

There's someone else who doesn't appreciate my little jokes.

I did ever such a silly thing this morning. I bought your tartan dressing gown back off the Oxfam shop. I did. Only £2.15 – quite a bargain, considering what I paid for it in the first place. It was a Christmas present, if you remember. I got it at the Scotch House, same time as I bought those Edinburgh Castle coasters and table mats for your brother Derek and Marion's silver wedding anniversary.

No, only I'd steeled myself to go into Oxfam and ask if they wanted any part-time help. As it so happens the lady was busy serving somebody, so I thought I'd just have a mooch round the shop and see if they've sold all the stuff of yours I fetched in soon after you passed away. They have, most of it. All four of your suits have gone, including as we know The Suit, and all the jackets and trousers – as they should have done, it was all good stuff and well looked after. The shoes I'm not sure about, because frankly I can't tell one pair of shoes from another, even yours. The casual wear I couldn't swear to either, whether it's gone or not, because all the pullies and sweaters and what have you are all in a heap where people go constantly rummaging. There was a red V-neck that could have been one of yours, and I'd just picked it up to have a skeg at the label when I saw your dressing gown, hanging up on its own on a hook next to an inner door, for all the world as if you'd just popped in for a quick bath.

Oh, my heart did jump. It does me no good at all, y'know, all this pounding and lurching and pummelling in my chest, I shall finish up one of these days with a heart attack like you, if this goes on.

It did look forlorn, though, all on its lonesome against that bare distempered wall. And a bit seedy and shabby in the glare of the fluorescent light. Well, you'd had it over five years after all, and it's nobody's business how much cigarette ash and spilled whisky and bacon fat it's absorbed.

Even then, I didn't mean to buy it. I mean to say, what would I want it for, why would I have given it away in the first place? It's far too big for me, and the only constructive thing I could do with it would be to take it up the street to the Sue Ryder charity shop, which would be downright bloody ridiculous.

But I just had to touch it, feel it, and that's what I was doing when the lady comes up behind me. Of course she doesn't remember me fetching it in in the first place, no reason why she should, if it comes to that I don't remember her either, they presumably have a rota which of course was what I had come to ask about.

She says, If you're interested in that I should point out it's a man's dressing gown in actual fact, but there's no reason why it couldn't be unisex I suppose.

I found myself saying, Yes, I know it's a man's, it's for my husband.

Why I said that I shall never know.

But now that it had come to it I found I couldn't get the words out that I'd been rehearsing to myself all morning, I just couldn't bring myself to say, Oh, while I'm here, I'm wondering if you ever need any help at all, I've got time hanging on my hands these days and I'd be more than happy to come in for a few hours a week, whether it's serving or sorting out the stock or whatever there is needs doing, I couldn't help noticing you seem a bit short-staffed if you don't mind me saying so.

Because what if she'd said, Oh, delighted to have you aboard, you can start tomorrow as far as I'm concerned? And then when tomorrow came she said, And how does your husband like his tartan dressing gown?

So instead I said, How much is it?

And that, our Sam, is how I come to be the proud possessor of your dressing gown. It's hanging behind the bedroom door again, where it belongs.

Whether it was with the notion of taking a part-time job being at the back of my mind or not I don't know, but I've had a sudden yen to go down to the office, and today I went through with it. You don't mind, Sam, do you? I didn't show you up through weeping and wailing.

I thought I'd take young Sheila to lunch, she's been ever so kind to me whenever I've rung up, and she was all for it, Any time, June, she says, just say the word, there's a very nice place I go to if you're into vegetarian food at all, it's only round the corner from here but why don't you come up to the office first, say hello to a few of your old mates?

So I did. And I was that pleased after I'd asked for Sheila at the front desk, because who should come down with her but Bob Carp himself? I mean to say the editor, coming down to the lobby in person, in his shirtsleeves – it's unheard of, except for the Prime Minister or Prince Charles or whoever, in which case of course he would have put a jacket on. But I was very touched, Sam. I was made to feel really welcome.

Though not by all and sundry, I have to say. We didn't go up in the executive lift, he shepherds me into the staff lift, so he could walk me through the newsroom. The pretty way, as you used to call it.

All manner of people came up to say hello as we passed through, I felt like the Queen on walkabout. People I've known for donkey's years, people whose names I've forgotten, people whose names I never knew. And it was all Hello, June, how nice to see you, how are you keeping, you're looking well, what have you been doing with yourself, what brings you to this neck of the woods or couldn't you keep away? That columnist you took on, Barbara, comes over and gives me a big soppy kiss and I don't think I've exchanged more than ten words with her in my life. They couldn't have been kinder.

But there were just one or two, naming no names, who were really embarrassed. The way they turned away or pretended to be studying their computer screens, you would have thought I'd just been let out of Holloway. One certain person, that I've had many and many a drink with in your office, leaps out of his chair when he sees me coming down the newsroom and bolts into the gents'. I like to think he's skulking in there still, in case I haven't gone yet.

I can't really say I blame them. It takes a lot of people that way, especially men – there's neighbours who'll cross the street sooner than stop and have a word. Death makes them feel awkward, it makes them tongue-tied. And even those who do speak are ever so careful not to mention you. It's always a case of We've not seen much of you, where've you been keeping yourself – never Are you still grieving for your Sam. Ah well, it takes all sorts as you would put it.

We get into Bob's office, your office as was, and that gave me a pang, I must say. He's changed it round, as he would, as all new editors do – different desk, and caricatures of his star turns where your framed newspaper bills used to be – but it's still got an air of Sam Pepper about it, I could see you sprawled in that swivel chair clutching your glass and pontificating. And even though it's a no-smoking office now, because of Bob's asthma not political correctness you'll be glad to know, there's still a whiff of nicotine in the air, the same as on that dressing gown I've brought back home. That's one thing about non-smokers – they don't leave smells behind them.

The drinks trolley is still the same, and without asking me whether I want one or not Bob pours me out a large vodka and another one for Sheila who I'm glad to say guzzles it back and has another, I was worrying that as we were going to a veggie restaurant she'd turn out to be teetotal as well, it's none of my business if people choose not to drink but they always make you feel like an alcoholic if you order a second glass of wine, don't they?

So we get chewing the fat, insofar as you can do in an editor's office with all the comings and goings, and everyone that pokes their head round the door saying, Hello, June, it is June, isn't it, welcome back to the madhouse, lovely to see you, will you be over in the pub later?

Then who should come down but Charlie Whittington himself. The editorial director no less, in a suit that must have cost him £500 if it cost a penny. And it's all kiss kiss and hug hug but then unusually for Charlie, in fact unique in my experience, he refuses a drink. Wonder of wonders.

No, he says, I'm running late, I've got the jamjar waiting, I'm having lunch with British Telecom, I just wanted to say hello to June, you've lost some weight, darling, it suits you, now I must dash but is there anything we can do for you, June, anything at all?

Kind of him to ask, I must say. He must've thought that was why I'd come, to beg a favour. And though the thought had been far away from my mind when I entered that office, I heard myself saying, just for the sake of saying it style of thing, There is one thing, Charlie, since you're asking, have you any idea how I can get in touch with Eric Grant?

He says, Eric Grant, what do you want to see that prat for, whoops, I hope he's not a friend of yours, June, I know he was certainly no friend of Sam's.

I says, No, he's no more a friend of mine than he was of Sam's, Charlie, but when he was so abruptly thrown out on his ear he went off with some of my property. Or rather, I says, Sam's daughter Pauline's property.

I caught Charlie trying to glance at his watch without me twigging it.

I says, There's a clock up there, Charlie, and I don't want to come between you and British Telecom.

That got him. He says, They can wait, June, what's the problem?

So I told him about Pauline's letters to you, Sam. I could just as well have told the story to Bob, I suppose, seeing as Charlie was in such a tearing hurry, but I thought as Charlie was your biggest pal out of the two of them, I'd burden him with it.

He says when I've finished, No, they're not Pauline's property, June, unless Sam specifically left them to her which by the sound of it he didn't, they're your letters as his next of kin.

I says, But Pauline wrote them.

He says, It doesn't matter who wrote them, June, a lot of people make that mistake, even experienced journalists. He says, The copyright belongs to Pauline, yes, but the actual letters, the paper they're written on, belong to you. He says, Anyway, I gather you want them back?

I says, Well I expect Pauline does, at any rate we don't want them in Eric Grant's hands, they're nothing to do with him.

He says to Bob, Where is the little scumbag, Bob, didn't he bugger off to Florida?

Bob says, That's where he was heading, last anyone heard.

Charlie says, Can we get New York on it, and when they've located him go down and kick his arse for him?

—No problem, boss.

Charlie says, There you are, June, it's sorted, now don't leave it so long next time, give me warning, we'll have lunch, rather a scarlet widow than British Telecom any day.

And with that he gives me another kiss and off he goes. He's a lovely man. Very warm-hearted.

And I must say it was a nice cosy feeling, having the paper's arms around me again, if that doesn't sound too sentimental. That's one thing I miss, Sam – knowing that if there was any kind of crisis, the paper would come to the rescue, whether it was getting you a new set of credit cards after you lost them in Rome that time, dozy article that you were, or like when we were on that swan in Dublin and I'd forgotten some tablets I had to take, and you got them flown out. It makes you feel protected, that class of treatment.

Bob was already raising New York when Sheila and I took ourselves off to lunch, so there's somebody who doesn't let the grass grow. It was a very nice lunch I must say, although since I only come up to Town once in a blue moon these days I could have done with something a bit more exotic than vegetable flan. Still, we had a nice bottle of Chardonnay and Sheila's good company. She didn't have much office gossip to spill, I suppose she's got to be careful what she says now she's the editor's secretary, but she chattered merrily away about nothing in particular. She's got a nice bubbly personality, Sheila, hasn't she?

I was that much enjoying myself I wouldn't have minded a second bottle but of course Sheila had her desk to get back to. Over the coffee she asked the same question as Charlie, was there anything she could do for me. I expect like Charlie she was wondering if I'd come up with a purpose.

I said, Well, that's very kind of you, Sheila, it's a long shot but I don't suppose you know of any part-time jobs going for a woman of my age, I mean voluntary, not a charity shop because I've gone off that idea but something to take me out of myself.

The reason I've gone off charity shops is that it suddenly occurred to me that if that's where The Suit's in the habit of buying his clothes, as it seems to be, it could be a bit embarrassing having to serve him.

She says, It's funny you should ask that, June, if you'd put the question to me last week I should have had to say no, but then of course it depends what you're calling a job.

I says, So long as it's not scrubbing floors I'm not fussy, anything legal style of thing, why, what did you have in mind?

She says, My Auntie Clare's been spending three mornings a week I think it is, stuffing envelopes for the Animal Trust, you know, that big pets charity, all the fund-raising bumph that they send out. She says, But she's having to give it up because of the rheumatoid arthritis in her hands, her fingers are all thumbs these days, I'm sure they'll be looking for a replacement. I could always ask her to put a word in, they're in Croydon so it's not all that far from you.

I said, I wish you would, Sheila, it sounds just what I'm looking for. I'm sorry about your auntie, though, it can be very painful, arthritis can.

She says, I won't forget, June, I'll give you a ring.

So all in all, quite a fruitful day. And before you start sneering and snorting, Sam Pepper, stuffing envelopes is right up my street. It's just the kind of mindless task I need to keep my mind off you. Go on – tell me that's a contradiction in terms, but I know what I mean even if you don't.

I thought I'd do a bit of shopping while I was up in Town. I bought some shoes if it's of any interest which I know it isn't, because I've bought shoes and bought shoes and worn them out and binned them before you've even noticed I've got them. Then I did something mad: I bought a box of Maltesers and took myself to the pictures. The Odeon Mezzanine in Leicester Square. Two people I've never heard of, although I expect they're big stars, in a film called *Hate Mail*. Complete tripe. Still, it passed the time.

It was well past seven when I got home. Your Pauline was already back, cooking herself a boil-in-the-bag. She was quite tetchy.

She says, Oh, so there you are, I wish you'd say when you're going to be out till this time, June, you had me quite worried, couldn't you have left a note?

Silly cat.

I said, I'm very sorry, Pauline, but I'm a grown woman who comes and goes as she pleases. I says, If I'd known in advance I was going to be this late then I would have left you a note. But, I says, it's not as if I've come rolling home at midnight, now let's forget it, shall we?

She says, Anyway, someone called Sheila from the paper's been trying to reach you, she'll have gone home by now but there's two messages she wanted passed on.

One was from the Animal Trust to say they'd be only too delighted to have some help with their envelope-stuffing, as many or as few hours as I'd care to put in and would I like to start next Monday or as soon as I found it convenient? So that's that settled. I was quite excited, like when I got my first job at the *Manchester Evening News* after coming out of typing college.

The other message was from Bob Carp. He's already heard back from New York and it turns out that while Eric Grant did land himself a job as a down-table rewrite man on a supermarket tabloid, he'd failed to check some story about Elvis Presley being seen on the moon or something – I think they were making that bit up – and so the upshot was that to everybody's delight he's been fired again and now he's back over here.

Pauline said, This Sheila's given me his address, his address for you I should say, but there's one puzzling thing, she said something about some letters.

I said, Yes, he's apparently taken possession of a bundle of letters you sent to your father at the office when you were a schoolgirl.

—So I've been informed, but what I can't understand, June, is why did I have to learn about it from the editor's secretary when you've known all along?

Ooh, she can sound nasty when she likes, your Pauline. But she did have a point, I had to admit it.

I says, I'm very sorry, Pauline, I should have mentioned it I know but for one reason or another it slipped my mind, anyway, now that we know where he is at long last I shall drop him a line and see that he returns them.

She says, very carefully as if she's addressing a geriatric, *No*, June, *I'll* get them back.

I did remember what Charlie Whittington had told me, that under the copyright laws they belong to me, not her. But then I thought, what am I trying to prove? Whatever the law says, they're her letters, she wrote them to her daddy, and they're nothing to do with me.

But why did the title of that film I'd been to see, *Hate Mail*, come to mind?

I said, You suit yourself, Pauline.

She said, looking pleased with herself as if she'd won an argument, Now can I make you some supper, June, an omelette or there's some pressed turkey breast or there's—

I says, Yes, I know what's in my own fridge, thank you very much, Pauline.

She says, And do you know the door's practically hanging off its hinges, I don't know what you've been doing to it but unless you get it seen to you're going to find your fridge isn't properly insulated and your food's going off, now will you let me put something on a plate for you before I sit down myself?

I says, No thank you, Pauline, I'll have a cheese and pickle sandwich later. But first, I says firmly, I'm going to have a very large vodka.

Been a long day, Sam. Not often I get them, nowadays.

Right: I am now the proud possessor of a brand-new fridge.

I came down in the middle of the night for a glass of mineral water and wouldn't you just know it, the flaming fridge door came away in my flaming hand.

Nothing to be done about it. Kitchen swimming in water next morning naturally, little note from Pauline saying, I did point this out, June. Thank you for nothing, Pauline.

And thank you for nothing, The Suit. Why does one imagine always that people who volunteer to do things will know what they are doing? Still, he meant well.

So yesterday morning I trolled down to Grisby's and bought a new fridge. Smaller. That's another little shift in a widow's rich full life, Sam – we're only freezing for one now, eh? They agreed to take the old one away and that I could take delivery this afternoon. I was amazed when they turned up on the dot because you know what they're like, delivery men – in the past I've always had to threaten them with the power of the press. But no, in they came, took the thing out of its wrappings, installed it, the lot. And did you know, Sam, that on the latest models the freezer cabinet is now at knee level instead of eye level, on account of you don't use it as much as you do the regular fridge? That's the kind of detail that used to fascinate you.

The other interesting detail is that of course the bloody fridge door opens to the right, so that once again it bangs against the wall and scrapes my knuckles. If The Suit should die and go up to heaven or wherever you find yourself, don't mention it for God's sake.

There's only one thing to be said for stuffing envelopes, kid – it beats roaming the streets of a morning staring in shop windows and reading framed menus.

It doesn't have a lot going for it otherwise. I mean, I thought it would be a social activity style of thing. Chatting. My turn to make the tea. Rows of middle-aged women sitting at trestle tables gossiping away twenty to the dozen, like the girls on their sewing machines in Mike Baldwin's factory that he used to have in *Coronation Street*. No way.

The Animal Trust turns out to be in a three-storey Victorian terrace house in some run-down street – I'd thought, Croydon, well at least it's got to be in a modern building even if it's only an egg-box, but no, it's practically a slum. And the envelope-stuffing department is down in the basement, so for openers you don't get to meet anyone else as you pass through the building, because you don't pass through the building.

I was met by Sheila's Auntie Clare who introduces me to a woman whose name I didn't even catch, and then she takes me straight downstairs to show me round, as she puts it. Much there is to be shown: there's a little partitioned-off office where someone called Helen is batting away on a computer keyboard, she says, Oh, welcome aboard, Mrs Er, good of you to help us out, we're very short-staffed at present as you can see, Clare will show you the ropes, there's a coffee machine in there always on the go, anything else you need you've only to say the word, ladies' room that door over there.

And that was all she had to say for herself. Mail-shot supervisor she's supposed to be, all she seems to do is come out and say, Are these ready to go off, Mrs Er?, then she carts them into her office and puts them through the franking machine. I've told her to call me June but it makes no difference. She's one of those people who gives the impression she's always got something on her mind, youngish she is, about Pauline's age, probably just been through a divorce I'd say, or a split-up of some kind. That's why they come to work in these places.

But I'm getting ahead of myself. Sheila's Auntie Clare has taken me into the next-door room, a bigger one, what used to be the kitchen by the look of it, and sure enough there's the expected trestle tables, half a dozen of them, but nobody sitting at them.

She says, They're short-staffed at present as Helen explained, ladies come and go all the time so quite frankly I'm not sure what the position is at the moment, you'll just have to see who turns up, anyway, sit where you like, I'm afraid they're a non-smoking office, June, but apart from that make yourself comfortable.

I noticed she said they and not we, indicating that she meant to be off the moment she'd shown me what to do. Still, I'd been told that. But I didn't realise I'd be left running the envelope-stuffing department more or less on my own.

There's nothing to the job whatsoever, a girl of ten could do it – you bung an assortment of leaflets and forms from different piles into a buff envelope, you slap a pre-printed sticky address label on the front of it and sling it in a cardboard box, and so it goes on, all through the morning. All through the day if you've nothing better to do with your time.

I says, Yes, I've got the hang of it, Clare.

She says, It's repetitive as you can see, but it's something to do, isn't it? And then she says, I believe I'm right in saying you've endured a loss?

I was quite cross with young Sheila for telling her, no reason on God's earth why she needed to have done, all she had to say was she knew someone who wanted a bit of voluntary work. Still, I can't blame her. She wasn't to know I wouldn't want it spreading around.

I says, quite starchily for me, Yes, I lost my husband some time ago as Sheila may have mentioned; but we don't make a song and dance about it.

She says, No, Sheila's said nothing about it as a matter of fact, some of us can tell these things, call it instinct if you will although insight would be a better word in my opinion.

Now I don't dress like the Black Widow as you know, Sam, and I don't go around with a face as long as an ironing board. So how she twigged it I couldn't say.

I said, making light of it, Fancy, but tell you the truth it's not the kind of gift I'd like to have myself, thank you very much.

She says, all prissy, We must make use of the gifts God has given us.

And I thought, Oh my godfathers, she's bloody psychic!

And was I right? Because she goes on, Can I ask you, are you in touch with your late husband at all?

I says, No, I'm not, not in the way you mean anyway, I've never been a believer in that sort of thing.

She says, If you'll forgive me, June, it's not for you either to believe or disbelieve, if someone on the other side has something they want to say to you, then the message is there waiting, there's no getting away from it. Then she says, giving me an old-fashioned look, And I think you'll find there is one, waiting for you to pick it up.

I wish young Sheila had warned me her auntie was stark

staring round the twist, I'd've gone and signed up with the Oxfam shop after all.

I could see very well what the woman was driving at. Any encouragement and she would have had me sitting round one of those trestle tables touching palms with her and calling out, Is there anyone there?

I says, very firm, I think we'll just leave it there if you don't mind, we all have our own little ways of coping with these sort of things, you have your way and I have mine, so let's just drop it, shall we?

There was no way of putting her off. She says, dipping into her handbag, I'm going to give you my card, now if you feel in need of help or advice at any time, I want you to call me at this number night or day, I don't care what time it is. I don't care if it's three in the morning, in fact that's when many of my clients do call. Because, she says, I know your husband's trying to reach you, what did you say his name is again?

I says, all frosty, I didn't tell you his name and if you don't mind I don't think I'm going to.

Even so, I took the visiting card that she gave me. And under her name it said Spiritual Counsellor.

Now just listen to me, Sam Pepper. If anyone on this side ever tries to get hold of you – and we're talking about a thin little elderly woman with rimless glasses and her hair dyed ginger, Clare as her name is – then you have nothing to do with her. Anybody asks you to give two knocks for yes and one for no, you don't answer. No throwing glasses about, we had enough breakages when you were alive. No, Sam, we've made our own quite adequate arrangements for how to get through your demise, and I don't want anybody else interfering.

So why have I kept her visiting card, instead of binning it the minute she was out of sight?

Because this. She goes into the inner office where this

Helen is sitting, and she puts on her hat and coat and picks up her bits of shopping. Now during this she hasn't been out of my sight for a second. I mention this, our Sam, in case with your suspicious newspaperman's mind you think she must have made a quick crafty phone call to young Sheila. She couldn't have done. Not possible.

She comes back into the room and shakes hands with me and says, Well, June, I'll leave you to it, don't work too hard will you, oh, and you'll find tea bags, loo rolls et cetera et cetera in that filing cabinet, bottom drawer.

And just as she reaches the door leading to the stairs she turns back and she says, His name's Samuel Herbert, am I right?

Talk about spooky.

I was that shaken I had to have one in the Duke of Clarence on the way home to settle my nerves. And of course The Suit's there, reading the Situations Vacant columns over a half of lager and a bag of crisps.

I says to him, So I take it you didn't get that job you were applying for?

He says, No, I never thought I would for a minute, complete waste of time, I don't suppose you know of anything going by any happy chance, do you, June?

I says, The only vacancies I know about is for envelope-stuffers but unfortunately it's a charity, they don't pay.

He says, They can stuff their envelopes, then.

He seemed a bit down, first time I've seen him like it. I suppose it gets to you when you're looking for work and there's none to be had.

I told him about my little adventure working for the Animal Trust, missing out the detail of Sheila's psychic Auntie Clare, not a subject I'd care to discuss. He wasn't very interested, no reason why he should be, nothing to be interested in.

He says, politely, So you're keeping yourself busy, June, that's the main thing.

I says, I'm trying to.

He says, How's your daughter-in-law, Pauline isn't it, has she settled in?

I said, I'm afraid she has, only too comfortably, I don't know how long she plans on stopping.

He says, Like that is it, you sound as if you don't hit it off.

I says, She could be worse I suppose, it's just that we've never been friends and we've got nothing in common, it's like having an unwanted paying guest.

She does pay, then?

—Oh, she pays her way, Duggie, I'll say that for her.

He says, And it's not as if she's under your feet all day, she does work unlike some of us I take it, lady of her age, no kid, what does she do?

I told him about the nail clinic, what there was to tell, which seeing I've never set foot in the place wasn't much. Another topic of conversation that didn't exactly grip him. I tried to think of something that might cheer him up a bit, he was that low, but I'm afraid that after a morning's solitary envelope-stuffing and spiritual counselling I wasn't what you might call on top of the world myself. And he wasn't making it much better.

He seemed to sense he was having a depressing effect because he said, I'm afraid I'm not very good company today, June, take no notice, it's just that I told you a little white lie when you sat down, I did dare to think I might be in with a chance of that job, I've had everything crossed for a week but this morning I got the thumbs down, sorry, chum, right qualifications, favourable impression and all that, but the post has been filled in-house after all. He says, Between you and I, June, I was banking on it.

I says, I'm that sorry, Duggie.

And I put my hand on his sleeve, where he was resting his arm on his knee.

He says, Ah, well, these things are sent to try us.

And with his other hand he presses mine. Not in any lingering way, just a quick little squeeze. He's got very soft hands, first time I've ever noticed.

I didn't even ask him what this all-important job was, I thought if he got to talking about it, it'd only be rubbing salt into the wound. So I got us a drink instead, a large Scotch for him and a vodka for me. I says, Get this down you, lad, it might not make you feel better but it won't make you feel any worse.

It made me feel better, anyway. Tell the truth it was good to be feeling sorry for somebody else for a change instead of feeling sorry for myself. And I did feel sorry for him, Sam, he was that woebegone.

But with the whisky inside him he begins to chirp up a bit. He says, Anyway, June, that's enough about my troubles.

Now it's my experience that when people say that they mean they've only just started, and The Suit was no exception. I didn't mind, I'm a good listener as you know.

He says, Do you know how many job applications I've made so far, June?

I says, A good many, I'm quite sure.

—Over fifty, June.

I says, And there's some you hear about who've sent out a good twice as many.

—Not this chicken, June. Because I've never been one to push myself forward where I'm not wanted and enough is enough.

I thought for a minute he was going to start talking about throwing himself in the river, but no, in reality as I say he was brightening up.

He says, Y'know, looking at the situation realistically and trying to be constructive, June, tell me whether you think this is a good idea or a bad idea, because I'd really value your opinion. The thing is I'm considering abandoning looking for desk work altogether and striking out on something altogether different. He says, I'll surprise you now, but do you know what line I'm thinking of setting myself up in?

I says, You mean something self-employed?

He says, You've got it in one, self-employed handyman.

I didn't know what to say, Sam. I thought of that fridge door falling off its hinges and it was all I could do to keep a straight face. But at the same time I felt sorrier for him than ever. He looked so, well, the only word is vulnerable.

I says, clenching my cheek muscles to stop myself bursting out laughing, Well, if people know where to find you, there must be a lot of work in that line, have you looked into it or is it just something you're turning over in your mind?

He says, It's just gestating at present, but shall I tell you what put the idea in my head, June? He says, It was when I came in to switch your fridge door round.

I couldn't help myself, Sam. I'd just taken a sip of Guinness and he was very fortunate I didn't splutter it all over him. I was fair choking.

He says, Have I said something funny?

I says, thinking very quickly, because I didn't want to hurt his feelings, No, no, no, I was just remembering, how we were nearly caught red-handed by Pauline coming in, five minutes later and I shouldn't have known where to put my face.

He gave me a little smile – he has quite a shy smile on occasion, suits him – and said, Nor mine either.

I was grateful for that. Because he had the opportunity to say something really crude there, if he'd been like some men.

He says, Anyway, leaflets through letterboxes, trade card in newsagents' windows, word of mouth, there must be scores and scores of householders round here want little jobs doing, tap washers, garden gates rehung, cisterns lagged, glazing, painting, decorating, you name it, I can do it, and the beauty of it is, June, unlike most one-man businesses, there's no capital outlay whatsoever in any shape or form, so what am I risking?

I says, giving him a smile, Only your reputation, you could put on your cards Switching Fridge Doors Our Speciality.

He says, I could give you as a reference, all hunky-dory is it, working smoothly all right?

There was no way I was going to tell him.

I said airily, Oh, yes, couldn't be better.

He says, There you are, June, you were just in time, you just sneaked under the net, now if you'd brought me that problem tomorrow you would have got an invoice.

Then he says, So what do you think, do you think I should give it a whirl?

I says, Why not, as you say, you've nothing to lose.

He says, I'll tell you who I'd like to have as my first customer, now what about giving me a list of all the little jobs you've got that need doing, June, and I'll give you a favourable quotation.

I thought, Oh, my God.

Because much as I would have liked to have helped him out, and there's a score of things need looking at in that house as you very well know, Sam Pepper, how could I invite him back in? I couldn't very well bar him from the kitchen and as soon as he saw my new fridge and I'd confessed all it'd be a case of, Oh, June, June, that was a perfectly good fridge you had there, years of life in it yet, all it can have needed was the screws tightening, why didn't you tell me the door was hanging loose, I'd have been round like a shot.

No, I couldn't do it to him.

I says, thinking on my feet again, Oh, now if only you'd

asked me last week, Duggie, but I'm afraid as luck would have it I've just had a man in doing everything that needs doing for the time being, lawn-mowing and so on and so forth, Mick his name is, he used to do odd jobs for Sam and he just came round asking if there was anything I wanted done.

A complete fabrication as you know, although you once did have an Irishman over to push the lawnmower about, and he could very well have been called Mick.

He looked disappointed but he said, Well, at least it shows the demand is there.

I says, to encourage him, It certainly does and I should go for it.

But I thought to myself, For God's sake, though, keep away from refrigerators.

Now when he'd asked if there were any jobs I wanted tackling, naturally I thought he was trying to drum up a bit of custom there and then. I was even racking my brains to think how I could put something his way without asking him back to the house – for instance bringing in that old portable radio that's never worked since you threw it down the stairs, and asking if he could mend it for me. The back would probably fall off when I got it home again but at least I should have the excuse for slipping him a few bob without his taking offence.

But now, after we'd gone on talking about his brilliant new career as a handyman for a minute or two, he suddenly comes out with, Y'know, June, I'm sure we could find something that needs doing round at your place if we had a good look, I noticed two or three little things that need attention in the kitchen and living room alone, and I didn't even get a chance to look upstairs as we both know. And I'll tell you what, he says, seeing it's you I won't charge you, how about it?

And the penny dropped at last, as to what he was driving

at and why he wanted to come over. I can be ever so slow-witted sometimes as you know.

And the thing is, Sam, because I'll keep nothing back from you, what he wanted was what I wanted too. Whether it was with having been upset by young Sheila's Auntie Clare, or loneliness, or just simple appetite I couldn't say – no, it wasn't just simple appetite because unlike the other occasion I wasn't in any danger of being carried away by what you might call lustful thoughts, it was just that he seemed so down in the dumps I wanted to comfort him in some way; but yes, I wanted to comfort myself too.

But I said, No, I'm absolutely sure, Duggie, although it's very very good of you to ask.

If he'd made a better job of that fridge door it would have been a different story, I freely confess it.

I simply cannot fathom where that woman could have got your Christian names from. It bothers me. All right, Sheila just might have told her your first name, although she would have spoken of you as Sam not Samuel. But how many knew your middle name was Herbert? You never used it, ever. You hated it. It was printed on the order of service at the St Bride's do, of course, but people don't remember that kind of detail. Everyone has middle names but you don't take them in. It's a rum do.

I wish I'd never met young Sheila's Auntie Clare and I've certainly no desire ever to meet her again, I get goose-pimples whenever I think about her, which is often. So why won't I throw away the visiting card that she gave me?

If you feel the need for help or advice, she said. That'll be the day. When I want spiritual counselling I pour myself a vodka.

I do not and I will not believe in ghosts, Sam.

So who do I think I'm talking to, then? Where are you?

Here in my head, that's where. Where you belong, failing next to me in bed.

And I couldn't get you out of my head for long even if I wanted to – which truth to tell I do, sometimes. You're always there, like a headache. Always there, sticking your oar in.

Take the coffee percolator. Every morning I fill it and every morning the jug drips water on to the worktop, and every morning I hear you say, It has a design fault, that thing.

If you said that once, you must have said it a couple of hundred times. And sometimes you'd say, Typical British workmanship.

And I'd say, How many times do I have to tell you, it's not British, it's Swedish.

And you'd say, Typical Swedish workmanship.

And that was your joke for the day.

Then again: when I drip coffee on my napkin, as I sometimes do due to that self-same design fault you were for ever pointing out, I can hear you saying, as you always did, Why the thump don't you get some paper serviettes in, that dish rag you've got draped over your lap looks like something you'd find tucked into a plastic napkin ring in a Blackpool boarding house at the end of the Illuminations.

And I still say to you, Yes, I will, Sam, when I remember.

What else? When I hear the chink of the milk bottle on the doorstep, I also hear you chuntering away as you did so often if you happened to be at home, How much do you say we're paying for milk deliveries, you do realise in a few years you'll look back on the milkman as on a par with the muffin man and the pea and pie man?

And I hear myself saying, as I always did, I used to like a pie running in gravy and mushy peas.

And you saying, So did I, lass, still do when I can get it,

I'm not knocking it, all I'm saying is why can't you buy a carton of bloody milk from the corner shop?

And me saying, Because we don't have a corner shop.

Then there's the postman, if he chances to be a few minutes late:

—Why did they ever invent postcodes, just tell me that, because that post's slower with new technology than if it was being carried through the jungles of Borneo by cleft stick.

You've said that to me three times this week, and twice you've said, I'm going to start sending all this junk mail back to where it came from, I'm going to find out the names of the managing directors of all these firms and I'm going to post it to their private addresses marked Personal.

And how many times in a week do I hear you saying Age before beauty, Better out than in, Rather you than me, It'll all be the same in a hundred years, What a bugger, Why do they make sliced bread that won't fit in the bloody toaster, I'm going to put a notice on that clock saying This clock is five minutes fast.

Oh dear, oh doctor, I make it sound as if life with you was one long gripe, and in a way it was, but it was just your style, just your manner. I know this much: as I get my morning coffee on the go, I'd give anything to hear in the flesh what I hear in my head:

—It has a design fault, that thing.

Failing which, I do sometimes wish you'd put a sock in it, Sam.

Happy birthday, chuck.

You would have been fifty-four. Should have been fifty-four too, if you'd taken more care of yourself. Or I'd taken more care of you. Or that Tricia had taken more care of you. You don't know who to blame.

Silly me that I am, I looked up your horoscope. If Today Is Your Birthday. An additional responsibility may have caused you to postpone a foreign trip or new enterprise. However, now is the time to set the ball rolling again. Finances are still a sore point but there is now light at the end of what has been a long dark tunnel. Oh, and thanks to a potent Sun–Pluto liaison, a personal goal you have set yourself may now be reached.

So now you know.

I've been dreading this. This and Christmas. And our anniversary.

Yet what's so special about all these dates? A day's a day, it's what you have to get through like any other day – and it certainly doesn't have to be a red letter one to bring on a touch of the Memory Lanes.

It does occur to me, though: there's another anniversary for my diary now, thanks to your carelessness in dying. Well, we'll face that when we come to it.

I'm glad now you'd never have a fuss made of your birthday. Shut up, girl, I don't want to be reminded of it, you'd always say; and as for giving you a present, you always wanted something really boring. You'd say, If you want to give me anything, you can get me a pair of gloves, or a pair of slippers. But there's no need to bother, you'd say, it's just another day so far as I'm concerned.

Yet you'd come home pissed all the same, having pushed the boat out at the office. I didn't mind, if that was the way you wanted to play it. You always remembered my birthday, that was the main thing. Or somebody did. What are secretaries for, after all? I should know. Time was when I had to remind you of Tricia's birthday, Pauline's too, or don't you remember that? No, you wouldn't.

So apart from feeling a bit weepy, nothing unusual in that, I didn't plan on marking the day in any special way, I mean to say with no grave to put flowers on, what was I supposed to do anyway? I decided to treat it just like any other day if you want to know, Sam. I know it wasn't quite

just like any other day but that was my way of dealing with
it, all right? Nothing special, all right?

I'm saying nothing special, but there's one thing I ought
to tell you, pet, and that's that I'd made a sort of half-
arrangement to see The Suit in the Duke of Clarence at
lunchtime. Nothing definite, I'd just said to him a couple of
days previous that I might be in on the Thursday lunchtime.
And that was in case I had trouble getting through the day,
because there was no way of knowing in advance how I'd
be feeling. It was a kind of insurance if you like. Well, no
harm in it, was there? And it wasn't as if he was taking me
out to lunch at the Ritz, after all. You don't blame me, do
you, Sam? Do you?

Anyway, in the end I didn't go.

Which I have to say was in no small way down to your
Pauline, considering her attitude. I could tell as soon as she
came down to breakfast – because I was down ahead of
her for once, couldn't sleep – that she was going to make
a beanfeast of it. She'd already been having a bit of a snivel,
I could see that, and it was only eight o'clock.

Her first words were, Has the postman been?

I said, Not yet, why, are you expecting something?

She says, I'm not, no, but I've a confession to make,
because you know what day it is, don't you?

I says, Yes, of course I do.

She says, I've sent my dad a birthday card and I'm
wondering now if I should have done, because I'm not
too sure how you're going to take it.

I says, You've done what? I says, You've sent your father
a card, when he's been dead all these months? What do you
want to do a silly thing like that for?

Honestly, she's dafter than I am.

She says, There you go, I knew you'd take that attitude but what's silly about it, you tell me, I've sent him
a birthday card every year since he went off with you,

why should I stop now just because he happens to be dead?

There was no answer to that, or none that I would have cared to make. But I said, quite gently, You didn't used to send them here, though, did you?

She says, very abrupt, No, I didn't.

I thought on the whole I'd better change the subject, or half-change it at least. I says, Which reminds me, that packet of letters that Eric Grant is holding, it's none of my business but did you ever get them back?

She says, No, I've been round a couple of times after work but he's not been there.

I says, Oh, I see.

We both nibble toast. She's in a sulk and I'm in a sulk. And she's seething with it. Because after snapping the crusts off her toast the way you used to do, she comes out with, I'm very sorry if you think posting a birthday card to my own father is silly, June, but what exactly have you done to mark his birthday, may I ask?

I said, I haven't done anything, Pauline, what is there for me to do?

She says, You could have taken him some flowers.

I says, What's the point of taking flowers to a crematorium, where would I leave them? I says, The whole point of being cremated is to do away with all that rigmarole, that's why your father wanted it.

She says, crumbling toast, Or at least that's what we've been led to believe.

I wasn't going to be drawn into a row, not on your birthday. I kept my mouth zipped.

She's nothing if not persistent, your Pauline. She says, So you're not going out to the crematorium, then?

I says, getting exasperated, Of course I'm not, Pauline, what would I be doing there? You don't seem to know these places, it's not like a cemetery, there's no grave, where's the point in it? I says, Come to that, do you reckon on traipsing out there yourself?

She says, I can't, I've only got an hour for lunch and I have to go to the heel bar, that's why I sent him a card.

Then she crumbles a bit more toast and asks me, So how are you going to spend the day, then?

I says, The same as I spend any other day, when I'm not stuffing envelopes. I says, Busy doing nothing.

But she'd reminded me.

I said, That heel bar you have to go to, is it the one a few doors away from the Minimart on The Parade, just across from the Duke of Clarence?

She says, The Duke of Clarence, is that the pub I saw you coming out of with that fellow you gave Dad's suit to, who you say came round to mend the fridge?

—I didn't give him your dad's suit, Pauline, let's get this straight, he bought it from the Oxfam shop – and I don't as you put it *say* he came round to mend the fridge, he did come round to mend the fridge.

—He didn't make a very good job of it, then, did he?

I said, Anyway, if you are going to the heel bar, I wonder if you'd mind very much popping across to the Duke of Clarence and putting your head round the door, and if he chances to be there telling him I'm sorry I can't make it this lunchtime after all, you can say I don't feel up to it.

She says, You what, June, do you mean to sit there and tell me you'd arranged to meet this man on my father's birthday?

I says, I wouldn't say arranged, I'd call it half-arranged, but what's wrong with that, life has to go on, Pauline.

She says, Yes, I can see it does, June.

I'm sure we could have gone on in this vein until your Pauline had to go to work, but luckily for peace and quiet the postman was on time for once and we were interrupted by the slap of the letterbox.

Pauline's birthday card was all there was. There's never any post these days. They seem to have crossed you off all the mailing lists finally. I suppose they get the names and addresses off a computer and somebody's noticed you're no longer with us and wiped you off. It's probably somebody's sole job, to wipe the dead off the computer. It makes me feel sad for some reason. It's like obliterating them, erasing them, so that as well as having no future they've got no past either.

I fetched the card in and tried to hand it over to Pauline. But she says, No, I chose it and posted it, June, so I really think it's up to you to open it.

It was what you in your ranting way would have called Grade A slop – a picture of a cutesy little dog with its head on one side and a slipper in its mouth. Aw! Why a flaming dog? You never had a dog.

Then I remembered. Tricia had a dog.

I opened it out. Some scrawled words from Pauline and a row of kisses – Always thinking of you – and the printed message, Missing you darling Dad, ever in our thoughts on this your birthday.

I felt queasy. Do they really manufacture dead persons' birthday cards?

Or did she have it specially made, like one of those Thomas the Tank Engine birthday cakes you see in confectioners' windows?

It's on the mantelpiece if you want to see it. But it comes down tomorrow.

And I did get through the day, Sam. By thinking to myself, Now what was I doing this time last year? The answer being Waiting, waiting, waiting, the same as you are now, June, and the bugger didn't surface till four in the morning.

You'll not see me up till four in the morning this year, don't think it, lad. Beddy-byes. And onwards and upwards.

Do you know what I've a fancy for, all of a sudden? Ironing half a dozen shirts, the same as I used to do every Wednesday afternoon. Not yours particularly – and no, in case that's what you're thinking, not The Suit's either. Shirt-ironing for shirt-ironing's sake, that's what I'm craving at the moment, the way you sometimes have a mad yen for a Mars bar.

It was soothing, was shirt-ironing, with the radio on and the kettle whistling away and the tea and biscuits waiting. One of the pleasures of married life, for me. Small pleasures, true, and I know there's women, particularly in your line of country, who despise ironing and suchlike. They used to write TV plays about them, do you remember – there must be more in life than this style of thing? Not for me. When all's said and done, if you haven't got kiddies, and you're not going to see your husband till nightfall, and you don't have a career or any outside interests which I never had because with my talents what would I have done, raffia-work? – there's a rhythm of life to be got out of washing, cleaning, ironing, bed-making. A pattern.

It's like doing tapestry-work. Soothing. It was, but now all the stitches are coming out. I've seen it happen in others. My mother must have been one of the last women in England to black-lead her grate but it stopped the moment Dad died.

But you see what I mean: I'm letting things slip. I've bought a duvet now, did I tell you, to save me the trouble of making the bed? And I'll let two or three weeks go by before I'll change the sheets and pillowcases. Talk about Sloppy Alice. As for the dust, I'm just waiting for your Pauline to point out there's cobwebs on the landing ceiling. I shall say, Right, here's a feather duster, Pauline, go to it, and see how many more you can find.

But I really could do with a spot of ironing, Sam. Maybe I should have gone to work in a laundry. It would have beat stuffing envelopes.

Eric Grant's rung up a couple of times for your Pauline, but she's been out. I'm beginning to wonder if she's started seeing him. None of my business of course, but the last time I saw the pair of them together, when he gave us a lift back after your memorial service, I did wonder if there was something rumbling between them. And now of course she's got the incentive of paying Jack back in kind. Personally I'd rather go out with a one-eyed hunch-backed Chinaman but as I say, it's nothing to do with me.

I didn't ask him about the letters. That's something else that's none of my concern.

She goes on holiday a couple of weeks from now, thank goodness. Spain, somewhere. One of the Costas. I wonder if he's going with her. She cracks on she's going with a girl from work, but then she would say that, wouldn't she? I've said it myself, way back, and my mother didn't believe me any more than I believe Pauline. Paris. Remember? You'd better.

I could do with a holiday myself, if I could find someone to go with. Besides you, I mean. No one's come forward with the suggestion. Talk about the spectre at the feast – if folk don't want widows at their dinner parties, they sure as hell don't want to spend a fortnight with them in the Dordogne or wherever.

The Suit? I don't think so. Too near the deep end. Besides, I doubt very much whether he could afford it.

There must be somebody. Young Sheila? No. She'd say yes I'm fairly sure, but only out of pity. We don't want that. And everybody else is married. Three's a crowd.

Honestly, Sam, you feel like a criminal sometimes, being widowed. Anyone'd think I'd bloody murdered you. Yet of every two people who get married or live together, assuming they stay with one another, one's going to die first and the other's going to carry the can for it. It's heads or tails, supposed to be, although from my observation it's usually the man who goes first. Heads.

In fact I don't think I know any widowers at all. Agreed, in the line of country you were in men drop like flies, but without knowing the figures, and it's no use you saying, Check your facts, girl, check your facts, I've got the impression that it's general, there's a lot of widows about.

So I'm wondering why we don't keep in touch more, make a club of it style of thing. Widows Anonymous. I've been adding them up, and I can think of at least eight of your old colleagues who've departed this mortal coil in the last few years. So that's eight widows. But do they keep in touch? They do not. Not one of them was at the memorial service. One or two of them wrote bread-and-butter letters of condolence, but that was it.

Mark you, they could say the same about me, because I'm as bad as they are. It's been a case of meaning to get So-and-so's widow out for a bite of lunch but somehow never getting round to it.

Why is it? Do we feel we've nothing in common, apart from widowhood? Happen. We used to be good chums, some of us, we had a lot of laughs. Lorra laughs. But then husbands die and it goes. Do we think friendship snaps when the men who brought us together pop their clogs? It would seem so. Are we fickle, or what?

Envelope-stuffing session today, you'll be excited to hear. Actually, now I've fallen into a routine, Mondays, Wednesdays and Fridays, I'm getting to quite enjoy it, I like the long meandering bus ride and then I can always look forward to rewarding myself with a glass in the Duke of Clarence afterwards. Haven't seen The Suit all week, he must have got started on his odd-jobbing.

That Helen, now I've got her to start calling me June at last instead of Mrs Er, is a bit more forthcoming, she's started coming out to my work station as they insist on calling it to have her elevenses with me, and we've fallen into the routine of taking it turn and turn about to make the coffee. Still no sign of any other volunteers, though. They don't need them, tell the truth. It's amazing how many envelopes you can stuff in the course of a morning if you set your mind to it.

Do you know, I stick half a dozen leaflets into each envelope and I've no idea what any of them's about, apart from the pictures of muzzled dogs in quarantine and rabbits having dreadful things done to them which I don't want to know about. You'd think I would at least read them, wouldn't you, they could be sabotage instructions for all I know. But I don't, and have no desire to. It's all blissfully mechanical, I become like one of those girls in the Fruitimallow factory near where I used to live when I was growing up, sitting there all day long with the wireless blaring and sticking the six different flavours into the boxes, that's before it all went over to machine of course. It's therapeutic, Sam. I'll be chewing gum next.

She still seems a bit abstracted though, does Helen, as if she's got some problem nagging away at her. She's not the kind of person you'd care to ask about it, though, you can't draw her out.

Last time I was in I did ask about young Sheila's Auntie Clare, though. I says, Do you hear from Clare at all?

She says, No, not heard from her since she left, why do you ask, I didn't think you knew her?

I says, No, I don't, except through her niece, but did you know she's supposed to be psychic?

She says, There's no suppose about it, she is, she tells everybody, she makes no secret of it.

I says, And do you get the impression she's, well, it sounds rude to say genuine, but would you say she really does have these so-called psychic powers?

She says, I know she does, because as a matter of fact the first thing she told me within half an hour of her meeting me in this very office was that I'd lost my mother, which I have, three years ago. Now there was absolutely no way she could have been aware of that, there's nobody in this building knows it.

I says, And did she tell you your mother had a message for you?

She says, Yes, she did, since you ask.

I says, And did you get this message?

She's clamming up now. She says, Yes, I did.

She was getting shorter and shorter in her tone. I ought to have sensed I was intruding, but you know me, bigmouth June. Plod on.

I says, I wouldn't dream of asking you what it was, but would you mind telling me how it was, what's the word, transmitted?

She says, No, I'm very sorry, June, don't take offence but it's a very private matter, it's between me and my late mother and Clare as the medium, and nobody else.

Oh dear.

I says, I quite understand, I didn't mean to intrude, Helen, do excuse me.

She says, That's quite all right, think no more about it. But she says, If you want to know if Clare could get a message through to you should the need arise, which is what I believe you're driving at, I'm confident the answer is yes.

End of coffee break. I wish I'd never asked.

I'm afraid I've got some bad news for you, Sam. That's if you haven't heard it already on the grapevine, being where you are.

I was just going out this morning when the telephone rings. I wasn't going to answer it at first, I thought it might be Eric Grant and I've got so as I can't stand the sound of his voice.

But then I thought, Come on, June, you can't go through life leaving the phone to ring and ring just in case it's that slimy bugger, answer it and tell him, Look, buster, you must know Pauline goes out to work, why can't you ring her in the evening or over the weekend?

But it wasn't him.

It's a woman's voice, and she says, Hello, June, it's Marion.

Marion, Marion. I just couldn't place her.

I says, Excuse me – Marion who?

She goes, Marion! Your sister-in-law!

Whoops. Well I'm sorry, Sam, but can you blame me? Apart from having a few words with her at the funeral and the memorial service, I don't think I've spoken to her for two years. You and your Derek were never very close, were you, and his wife and me even less so. You're not what we'd call one big happy family, there's cousins of yours I've never even clapped eyes on.

I said, lying through my teeth, Ooh, you'll have to forgive me, Marion, you see I know three or four Marions and I couldn't place your voice for a moment, there's a lot of crackling on this line, is it the same your end?

She puts on the formal voice that you do on these occasions. I know: I've done it myself.

She says, I'm afraid I'm the bearer of bad news, June. Derek passed away at five and twenty past two this morning.

So farewell then, Derek. I can't in all honesty say I felt anything. I hardly knew him and I hardly know her. But you go through the motions, don't you?

I said, Oh, I am sorry, Marion, oh, you poor thing, oh, you must be devastated.

And then I did feel something, because it suddenly hit me

what she must be going through. The more so because like me when you went she was putting a brave face on it.

She said, Well, you've heard of bolts from the blue, this time last week he was as right as rain, then all of a sudden, Wednesday morning he's writhing about on the bathroom floor with stomach pains, perforated ulcer leading to acute peritonitis. Though why he had to die of it we still haven't got to the bottom of, there's a lot of questions to be answered, June.

That'll keep her occupied for a while. I'm not being callous, Sam – it will. Same as when a loved one dies in an accident or gets bumped off. You direct all your energies into how it happened or who did it. It gives you something to do.

I said, I'm more sorry than I can say, Marion, is there anything I can do for you, would you like me to come over?

And I realise that I'm repeating more or less the self-same words that she used when I had to ring and tell her and Derek about you. And I can't remember what I answered but it was probably very much on the lines of how she was answering now.

She says, It's very kind of you but thanks and no thanks, June, I've got a hundred things to do, hospital, registrar, undertakers, solicitor, well, you know only too well yourself, for the present I'm just ringing round all the relatives and close friends.

Two years older than you, wasn't he? Bit of a dry stick I always found him, on the rare occasions we've met. Funny family – him a tax inspector, you a newspaper editor. He always seemed on the edge of having a sneer at the tabloid press but it's my belief he envied you your life on the quiet. I think he suspected you were having all the fun and he wasn't. Anyway, you've both gone now. The moving finger writes, eh? I tell you, Sam, it's at times like this you wonder what's the bloody point of it all.

I says, Will you be letting Tricia know, or shall I get Pauline
to tell her, because it so happens she's staying with me at
present, Pauline I mean.

And not for the first time I wondered why she couldn't
go and stay with her own mother instead of me. Too far
away, she cracks on.

She says, If you would, June, I've not set eyes on Tricia
since – well, not for donkey's years.

Since you ran off with me, she means.

And she says, And of course I'll be sure to let you know
about the funeral arrangements in good time.

I'm dreading that funeral already. It's one thing I've not
prepared myself for, having to endure another funeral. I
don't know why – nobody's immortal. You thought you
were, Sam Pepper, and look at you now. There's no getting
out of it, I suppose, they came to yours, I shall have to go
to his. But I shan't like it.

When Pauline got home and I told her about her Uncle
Derek she surprised me by having a little weep. Turns out
that on occasion he used to drive over and take her on
outings to the Zoo and that. When you were too busy
for her.

She said, He was very kind to me. I think I was the
substitute for the daughter he would have liked himself.

It suddenly occurred to me what a forlorn little girl Pauline
must have been. I don't even want to think about it.

It's not often I go into the Duke of Clarence of a Saturday
morning, too much to catch up with now I'm envelope-
stuffing three mornings a week, but this lunchtime I did.
I'll come clean, pet – I was hoping to see The Suit. He
hasn't been there the last three or four times I've gone
in, and I've been wondering how he's getting on, whether
he's getting his odd-job career under way. I thought if he
has, Saturday might just be his day off, because husbands

tend to be around the house on Saturdays and they don't want handymen about doing jobs they could just as well do themselves if they stirred themselves, are you listening to me, Sam Pepper?

At first I thought he wasn't there but then as I treated myself to a glass of Guinness I saw there was a Sainsbury's bag next to the bar stool where he normally sits, and an unfinished half of lager on the table. So reasoning that he must be in the gents' I went and sat down.

I wasn't prying, but the way his carrier bag had fallen open you couldn't but help seeing the entire contents, few that they were. Melton Mowbray pork pie. Pair of Scotch eggs. Three tins of sardines. Beefsteak tomatoes – I could see him deluding himself they were better value than the regular size. A chicken and sweetcorn microwave dinner. Tea bags. Packet soups. Carton of long-life milk. Packet of custard creams. Sliced loaf, white. Carton of I Can't Believe It's Not Butter. All human life is there.

Do you know, Sam, there's nothing more pathetic than a single man's bag of shopping, or than of one who's become single. You can see his whole crummy bachelor life in one fell swoop, it's like a still life almost. The gas ring. The microwave, stained with gravy. The burned saucepan. The tins and packets in the waste bin. The wringing-wet tea cloth, from wiping up the same dinner plate over and over again rather than let the crockery pile up in the sink like it does in the cartoons. You were always a one-plate man if I chanced to be away anywhere, weren't you? A pity you thought rinsing it under the tap was the equivalent of washing it. And the biscuits that never make it to the biscuit tin but stay in their torn packet until they're finished, and the sardines destined to be eaten straight out of the tin with a cake fork, standing up. And the dead house plant on the kitchen windowsill, with cigarette burns on the saucer that's there to catch the water it never had.

—Anything there you fancy for your tea, then, June, you've only to say the word?

I did jump. He hadn't been to the toilet at all, he'd been on the pay phone right behind me. I bet I went bright red.

I said, to hide my confusion, I can see you're not a big believer in getting what you might call a balanced diet down you, are you?

He says, Oh, if you ask me there's too much fuss made about vitamins and carbohydrates and what have you, so long as I get my roughage and I'm not still hungry when I get up from the table, I don't worry, June.

I says, Well, you don't look as if you're fading away so it can't be doing you much harm. I says, I haven't seen you for a few days although I've popped in a couple of times, what have you been up to, have you got your handyman business off the ground or are you still weighing the pros and cons?

—It's all go, June, touch wood. Yesterday I had two tap washers, a sash cord and a broken loo window, and the day before I had a jammed fluorescent light tube, some loose bathroom tiles that needed glueing, and what else, oh yes, there was an old lady wanted me to scrub her kitchen floor for her, caked in grime it was but I'm not proud, June, I got down on my hands and knees and got stuck in. It doesn't sound much I know but you've got to begin somewhere and out of little acorns great oaks grow.

I says, Very good, you're off to a flying start.

I gave him a little smile and then I said, teasing him, No fridge doors want mending so far?

He frowned. Only a little crease of the forehead but a frown.

He says, There's some joke about your fridge door that I'm not in on, isn't there, June? Because your stepdaughter, Pauline, and oh, while I remember, thanks for asking her to drop in and let me know you couldn't make it that day—

I says, I hope you didn't mind, it was Sam's birthday and I didn't feel up to socialising, I hope she explained.

He says, She did explain and I quite understand, June, but I was grateful for the message, I could have been sitting here like a complete Charlie wasting good self-employed working hours. But he says, Getting back to your fridge, Pauline said something about she hoped I was better at mending a wonky carport door than I was at mending fridge doors, this being the job I'd told her I was going on to as soon as I'd had a quick bite.

I says, rather cold, Oh, you seem to have had quite a chat, the pair of you, she didn't tell me.

Nor had she. She just said that she'd found The Suit eating a ham bap and delivered the message, and that was all she did have to say.

Then I realised he must think I sounded jealous, my voice was that tart, so I went on, Not that there's any reason on God's earth why she should, she's a perfectly free agent.

He says, Come to that, June, you didn't tell me she has a taste for very large gin and tonics, I might not have bought her a drink if I'd known.

He was grinning but you could see it rankled, after all he does have to count the pennies.

Cheeky cat. Typical.

But that's something else she didn't mention, that she'd sat down and had a drink with him. More than one for all I know. So after banging on at me for thinking of having a drink with The Suit on your birthday, Sam, she ends up having one with him herself. I can't imagine why because I'm sure he's not her type, but then who is her type since she and Jack split up?

He goes on, Still, she's good company, once you get her chatting. I was surprised, from what I gathered from you I thought she was the complete opposite.

I says, all prim, It depends who the company is, doesn't it?

He says, Now, now, June.

Trust her to muscle in. And what she's said to him behind my back goodness only knows. I wish she wouldn't, Sam. The Suit's my friend, not hers. Anyway, she's already got Eric Grant in tow, or so I strongly suspect. What's she trying to do – build up a male bloody harem?

I get up and get a round in, hoping to change the subject, but as soon as I sit down again he goes, So come on, June, tell us the great fridge door joke.

He wasn't going to drop it, I could see that.

I says, Didn't Pauline explain what it was all about?

—No, she said you would.

Now I'd no way of knowing what she'd told him or what she hadn't told him, so I thought I'd better come clean, or more or less clean anyway.

I said, If you really want to know, I yanked the door open too hard when I'd had a few, I was after some ice. I says, And whether the screws had been working their way loose or what I don't know, but it wouldn't shut properly, it was hanging down, all out of kilter if that's the word I'm looking for.

Why I had to put it like that I do not know. To try and save his face, I suppose.

He says, I thought it came away altogether?

So she had told him, after all.

I says, No, no, no, I took it off its hinges, to see if I could get it hanging properly again.

He says, So you managed to do that, then?

Talk about Oh what a tangled web we weave.

—Only because I'd watched you doing it, Duggie. But in one way or another, don't ask me how, I seem to have succeeded in buckling it. So then I said to myself, Blow this for a game of candles, I'm overdue a new fridge anyway.

—You should have called me in, June.

—No point, Duggie, not unless you're a qualified panel beater on top of all your other talents.

And we left it at that. He seemed satisfied, at any rate he didn't go away with his feelings hurt. But bang goes my excuse for not having him round to the house. I shall have to watch my step, Sam.

Another phone call. Getting popular, I must be.

—Hello, is that Christine?

—There's no Christine here, this is 4723, you must have the wrong number.

—Not Christine, oh, sorry dear, my mind's gone blank, who's that speaking?

—Never mind who's speaking, who do you want?

—Mrs Pepper.

I says, very dignified, This is Mrs Pepper, but the name's not Christine and never has been, it's June.

He says, Of course it is, June, a thousand apologies, June, I don't know where I got Christine from, June, I'm losing my marbles, must be, June.

I thought, if he goes on calling me June at the rate of once every ten seconds, I'm going to hang up. And I wouldn't care, but I still didn't know who it was.

He burbles on, Anyway, June, it's Ted Cargill this end.

Ted Cargill, Ted Cargill. Never heard of him.

But you never admit it, do you, don't know why. I says, Ted Cargill, now I know you, Ted, remind me.

He says, No, as a matter of fact you don't know me at all, June, in fact we've never met, and I very much doubt whether Sam ever mentioned me.

I could have murdered him. You feel such a fool.

I says, Well, if I don't know you and you don't know me, as it seems seeing you appeared to think I was called Christine, do you think we could somehow get to the point?

He says, Absolutely, June, but first let me say how sorry I was to hear about Sam, it came as a great shock.

I begged leave to doubt that, but I murmured the kind of things you get into the habit of murmuring in this situation, the funereal equivalent of what I imagine very minor TV personalities say when people come up to them and ramble on about how much they've always liked their programme. I was right, too. He never knew you at all.

He says, I can't pretend I was big mates with him either, June, but we did used to have the odd jar in the Three Feathers, remember the Three Feathers, that was when I was on the old *Daily Post*, what days they were, eh, seems like a different age as indeed it was. Of course I'm long retired now.

I began to think, if new technology made it possible to strangle someone long distance with telephone flex, he'd be on his way out by now. He'd be writhing on the floor.

I says, lying of course, Excuse me, this is all very interesting but I've got a cab ticking away outside waiting to take me to the foot clinic, in fact thirty seconds more and you would have missed me, can you tell me what this is all about please?

He says, I'll come directly to the point, June, do you still have Sam's address book by any chance?

I says, Yes, of course I do, it's still in his desk, why do you ask?

He says, Would Eric Grant's present number be in it by any chance do you think? I wouldn't trouble you but the paper won't give it out, I can understand that, it's policy, in fact I'd hell's own job getting your number out of them but I managed to persuade them I was a family friend

Thank you very much, whichever dozy secretary it was. Not young Sheila, I'm sure.

I says, I know for a certain fact we've got his present

number, but pardon my French, what is it you want to get in touch with that little tripehound about?

He says with a chuckle, Well spoken, Christine, I should say June, he owes me a sum of money wouldn't you know, fool to myself, chanced to run into him in Soho, the respectable end I hasten to say, just after he got back from Miami on his uppers, I won't repeat his tale of woe and I won't say what I had the honour of being asked to lend him for two weeks maximum, but not having heard from him from that day to this I thought hello, it's time to take this up, brother, you can't afford to let these matters slide at my age, no way.

I said, No, I should think not.

Privately, while I looked up Eric Grant's number, I thought, Silly sod, fancy lending a prat like that money and not even knowing how to keep in touch with him. Prat speaking to prat, if you ask me.

I give him the number and he says, Thank you very much June, Christine, June, I beg your pardon, I'll get it right one of these days, speak to you again.

And he rings off.

And do you know, Sam, I felt that affected after I'd put the phone down, I sat down and trembled in my chair. I did. I felt – I won't say used, I certainly wouldn't say abused, I don't use these emotive words, but what is it I'm trying to say?

Bloke rings up. Hello, that the widow, got a minute? Still have his address book, do you? That's good, give us So-and-so's number, there's a darling. And rings off. Wham bam, thank you ma'am. That's what it comes down to, doesn't it?

It's like that old joke, one of your favourites, I've heard you tell it a million times. Two blokes, one of them has a decorating job to do, other one offers him a spare can of paint. Goes round to his house, knocks on the door, woman comes out, Oh, hello love, is your Harry in? No, have you not heard, he was run over by a brewery lorry last night, I'm very sorry to say he's dead. Oh dear me, did he say anything about a can of paint?

Tell me one of your jokes, Sam. I'd laugh. I would. Firm promise.

Six months gone by already. And it still seems like yesterday.

How am I doing? I'll answer that, lad: I'm surviving. Which is enough. But how I wish I could turn the clock back. Just a rerun of our last year together, that's all I ask, so I could savour it and appreciate it more.

Not that it was a vintage year – did we have any vintage years? – and not that I would do anything any differently. We would still have the odd stupid spat, I'd still let you come in pissed at three in the morning without putting my foot down, and you'd still fritter away your days off instead of us doing something more interesting. But that was our life. No regrets. But why can't time run backwards? It might as well – it'd make just as much sense as running forwards.

I'll tell you something I've come to realise these last six months, Sam. Death doesn't mark the end of memory. For some reason I'd always assumed that it did, that with one partner gone, all the other partner's memories and recollections would be of the time they spent together. Not true. The curtain comes down all right but then it goes up again. Act Two. Different set. I've memories as sharp dating from the day you died as for the six months before you went. Sharper. But all of them to do with you. The Suit entering my life. Your Pauline turning up. Going down to the office that day. Young Sheila's Auntie Clare. All vivid in my mind. So that's something I've learned. I thought life would become a haze, and it hasn't. Sometimes I wish it would.

I do think back to when you were alive of course, often

and often. Particularly those last few days. Shall I tell you what I keep coming back to? That time you were lying in your hospital bed and you said, or I thought you said, that you had to get home because there was some stuff you had to get rid of. Now as I say, I was punch-drunk with tranquillisers and lack of sleep at the time and I can't be sure from that day to this whether you actually did say that or whether I dreamed it or imagined it. But believing you might have said it is the same as your having said it, to my confused mind. And every so often I'll turn out a drawer or a cupboard in case there's a skeleton lurking there. I nearly had that squeaky floorboard in the bedroom up last week, then I thought, Don't be so daft, June, you want putting away. But I do wonder.

I was merrily stuffing envelopes this morning when Helen passes through and goes into the loo. Minutes later I hear this snuffling sound. I listen, and she is, she's sobbing her little heart out behind the loo door.

I thought, Oh my godfathers, this is all I need, if she starts pouring out her troubles it's going to put the tin lid on this day for me.

Because to tell the truth, when I say I was merrily stuffing envelopes, there was nothing merry about it. I was mechanically stuffing envelopes. It was one of those days. What I call my gloompot days. One of those days when you can hardly bring yourself to get out of bed, and when you do stir yourself you wonder what was the point of getting up. Black Monday, except it happens to be Wednesday.

She comes out of the loo, doesn't flush it, so I know she's only gone in there for a weep, and I brace myself for her to say something on the lines of, Excuse me turning on the waterworks, June, only I'm afraid I'm going through a bad patch just at present.

And then it would all come out. Man trouble, most

probably, usually is. Sorry, Helen love, not in the mood for true confessions.

But whether it was because she caught my discouraging look, or whether it was because I was frantically stuffing envelopes fifteen to the dozen, she stalked back to her own desk without a word. Out of the corner of my eye, I could see her putting fresh make-up on.

Contrary me, I felt sorry for her then. Only a minute ago I was burning with resentment at what I thought was going to be the intrusion of Helen's problems, but now of course I realised that she's not one to burden other people with her cares and worries. She keeps herself to herself.

But she looked so woebegone that come lunchtime, after I'd put on my coat, I hesitated for a minute and then went across into her little office. And I said, You don't fancy a glass of wine by any chance, do you, Helen?

She brightened. She says, Do you know, June, a glass of wine is exactly what I do feel like, I don't usually drink at lunchtime but I think for once I could do with cheering up.

I thought, Right, you've asked for this, June, you've no one to blame but yourself.

She goes on, But where could we go, all the pubs look so grotty round here?

I could have got out of it there and then. I could have said, You're right there, Helen, come to think of it, I was forgetting, it's not exactly Covent Garden around here, is it, ah well, it was just a thought.

Instead I said before I could stop myself, I happen to know where there's a very nice wine bar tucked away, only three streets from here, that's what comes of having been wed to a newspaperman, you get a sixth sense for where there's a good watering hole, Come on, Helen, you look as if you need one.

I do sit up and beg for it, don't I, Sam? But she did look as if she wanted to talk about something, and tell the truth, I'd be glad to get my mind off my own woes for half an hour.

So we get settled in with a glass of Chardonnay apiece, then after a few minutes' chit-chat I said, Now tell me to mind my own business if you're so minded, Helen, and we'll talk about knitting or whatever, but you've got something on your mind, haven't you?

She gave me a rueful little smile, then she says, Believe you me, June, knitting's the very last thing I want to talk about right now.

The penny dropped. I may be silly but I'm not slow.

I says, Oh, I see – you're pregnant.

She says, It very much looks that way.

I says, And again shut me up if I'm intruding, but have you had a chance to make your mind up what you're going to do about it?

She says, Oh, have it, definitely, no question. She says, I'm nothing if not pro-life.

I says, And do you want a baby?

She says, I do, June, yes.

—So what's the problem, Helen, doesn't the father want it or what?

—He doesn't know, June.

—Don't you think you ought to tell him, love?

—You asked me what the problem was, June. The father doesn't know because I don't know who the father is, that's what the problem is.

I was shocked. I was. I mean, I hope I'm broad-minded, Sam, you have to be, mixing with some of the characters I've had to mix with as we've gone through life, but I do draw the line somewhere. Besides – Helen of all people, her that looks so prim and proper.

She treats me to another of her wry little smiles.

—It's not quite as bad as it sounds, June. I chucked the guy I was more or less living with because he was drinking a lot and playing away as the charming expression has it, then took up with someone else on the rebound. So I don't know which one of them it is, simple as that.

I says, Oh dear me.

It was all I could think of to say. Then I thought, Come on, June, that's not very constructive is it, so I go on, Of the two, which would you like to be the father?

She says, The first one, even though he has let me down, the second was just a ship passing in the night, in fact he's passed. And anyway, the chances are ten to one the first one's the father.

I says, Well there you go then, love, it's nothing to do with me but at the risk of sounding like Auntie Agony I know what I'd do in your place, and that's go to this first chap and tell him you're expecting his child and what does he intend to do about it? I says, That's unless there's any chance of it being a different colour.

She laughs out loud. A bit too loud. Hysterical, nearly.

—Oh, June, what a thing to say!

I said, Well, I'm afraid these things have *got* to be said, in this day and age. I said, Now do you feel better, for having got it off your chest, because I couldn't help hearing you have a good cry in the loo this morning?

She says, I do feel better, June, and what have I got to cry about anyway, I want the baby and if he doesn't he can just do the other thing, now what about the other half before you wend your way home and I have to get back?

She was putting a brave face on it but I noticed there was a little catch in her voice.

And I thought, Funny old world, isn't it – here's me, wake up in a gloom this morning because there's one person's life ended, and here's her, sobbing her guts out because someone else's life is on the verge of starting. You just can't win.

I'll tell you one thing, Sam – I never want to go to another funeral like your Derek's. I never want to go to another funeral again full stop, come to that. Ooh, I was depressed, going. It brought it all back to me. Not that it's ever been far away.

It was all happy-clappy style of thing. Lord of the Dance and all that. No organ for a start – they don't use the organ any more, apparently the vicar says it's too gloomy, he's had a synthesiser wheeled in. No choir either, or not what I'd call a choir – just a dozen kids in scruffy jeans with guitars and tambourines.

I says to Marion after the service, if you can call it a service, I didn't know you and Derek were evangelists or born-again Christians or whatever it is, when did this happen?

She says, Oh, we're not, far from it, June, don't go away with the wrong impression, no, it's all Ron's doing.

I says, Ron, who's Ron?

She says, The vicar, that's what you've got to call him. She says, This is how he does all his services these days, weddings, funerals, christenings, ordinary services when he has them, they're only every three weeks these days, because with all the cutbacks that they've had he's got three churches to run. Oh, yes, she says, it's very much take it or leave it, I'm afraid, unless you want cremating which unlike your Sam my Derek didn't, he couldn't be doing with it, still, everyone to their taste.

I says, Well all I can say is that he takes a lot on himself, this Ron.

She says, Oh, I don't know, June, it takes a lot of the pressure off, knowing you're sending his friends and relations away cheerful not tearful. That's Ron's phrase not mine, he says he wants them to come out of the church whistling.

I thought, Well, it's your funeral, Marion. It wouldn't have done for me. It wouldn't have done for you either, Sam. You'd have been that angry if you thought this was the kind of farewell do you were going to get, you'd probably have stayed alive out of spite.

Ron, as he calls himself, arrives five minutes late – on a motor-bike if you please, because he comes down the aisle carrying his crash helmet under his arm. His cassock has caught up over the top of one of his boots and you can see they're cowboy boots. At least he had the grace to apologise – he's just had a christening over at one of his other parishes. He says, as though it's a brilliantly original thought that he's had, And so, friends, as one door closes here at St Chad's, another one opens over at St Michael's Without The Wall, and there's humankind's immortality in a nutshell.

The self-same thing as I thought when Helen told me about being pregnant, but I didn't make a sermonette out of it.

Anyway, Sam, if this interests you at all – you could have got the full story from your Derek for all I know – the first thing we have to do is everybody has to turn to their neighbour and give them a big hug. God, I hate that sort of thing – you feel such a fool, embracing somebody you've never clapped eyes on before.

Except it wasn't someone I'd never clapped eyes on, it was young Sheila's Auntie Clare, dressed all in black like that old Keep Death Off The Roads poster, do you remember it? But with her ginger hair sticking out from under a black pillbox hat and veil. She looked like a madwoman.

I nearly shrieked. I did. I was trembling.

The row of seats I was in had been nearly empty when I came into the church, and while I knew someone had sat down next to me I hadn't even given them a first glance, let alone a second one, too busy reading the order of service.

I didn't know what to say. I just babbled. I go, Of all people, ooh, I'm sorry, you startled me, you're the last person I expected to find sitting next to me, what a coincidence.

She says in that knowing voice that she has, Oh, it's not a coincidence, June.

The happy clappies were tuning up their guitars so we had the chance for a word or two. Why they couldn't have done what they had to do before the service got under way we shall never know, but there you are.

I said, I didn't know you even knew Derek.

She says, Oh, no, I don't know him, June, at least not yet. No, I come to a good many of the funerals announced in the *Croydon Advertiser*, and of course Ron's church is practically on my doorstep.

I thought, Yes, I see – touting for trade, eh?

And was I right or was I right? She says, He's here, of course, Derek, and so is Samuel Herbert, they're together again.

And I'm thinking, For your sake, Sam, I hope and pray you're not here, you used to say you'd got the most boring bloody brother in the universe. And that's swearing in church. If you had been there, you'd have had another heart attack. I can just hear you saying, I come down from Manchester to avoid the bugger and he follows me here, and now I can't get him off my back even by dying, he's got to follow suit. Oh dear, oh doctor. You've got to laugh.

The service got started, after a fashion, with the kids in jeans singing a couple of songs, I refuse to call them hymns, about Jesus bringing home another friend and the Stairway leading up to Heaven. Hardly anybody joins in because although we've got hymn sheets we don't know the tunes, except for a group of about a dozen young people in casual dress, far too casual for church in my opinion but what do I know. Turns out they're some of Derek's colleagues from the Inland Revenue and they know all this stuff, they're into it as they say. Takes all sorts, I suppose.

In between these numbers, as he calls them, Ron treats us to a couple of what I think were supposed to be prayers,

I can't remember what he was banging on about but I did hear him say Y'know, God a couple of times, which in my humble opinion is taking familiarity too far.

Then we have the address, or the sermon, or whatever it's called, with Ron drivelling on along the lines of, Y'know, none of us knows for certain where our brother Derek has gone . . .

Young Sheila's Auntie Clare nudges me and whispers, Oh, but we do!

I whisper back, Ssh!

Meanwhile Ron is going on about while we know there is a God we don't know what form this God takes and though we've been singing about the Stairway to Heaven we none of us knows where that stairway really leads

I didn't dare look across the aisle to see how Marion was taking all this. If it had been me in her place I should have cracked up, I'm sure I would.

Anyway, mercifully there's not much more of this, in fact he's glanced twice at his watch while he's chuntering away so probably he has to vroom off to a wedding or whatever. We have the Lord's Prayer, with most of the congregation mumbling one version and Ron bleating another, then he consigns your Derek to wherever he might be going and after another clappy-happy hymn about the good morning coming we all troop out, leaving your brother there in his coffin.

Because this is the weird thing, Sam. As they no longer do burials in the churchyard, I suppose it must be full up by now, they cart the coffin over to a cemetery ten miles away and just quietly bury it. You see, Ron won't do a graveside service, ashes to ashes and all that, he says it's pagan. So it's another question of never mind what the relatives might want or not want, this is how it's done.

Being a northerner like us, Marion had laid on a ham tea for a few of the relatives and friends. I couldn't help remembering that I hadn't bothered after your funeral – the last thing I wanted after seeing you off was to sit around scoffing sandwiches and exchanging small talk. I hope Marion didn't expect it – too late now, June, even if she did.

I was surprised to see young Sheila's Auntie Clare getting out of one of the cars. I'm sure she must have invited herself, but I suppose there wasn't a lot Marion could do in that situation, not without making a scene.

I get myself a cup of tea and I'm chatting with your cousin Leonard when Marion comes across the room with two of the kids from the happy-clappy choir, as I thought. But no, turns out I'm mistaken.

She says, introducing us, Roz and Steve, this is my sister-in-law June, June, I'd like you to meet Roz and Steve, they've been very helpful to me, haven't you, Roz and Steve?

Then she goes off to help cousin Leonard to a sausage roll, leaving me to talk to the two kids.

I said, So are you neighbours of Marion's, then, or—?

Roz says, No, we're with the social services, June.

I didn't like being addressed as June by this slip of a girl, I can tell you. She only looked about fifteen, though she must have been older. But I wondered what Marion was doing with the social services. Had they been doing her cleaning for her or what?

I must have looked puzzled because Steve, who looks even younger than she does, laughs and says, No, we haven't come to take Marion into care, June, we're what's known as life counsellors.

I says, You're what?

Roz says, You're probably more familiar with the term grief counsellors or bereavement counsellors, but we don't use that job description any more, June, we're dealing with clients who've got to pick themselves up and get on with their lives, so in our book that makes us life counsellors.

As in Tomorrow is the first day of the rest of your life, June, says Steve.

I says, Life counsellors, grief counsellors, whatever you like to call yourselves – get away, you're not old enough!

This time Roz laughs. They both had such patronising laughs – I tell you, if they'd been counselling me instead of Marion I'd have banged their heads together.

—It's a young vocation, June. We know there's a lot of older workers in the field, but in our experience the biggest majority of death-deprived clients prefer someone much younger than themselves to lean on, because they know we'll be less judgmental.

I says, How do you mean, what's there to be judgmental about over somebody being dead? Unless you've stabbed them with a bread knife, I says.

Not quite the thing to say straight after your Derek's funeral, but I'm afraid I couldn't take them seriously.

Steve says, Oh, you'd be surprised, June, when a partner dies the reaction of the survivor is often one of guilt, guilt at not having done enough, guilt at not having cared enough, guilt at not having cherished enough, and that guilt transmits itself to other people so that unless they happen to be qualified counsellors who know about these things they tend to take the survivor at his or her own valuation. You see if somebody holds themselves in low esteem, others are likely to do the same, it rubs off, it's how we account for promiscuity for instance, the facts are all there, June.

I says, you know all the answers, don't you?

Roz says, with a smug smile, Not all the answers, June, only some of them.

I noticed that they took it in turns to speak, like two cross-talk comedians. I suppose it's the way they're taught to do it on their course.

So Steve pipes up, If we had all the answers, June, we'd be Superman and Superwoman respectively, and we're very far from that, I can assure you.

Roz says, Of course, some caseloads can be more difficult than others, we're not allowed to talk about individual clients but I think I can say that with Marion it's been quite easy so far touch wood, we were very fortunate in getting to her when we did.

I said, just to be polite, Which was when?

They surprised me then.

Steve says, Three days before Derek died.

Roz says, So you see we had time to help Marion prepare herself and come to terms with the inevitable.

I thought, My God, they're a pair of bejeaned bloody vultures!

I says, But how did you hear about Derek, did Marion call you in when he was taken to hospital or what?

Steve says, Oh, no, it's not often that clients will call us in, we offer our services and it's up to them whether they choose to avail themselves of those services or not.

Roz says, But we keep in constant touch with our hospital outreach worker, and Debbie lets us know when she thinks we can probably be of use.

I couldn't believe what I was hearing. I said, So do you mean to say that you start counselling people before their partners as you call them are screwed down in their coffins?

Roz puts on a glassy smile and looks warningly at Steve, who says, I *think* considering what day it is and where we are we'd better change the subject, June.

Which was all right by me, I can tell you.

Some idea of changing the subject they had, though, because straight away Roz says brightly, in a falsely cheerful voice, Marion tells us you yourself suffered a loss recently.

Oh, she did, did she? She takes a lot upon herself, I must

say, talking about my affairs to two total strangers, and both of them just out of their teens.

I said grumpily, I wouldn't say recently, it was six months ago now.

Roz says, Not very long, June, in the healing cycle.

Steve says, And did you accept counselling, June?

I says, I most certainly did not, the doctor gave me a helpline number but I've never had call to use it.

Roz says, Not yet, June, but that day may still come, have you had your crisis yet?

I says, Crisis, what crisis, life's one long bloody crisis and that's swearing.

Steve says, Clearly you're still under considerable strain, June.

I was. I could have murdered a double vodka.

—That's because you've never allowed yourself to properly come to terms with this very important event in your life. But by crisis, what Roz means, it's a bit like a fever, June, when your temperature reaches its high point like a kettle boiling over, and then it begins to come down again. I shouldn't say this without having got a complete profile of what you've had to experience so far, but from where I'm standing I'd say that your crisis is still to come.

I says, I sincerely hope not.

Roz says, I'd agree with Steve, you really should accept some counselling, June, it's not too late, it could be damaging if you don't.

Steve says, It's never too late although it does make it more complicated for us in the field, still, that's what we're here for, to pick up the pieces. Now you say you've never called this helpline number, June?

I says, No, and I've no intention of doing so.

Roz says, You should, I really mean that.

—Or there are other numbers I could give you in your area, June. We're on a web site, now, I could easily surf the Internet and find a counsellor exactly tailored to your needs.

I'd had enough of this.

I says, No thank you, and it's time I wasn't here.

I was about to cross to where Marion had been collared by young Sheila's Auntie Clare. But then I turned back.

I said, And if you'll let me give you two a tip – I know your hearts are in the right place and you mean well, but never ever tell anybody that they've got to come to terms, because all that expression shows is that you haven't the first idea what you're talking about.

Roz gave another of her irritating smiles.

—I think if you gave us a chance, June, you'd find that we do know what we're talking about, very much so.

And Steve chimes in, Whenever you need us, June, Marion knows how to get in touch, and we in turn will put you in touch with someone who knows how to help.

I went across to Marion feeling as if I'd lost an argument.

I says, Could we have a word before I go, Marion?

I'd nothing in particular to say but I thought I'd be doing her a favour getting her out of Sheila's Auntie Clare's clutches. I steered her away and chit-chatted about how well the service had gone, which was just about all I could bring myself to say about it. But all the while I'm yakking away I notice that Marion keeps glancing over at Sheila's Auntie Clare who by now is chatting up your cousin Leonard.

And before I'd time to say my goodbyes properly she says, Well, if you really have got to go, June, thank you very much for turning out, do keep in touch, there must be other occasions when we could meet besides funerals, now I must have another word with that lady before she wanders off, I believe you know her?

And with that she's propelling me towards Sheila's Auntie Clare. I'd no intention whatsoever of getting into another conversation with that one so I said, I'll leave you two together, then, thank you again, Marion, lovely service, and a lovely tea.

Sheila's Auntie Clare shakes hands with me and says in a meaningful voice, We shall meet again, June.

I says, I very much doubt it.

She says, Oh, but I know we shall.

I was seething as I went home, Sam. Seething. I felt imposed upon. First by that screwball Ron's happy-clappy funeral, then by those two insufferably patronising kids, and then by that crazy Auntie Clare. I felt that between them they were all trying to manipulate my life, to change me round to their own way of looking at things, to mould me into something I wasn't.

But do you know, Sam, after I'd poured myself a much-needed large vodka and begun to simmer down a bit as I told myself, Now come on, June, this isn't your day, it's Marion's day, I started to think.

And what I thought was this, it was how well Marion was bearing up – appearances can be deceptive I know but she looks in ten times better shape than ever I was in after your funeral, she was radiant where I was just playing tough. And I thought, Well, June, maybe those two kids have done her some good after all, all right, they may not have done for you, June, they'd've driven you up the wall, but we're not all the same, are we? And I thought, And that service, to me it was rubbish quite frankly, I hated every minute, but the effect on Marion seems to have been I can only call it uplifting, she really seemed to get something out of it – which is more than I did at your funeral, Sam. And I thought, And young Sheila's Auntie Clare, Marion seemed very keen to talk to her, so maybe she's getting something there too, well very good luck to her.

I left her in much better shape than I'm in at this moment in time, I can tell you, because as I was thinking these thoughts a really black mood crept over me. I was jealous, that was the size of it. Jealous that Marion was coping better than I did – letting it happen rather than brazening it out. Or maybe it was just the vodka.

One thing I've learned today. Everyone has to handle these things their own way. Marion's way isn't my way – but she left me wishing it was.

And yes, I have had a vodka too many.

I wonder why The Suit always wears The Suit. It's not as if he can't have any other clothes, but I've never seen him wearing anything else – although you'll recall I did once come damn near to seeing him not wearing it.

Sorry about that, chuck. The joke, I mean.

Yet it's always spotless, and the trouser creases like knife blades. He must sponge them and press them of an evening. I can just see him standing over the ironing board in his shirt and his Marks and Sparks knickers. His shirts are always spotless and nicely ironed too. Launderette, I shouldn't wonder, although that would be expensive for him. I'm not going to ask, it's just idle curiosity. If I did ask, he'd maybe think I was volunteering to do his laundry. No way.

One thing I did ask, when I saw him in the Duke of Clarence a few days after Derek's funeral, was how his little handyman business was coming along.

—Rushed off my feet, June, rushed off my feet – I tell you, if your fridge door fell off tomorrow morning, it'd be the back end of next week before I could get round to it.

I said, I'm very glad to hear it.

I was very glad, too, that the fridge door has become a shared joke rather than my own private joke.

He says, But there's just one snag, I was wrong when I said the business doesn't need capital outlay because it does, I've got to have transport, I need a small van, I'm having to turn work away on account of I just can't reach it in the time available, it's ridiculous.

I says, Get yourself a van, then, I'm sure there's plenty of cheap second-hand ones on the market.

He says, Oh, there are, June, there are, most definitely, but unfortunately there's a certain shortage of this . . .

With which he rubs his thumb and forefinger together to simulate peeling off bank-notes.

I'll tell you, Sam, I had just the faintest feeling of uneasiness. Was he going to try and tap me for money? I did hope not. Knowing me, I'd probably have finished up lending him the price of a second-hand van but I shouldn't have liked it. I shouldn't have liked it at all.

But I'd misjudged him.

He goes on, No, there's only one route to take, June, and that's to chat up the bank manager or customer relations executive or whatever they call themselves these days. I'll leave it for a bit and as soon as I can show I've got a regular healthy cash flow I shall go for it, the old business loan, charge you Shylock's rate of interest but it should be well worth it in the long term.

Even then I wasn't one hundred per cent sure it wasn't me he was asking for his business loan in a roundabout way, but he must have seen I was looking a bit tense, he does notice these things, Sam, because he says, And in case you're thinking I'm working my way round to asking you to tide me over till I win the Lottery, June, put it right out of your mind, that's not what friends are for, in fact it's the best way to lose them, now let me get you another drink.

So that was all right, then.

I said when he came back with my glass of Guinness and his own half-pint, Do you mind if I ask you something, Duggie?

He says, Go ahead.

I says, If you think it's too personal, don't answer, but I can't help wondering sometimes why you always wear the same suit?

He says, I thought you liked it, June, it's a suit that means something to you, I thought you'd be glad to see it being worn.

I says, Oh, I do, and it does, and I am, if I've got all that in the right order. But I says, Most men like a change from time to time, not as much as women granted, but they do get tired of wearing the same old thing day in day out, and you can't tell me you've nothing else in your wardrobe, you didn't used to walk around in a barrel before you found Sam's suit in the Oxfam shop.

He says, joking, Ah, now you don't know that, June, do you, the case comes up on Monday. No, he says, I'm a blazer man, actually, blazer and slacks as we used to call them, I've got three blazers but only the one other suit besides this, funnily enough I'd hardly ever wear a suit before this one came into my life but I'll tell you the truth now, June, since you've put the question, I wear this suit because it brings me luck.

I says, It doesn't seem to have brought you much luck so far, all the jobs you've been after and they didn't even have the decency to reply.

He says, It's brought me two pieces of stupendous luck, June, number one it's set me on the road to running my own successful business because this is going to work, June, I've got a good feeling about it. And number two and even more stupendous, having the privilege of wearing this suit was instrumental in my meeting one of the nicest and most delightful persons I've ever come across and I do mean that.

Wasn't that kind of him, to say a thing like that?

I leaned over and gave him a little peck on the cheek.

I said, Thank you, Duggie, and I couldn't imagine that suit going to a nicer man.

Then into the pub trolls your Pauline, to spoil it all. She cracks on she was passing on her way to Boots to pick up a prawn mayonnaise sandwich for her lunch when she saw us through the glass. Now you cannot see anyone through that glass, Sam, for the very good reason that it is frosted. She came in on the off chance of finding us together. She was spying, that's the top and bottom of it. Whether she saw me giving him that little friendly kiss I didn't know and I didn't care. She should keep her nose out of my life.

The Suit has to buy her a gin and tonic, of course. She says to me while he's up at the bar, The regulars are going to start taking you two as a couple if you're not careful.

I says, There's nothing I need to be careful about, Pauline, thank you very much, and even if there was it'd be my business and nobody else's.

She says, I was only winding you up, June, no need to snap my head off.

Well, maybe she was and maybe she wasn't.

The Suit fetches over her g-and-t and by way of conversation asks her, All set for your holiday then, Pauline?

She says, Just about, as soon as I've got my pesetas and a swimsuit I can get into.

And we start talking about all the little ins and outs and ups and downs of setting off on holiday. As you do. But then as we were rabbiting away about the merits of Gatwick over Heathrow I suddenly thought to myself, Hello, just a minute, June, hang on, how does he know she's going to Spain next week because I'm quite sure I've never mentioned it?

So perhaps she mentioned it herself, when she had that drink with him on your birthday. Long memory he must have, then.

I still wonder if it's Eric Grant she's going off to Spain with and I'm searching for a way of dredging his name up while we're still on the subject of holidays, in case she inadvertently gives away some clue, when she drains off her g-and-t and saying, Time I wasn't here, thanks for the drink, Duggie, see you tonight, June, off she blows.

No thought of getting a round in, it goes without saying. But Duggie, I noticed she called him. Someone else with a long memory, because I certainly never mention his name at home.

By this time I've got to make a move myself – hair appointment. I'm going to have it dyed strawberry blonde. Don't look like that, Sam, if you are looking like that, I'm only joking. Just the usual cut and blow-dry.

The Suit says, all rueful, Sorry about that little invasion, it was none of my doing.

—No sorrier than I am, Duggie. Thanks for saying what you did.

Something's been nagging away at me and I wanted to talk it through with young Sheila. So I rang up and invited her to another lunch. After all, she'd said call any time you like, June, always pleased to see me style of thing.

Surprise, surprise, Sam, I got definitely bad vibes. I know how you used to be able to sense an atmosphere on the other end of a telephone, how you could tell what was going on even if the person you were speaking to was six thousand miles away. You knew if they were pretending whoever it was you wanted was out, or whether they were being evasive, or that while you were keeping them talking they were racking their brains for the first excuse to hang up and it was your task to stop them doing it. Well, something of that instinct must have rubbed off on me after all these years, because I could tell from the start that I was bad news to Sheila this time round, fulsome though she was. Over-fulsome, I'd say.

How shall I put it? It was a sensation of her thinking, Oh, my God, it's her again, she's already been back once and everyone was very nice to her, what does she want now, does she intend making a habit of this, is she going to be turning up like a bad penny every few weeks?

Anyway, she couldn't very well refuse point blank to have lunch with me and I did need to see her, so we made a date and I said I'd pick her up at the office.

Talk about cat among the pigeons. She says very quickly, Or June, better still, why don't we meet at the restaurant, unless you want to try somewhere different, not that there's very much choice around here.

Doesn't want me to come to the office, you see.

I says, No, the restaurant will do fine, it's just that I'm not too sure I shall know how to find it. And I should have to pass the office anyway on my way there, so why don't we meet in the lobby?

She says, Whatever suits you, June, just ask for me at the front desk as you did before and I'll come down.

She'll come down, do you notice? Not she'll invite me up to say hello to Bob Carp and he'll offer me a drink.

So come the day, that's what I did – I speak to the commissionaire, he calls Sheila's number, and after telling her I'm there he hands the phone over to me and says, She'd like a word, Mrs Pepper.

I says, Hello, Sheila, are you coming down or shall I come up?

She says, June, are you sure you can't find the restaurant on your own, it's only round the corner?

I says, I wouldn't like to risk it, Sheila, I'm lost round here on foot, why, can't you get out at the moment?

She says, The thing is I'm in the middle of a long memo to the lawyers that Bob wants on his desk before lunch, I shall be about ten minutes, tell you what, ask the commissionaire to give you the *Evening Standard* to read and make yourself comfortable, I shall be down as soon as I possibly can.

I was that narked, Sam. Why couldn't she have asked me up? Did she think I'd start distracting her by chattering while she's trying to finish her memo? Does she not know

I've been an editorial secretary myself in my time? It's humiliating, almost.

I sat down on a sofa in the lobby, having a little fume to myself. I picked up a copy of the *UK Press Gazette* but I'm afraid its contents are of little interest to me these days, so I put it down again. I hadn't asked the commissionaire for the *Evening Standard* but after I'd twiddled my thumbs for a couple of minutes he brings a Metro edition over.

He says, after I've thanked him, You'll be Sam's widow then, Mrs Pepper.

It wasn't a question, it was a statement, so he must have recognised me. I says, Yes, that's right.

He says, Excuse the familiarity, but that's what we all called him.

I says, Oh, I know, he never stood on ceremony. But I says, I just can't place you, and I thought I knew all the commissionaires.

He says, No, I'm new down here, Mrs Pepper, I used to be one of the messengers, eighteen years in the tape room for my sins, but now they've put me out to grass.

I still didn't know him from Adam but I said, Of course you were, it's seeing people out of context, it's always confusing.

He says, He's very much missed, Mrs Pepper, some said he was a tyrant but he was always very good to me, I did come along to the memorial service but you won't have noticed.

I says, apologetic, There was such a throng.

He says, It was a very good turnout, it's Fred by the way.

I says, I know it is, Fred, very nice to see you again.

He says, I'm glad you're keeping in touch, Mrs Pepper.

His phone's ringing so he goes back to his desk. I must say I felt much, much better, Sam, for that little interlude. Aren't some people nice? He needn't have said anything – he knew very well I didn't recognise him in his uniform (I wouldn't have recognised him out of it, come to that) so he needn't have come over. I felt a glow.

Which didn't last for long, I can tell you. Because out of the executive lift steps Charlie Whittington, with one of those power-dressed thirty-something women who get to be assistant editors these days; I didn't know her. And I swear to God, Sam, that he nearly leapt straight back into that lift when he saw me sitting there.

It was the same as it had been when I rang young Sheila. If looks could speak, his would have said, Oh, bloody hell, not you again, look love, I thought we'd got you sorted, this isn't a flaming citizens advice bureau you know, what do you want now?

But he switches on a big smile, like you'd switch on a fluorescent light, and comes over and shakes hands, although none too warmly. Shakes hands, I said – no kiss this time. He gave me a kiss on the other occasion and he must think it only encourages me.

—June! You always catch me when I'm doing a runner, is someone looking after you, oh, this is Melanie who's just taken over from Gabby, Melanie, this is June, Sam Pepper's widow.

Since I didn't know who Gabby was I didn't know who Melanie was either, obviously snake-bite executive material. She gives me a fishy handshake and a glossy, dead-eyed smile that says, You're not even B-list, baby, you're a has-been never-was, what are you hanging about round here for?

That's how I translated it, anyway, and I don't think I'm doing her an injustice.

And with some more come-back-and-see-us babble from Charlie they're off into the Jag outside, that silver job with the mini-bar in the back that I've had many and many a ride in.

No sooner have they gone than the other lift comes down

and three of the newsroom chaps pile out. Like Charlie, they'd all greeted me warmly enough on my first visit, but not now, oh dear me no. It was, Hullo, June, back again? and Can't keep away, eh, June? and Keeping well, June, gooood (this before I'd a chance to reply, No, I've got terminal cancer since you so very kindly ask), and they were through those revolving doors like spinning tops.

I felt that depressed. It was all so different from that warm reception I'd had the other time. Would you like to know what I was made to feel, Sam? I was made to feel that sympathy's rationed and friendship's rationed, that they all mean everything they say at the time that they say it but they don't want you coming round for a second helping like Oliver Twist. They've done their bit. And of course, with being a widow, you've no longer anything in common with them. Face it, you were an adjunct at the best of times. They would never have given you a second look if you hadn't married into their magic circle so why should they give you a second look now you're widowed out of it? Think yourself lucky they've been kind to you, but don't push that luck. That's how I was made to feel.

I remembered how that other time Bob Carp himself came down in his shirtsleeves to escort me up to the newsroom personally. Queen for a day, I was. I didn't expect that treatment again but I knew he must be up there because he's waiting for the memo that Sheila's typing up for him. All right, so he's busy, got a lot on his mind, could even be in conference. But has he got a paralysed hand, Sam? Couldn't he pick a phone up, just to say, Hello, June, sorry I can't come down, I'm right up to my eyebrows just at present but do come in another time, and sorry Sheila's had to keep you waiting. Couldn't he have said that?

I don't know what I was so put out about. It's the way of widows the world over, must be. You're only Queen for a day the once. But I did think our lot were that little bit different. I don't know why I should think that, I'm sure. If they've forgotten you already, Sam, which I'm sure most of them more or less have by now, because that's the name of the game, why should they want to remember me?

Sheila comes down at long last, only twenty minutes late if you please. She does have the decency to apologise, in fact she goes over the top with it, but then no sooner are we through the revolving doors than she comes straight in with, Now I'm afraid I've got to make it short and sweet today, June, Bob wants me back double sharp in case he's got to redraft his memo, poor devil, no Savoy Grill lunch for him today, it's a sandwich at his desk, you feel sorry for them, don't you?

In other words, Say what you've got to say, June, then get off my back.

So I did. I can take a hint. Especially since before we'd even got our first glass of wine down, Sheila was asking more or less point blank what it was I wanted of her. She starts out by saying, So were you able to locate Eric Grant, June?

After us going to the trouble of finding him for you, she means.

I says, I know where he's to be found, Sheila, if that's what you mean, but it's not up to me to make a move, it's up to Pauline, Sam's daughter, if she ever wants that packet of letters of hers that he's taken possession of back.

She says, So is there anything else on your mind, June?

Couldn't put it plainer, as they say.

I said, Well, there is and there isn't.

Then I told her about my weirdo conversation over the envelope-stuffing with her Auntie Clare, and how she'd turned up at your Derek's funeral and at Marion's house later.

Sheila said, Oh, yes, that sounds like Auntie Clare, very much so.

I said, Well, what I wanted to ask, if you don't mind

giving me a straight answer, is whether she's completely – you know what I mean, Sheila?

Sheila gives a trilling little laugh. I have to say this in her favour, Sam, that in spite of blatantly prompting me to state my business style of thing as she did, she did seem perfectly happy with my company. Perhaps she genuinely did have to get back to the office, I mean I'm not knocking her, Sam, she's a very nice genuine girl, it's just that I know perfectly well she would have been very glad to have been somewhere else, because I now come under the heading of Been there, done that, got the T-shirt.

She says, If you mean is she a hundred air miles short of a trip to Barcelona, which of us isn't, June?

I says, Not me for sure, certainly not since Sam went, but all this psychic stuff, Sheila, I mean do you believe in it?

She says, I neither believe in it nor disbelieve in it, June, let me put it this way, there's certain members of my family swear by Clare, they think she's magic, but then if you've lost somebody you tend to believe what you want to believe, don't you, I mean I don't mean you personally, June, but it's how some people react.

I says, Yes, I can see all that, Sheila, and it must be a great comfort, having that belief, but what is it that she actually does for these believers, I mean does she claim to be able to get through to the other side as they call it or what, because that's what it certainly sounded like to me.

Sheila says, Oh, she can, June, for some people, there's no doubt about that, I mean I've got proof.

I says, So you do believe in it?

She says, It's difficult not to, when your Uncle John has been told he's got a message from someone called Madge, and no one in the whole family was aware he'd ever known anyone called Madge, not my mother, nobody, because it was years and years ago when he was in the RAF down in Oxfordshire, June, that he had this relationship, and he'd played it pretty close to his chest as seemingly there was a baby involved, so how could Clare ever have known he'd known a Madge? Unless she genuinely is psychic?

I says, But how does being psychic tell you other people's names, and why?

—Don't ask me, June, you'd have to go to Clare for the answer to that one.

—The reason I'd like to find out, Sheila, is how the thump does she come to know my husband's full names were Samuel Herbert, I mean did you happen to mention it, no reason why you shouldn't?

—Absolutely not, I might have told her he was called Sam, June, she'd know that anyway, it was a generally known fact while he was editing the paper, but as for the middle name, Herbert, she couldn't have got that from me because quite frankly I didn't even know Sam had a middle name, so far as I was concerned he was Sam, Sam, pick up tha musket as you used to say when you wanted him to finish his drink and get him off the premises, and that was all.

I said, Thank you, Sheila, I'm sure this is very boring for you but I'm looking for a logical explanation, though who knows but that there might not be one, not that we'd call logical anyway. But I says, Now just bear with me, can you tell me something else now, when she gets through to these dear departed spirits who've got all these messages for us, how does she set about it, is it seances or twiddling around with ouija boards or playing around with tarot cards or what?

Sheila says, Ah, now I've never actually been to any of her sessions, I've had no occasion to because I've never lost anybody close unlike some in my family, but from what I gather she's in very close touch with a Red Indian spirit guide called Hawkeye.

I says, A Red Indian spirit guide called what?

—Hawkeye. He's put her in touch with a lot of spirits so

she tells her believers – Gandhi, John Lennon, Picasso she's had, because she told this Hawkeye she was interested in painting. Then there was Churchill on one occasion, Greta Garbo – oh, it's like the Hall of Fame, June, believe me.

I says, I'll believe you, June, but with great respect I'm not so sure I'll believe your Auntie Clare, So it's this Hawkeye who passes on these messages from her clientele's deceased relatives, is it?

She says, Yes, he's her spirit guide, he's her only means of getting through.

And I says, So if I went to her myself, now don't think I'm knocking a member of your family, Sheila, because I'm sure she does a lot of good; but I'd be getting a word or two from George Bernard Shaw or Charlie Chaplin or whoever by way of a warm-up, would I, and then I'd get Sam's news, is that about the size of it?

She says, Something like that, June.

And I thought, And then the bill.

But all I said was, Thank you, Sheila, you've answered all my questions except one, which is why are all the spirit guides you've ever heard of Red Indians, I mean have they cornered the market or what?

She says, Looks like it, June.

She's glancing at her watch. Ever since I've been widowed I seem to have been surrounded by people looking at their watches.

So I let her off the hook. I said, Now I know you've got to get back, Sheila . . .

She'd picked up her handbag before I'd even finished my sentence.

I walked her back to the office. There was plenty of Lovely to see you again, June, you're looking very well, have you had a holiday yet, you should do – oh, yes, plenty of that. But this time, no Don't leave it so long next time, June, drop in any time, we're always delighted to see you, now you know I mean that – no, a distinct shortage of that.

It was kiss kiss with young Sheila and I know I've seen her for the last time ever. But that's life. No, it isn't life, is it? It's death.

Do you know, Sam, I never cease to be amazed at some of the things that some people come out with. I was watching one of those rubbishy game shows tonight – ooh, I wish you'd been there. Because they wheel on this gentleman who's been blind since he was a lad – meningitis I should think it was. And after the MC's asked him a few banal questions, he says to this blind chap, But it's your handicap that keeps you up and running, isn't that right, Les? And the audience applauded. I mean, what the thump was he blethering on about? They could have me on next week. So it's being a widow that keeps you so cheerful, isn't that right, June? Honestly!

Well, chum, we've established one thing today, and that's that whoever your Pauline's trolled off to Spain with, it isn't Eric Grant. Not that I give a toss if it's Guy the Gorilla. Because no sooner has the mini-cab set off to take her to Gatwick than the doorbell rings and blow me if it isn't Eric himself.

I made no effort whatsoever to look pleased to see him, I mean why should I, slimy sod that he is?

I said, all distant, You've just missed her, she's gone on holiday.

He says, Yes, I know that, June, I deliberately waited until Pauline was out of the way because it's you I wanted to see, June. He says, And neither at this hour of the morning nor in the evening which are the only convenient times to call round as far as I'm concerned is there any guarantee she won't be here.

I says, You've not put your feet across the threshold yet, Eric, and already you're building up a mystery, do you do it on purpose for the thrill of it or is it that you've got such a devious corkscrew mind you can't help yourself?

That was telling him, Sam lad, and I felt better for it.

He says, There's no mystery, June, but do we have to conduct our business on the doorstep?

I says, I didn't know we had any business to conduct.

He says, I think we have, June.

Yes, I know, Sam. I know I should have slammed the door in the little rat's face, but having just given him a piece of my mind had made me quite pleased with myself, so stupidly I let him in.

I said, as we went into the living room, I suppose it's about those letters.

And I noticed a bundle of tattered envelopes sticking out of one of his side pockets.

He says, darkly, That and another matter, June.

Trust Eric Grant to start going round the houses. I wasn't having it, Sam.

I says, What other matter, and if you say to me All in good time, June, I swear I'll throw that mug of coffee over you and it's still hot so be warned.

You'd think he'd look insulted, yet he never does, does he, no matter how offensive you are to him? He missed his vocation, did Eric Grant – he should have been a foot-in-the-door encyclopedia salesman.

He says, Have it your way, June, we'll dispose of the other matter first then if that's what you want, now do you mind if I ask you a personal favour?

I says, I'm doing you no favours, Eric Grant.

He says, Bear with me, June, you don't have to do anything, the reverse in fact, all I'm asking is in future would you mind not passing out my phone number to all and sundry?

I had to think for a second or two what he was going on about. Then I remembered – the call out of the blue I'd had from that Ted Cargill fellow, if that was his name, wanting Eric's number because he said he owed him money.

I says, with a big happy smile, Oh, so Ted Cargill's caught up with you at last, has he? I says, And did he get you to pay up?

He says, I don't think you know Ted Cargill, do you, June, you should take what blokes of that calibre say with a pinch of salt, if you knew the real story you'd realise that the boot's on the other foot.

I says, catty as they come, Oh I see, so he's chasing you because he owes *you* money, is he, wants to give it back, does he?

He says, All right, June, have your bit of fun, all I'm asking of you is please please please don't ever give out my number, because there may be others out there after it and Sam Pepper's widow's an obvious source. Quite frankly not being a brown-noser like some I could mention, I do happen to have made a certain number of enemies in this business and there are people I'd sooner avoid, if I'd wanted them to have my number they would have already had it from me.

It's not often I get the chance to kick a complete bastard in the goolies as you would have put it. Not often that I'd dare to. You would have been proud of me.

I says, I'm quite sure you have more enemies than even you know about, Eric, but let me just say that anyone who rings me up wanting your number is more than welcome to it, and do you know why? Because I think you're the biggest shit I've ever come across, in fact you're less than shit because that has a useful purpose, you're just scum.

Was I overdoing it, Sam? I don't think so, and you'll know why in a minute.

If he's in any way put out, he doesn't show it. He shrugs

and says, Oh well, I was just trying to save myself the bother of changing my number, play it any way you like, June.

I'd told him what I thought of him, and now I just wanted him out of the house double quick.

I said, Right, now we've cleared the air on that, what about these letters?

He says heavily, taking the packet from his pocket and placing it very carefully on the coffee table, The letters, June, yes the letters.

I seemed to remember they were tied up with ribbon the last I'd heard of them. They had a thick rubber band round them now. Make of that what you will.

I says, You've taken your time about delivering these, haven't you, I mean how many weeks, months even, must it be since you came round here and admitted you'd got them?

He says, Admitted's a strange word, June, I simply came out and said I'd taken possession of them, I don't suppose there's any coffee on the go is there, I'm gagging for one.

Talk about having the hide of a rhinoceros. I says, No, there flaming is not. I says, And by the way, can we get one thing straight, are you seeing Pauline at all?

He says, I think that's my business, June.

I says, It's certainly not mine, and I should never want it to be. But I says, I believe you are seeing her, because otherwise how would you have known she's gone on holiday?

He says, Oh, nice one, June, but the fact that we keep in touch doesn't mean to say we're quote seeing each other as you put it, that's if I understand the phrase right.

I says, It doesn't matter a toss to me whether you're seeing each other or not seeing each other or what the phrase means or what it doesn't mean, what I want to say to you, Eric Grant, is I never want you ringing my number and asking for Pauline ever again. I'll make a bargain with you, I don't take phone calls for you, and in exchange for that I don't take your phone calls for her, you can ring her at work. And I says, And I don't want you ever turning up on that doorstep asking for Pauline, because I shall slam the door in your face.

He says, June, June, we don't have a problem, now can we get down to business?

I says, Business, business, why do you keep on calling it business, you sound like a bloody blackmailer.

He says, Oh, come on now, June, calm down, calm down, I've brought the letters, haven't I?

I says, Yes, I can see that, but why have you waited till Pauline's out of the way, and come to that why did you never give them to Pauline herself, I mean how many times must she have asked for them?

He says, I'll surprise you now, June, she's never asked for them at all.

I says, Don't be so ridiculous, are you saying that the number of times you've spoken to her, either on the phone or in person, she's never once said, By the way, Eric, what about those letters of mine my stepmother says you're holding?

—Let me put your mind at rest on that one, June.

—My mind isn't troubled, Eric, just get on with whatever you've got to say.

—Very well, June, I'm going to tell you two things. First off, these letters are not Pauline's property, they're your property.

—Yes, we know all about that, I've had it all explained to me. But I've told Pauline that so far as I'm concerned they're her property, they're her own letters to her own father damn it all, and I want nothing to do with them.

—Which she's quite willing to accept, June.

And suddenly it comes home to me that he's discussed this whole thing with Pauline herself.

I says, So in that case why are you bringing them round to me?

He says, Ah!

I says, Yes, you may well say Ah, but what is it that you're up to, you admit that Pauline wants the letters back herself, yet you wait till she's out of the country before bringing them round to me, just what is your bloody game?

He says in what I can only describe as a silky manner, I'll be frank with you, June.

It's unbelievable, isn't it?

He says, We have two problems here, June. The first is that regardless of the ins and outs of the situation, Pauline didn't want the letters brought round here, in fact she specifically asked me to hang on to them until she's found a flat

Found a flat. First I've ever heard about her looking for a flat, I was beginning to fear I was saddled with her for life. I was mightily relieved to hear it, I can tell you, Sam, though why your charming daughter couldn't have had the courtesy to mention she was flat-hunting I do not know, I'm sure.

He says, But the question is, was I in a position to do what Pauline wished, to which the answer is I'm afraid not.

I says, What do you mean?

I can be thick sometimes. It was perfectly obvious what he meant.

He says, Because legally these letters belong to you and you alone as part of Sam's estate, June, and it's my bounden duty to deliver them to you, otherwise I could be in hot water.

I says, Hot water my eye, I know what you're up to.

He says, Up to, June, all I'm up to is handing over your property, whether you then hand it on to Pauline is entirely a matter for you.

With which he formally hands over the packet of letters with, I won't call it a smile, it was more of a smirk. A winning smirk.

And of course I did know what he was up to like I said. I'm

not totally stupid, Sam. Why should he wait until Pauline is out of the way before giving the letters to me, eh? For no other reason than that he wants me to read them. And it's because Pauline doesn't want me to read them that she wanted him to look after them until she'd found a flat.

What a vicious swine he is.

Still, I'd done enough name-calling for one day. There was nothing else to be said so I got him off the premises as quickly as ever I could, then I sat for a long time with the bundle of letters.

Fifteen of them there were, the envelopes a bit grimy by now as you might expect, but the rounded childish handwriting surprisingly unfaded. Maybe ballpoint doesn't fade, never thought of it. There were half a dozen picture postcards from seaside resorts where she'd been on holiday with Tricia – Cornwall, The Isle of Man, Guernsey, St Malo: farther and farther afield as she got older. These I read of course. Wish you were here Dads, this morning went shrimping, I have made a friend called Karen who comes from Blackheath, swam three lengths, I have got sunburn, big hugs and kisses, that sort of thing. Nice. But I didn't read the letters. I wanted to but I didn't. I replaced the rubber band, carefully easing it back into the ridge it had made in the top and bottom of the bundle, and took them up to Pauline's room, where I put them in her underwear drawer. And I thought, There they stay until she gets back.

I've been thinking on and off about selling the house, moving into a flat somewhere. Although not – this is yesterday's afterthought – until your Pauline has found a pad of her own. I don't want to find myself living in the same block or even in the same street.

Do you know where I've been fancying? Those thirtyish flats they've been doing up overlooking the park, pity about the two-way three-lane expressway or whatever these roads are called between them. I took a walk round that way the other day and they do look very smart with their little balconies and Nile green ironwork and all the stucco gleaming wedding-cake white again. But I've not seen inside them. Very pokey rooms, I shouldn't wonder, and of course they're north-facing.

But then today, when I'd half made my mind up to drop in at the estate agents and pick up a brochure, I began to wonder, well do I want to sell up and move or is it something I'm willing myself to do, something to pass the time?

And I realised that that was just exactly what I was doing. There's nothing wrong with this house, nothing wrong with this street, nothing wrong with this neighbourhood – that's why we bought it. Not a family house of course, we weren't looking for a family house, which is why it came relatively cheap – it suited two people and with Pauline out of the way, touch wood, it'll suit one. No, Sam, you'll possibly be relieved to hear with your horror of domestic upheavals (you never minded office upheavals, you thrived on them) that I shall most likely leave here when I'm carried out in the wooden box.

Though I've even thought, in the course of these ruminations, about going back to Manchester. But then why? I barely know anybody there these days, I shouldn't think I could even find my way about, it must have changed so much. And then I've wondered, in a drifting sort of way, about living abroad. Malta, Spain, Cyprus, little flat – I could probably just about afford it with what you left me if this place fetched the going rate. But to what purpose? Meeting and maintaining a young gigolo? Falling in with a bunch of blazered and peroxide-blonde expats and whiling the evenings away in a fake English pub called Ye Mucky Duck? I don't think so, Sam. As you've pointed out often and often, we've got fake English pubs less than fifteen minutes away.

No, it would be to the purpose of not being bored out of my skull for a while, that's all. And that's depressing. I can understand people moving house out of the nomad instinct, because they've got within them the desire to move on, but I haven't got that need in any sort of way whatsoever. The only reason I've thought about moving is to give myself something to do. Occupy the time. Pack. Unpack. Take down the pictures, put up the pictures. Stack all the books in cardboard boxes, replace the books on different shelves. Wrap the crockery in newspaper, unwrap the crockery and stuff the newspaper in plastic sacks. This could take a fortnight. Plus all the wonderful hours spent in showing prospective buyers round the house, looking at flats, seeing the lawyers, reading the surveyor's report et cetera et cetera, that could occupy a good six months of life. How wonderfully it could drift by. How to pass your time when all you have to do is pass the time.

But equally I might just as well pass it painting the walls of the house purple from top to bottom or paving the garden with mosaic tiles, or taking up tapestry, or learning to drive, or stuffing yet more envelopes. Learning to drive I wouldn't mind having a crack at but what holds me back is that I know my motivation for doing it wouldn't really be wanting to pass the test but needing to pass the time.

Why do we have to pass the time? I mean it passes anyway, of its own accord. Why do we wish the days away? Why do we look at clocks and say to ourselves, Nearly eleven, girl, morning's practically gone, another hour and you'll have the whole afternoon to look forward to? Why do we welcome tiredness and the blessedness of sleep, and fear waking up and misreading the clock when it's four something not seven something? Why do we scratch around so pathetically for something to put in our diaries? Tuesday, 10.30, dentist. Ten thirty's a good spot for time-passers, I can tell you. The morning's half gone before you're into your appointment and more or less over by the time you're out on the street again wondering if it's too early for a refresher at the Duke of Clarence, or should you have a very slow walk around the block? And why do we start surreptitiously, shamefacedly looking up the telly programmes for the evening at before four in the afternoon?

For we, us, read widows, Sam, or some of us. Those of us who've never plunged back into a career to give ourselves something to do or who didn't have one to plunge into in the first place. Those of us who thought, stupidly, that there'd always be a husband coming home no matter at what time and no matter in what state, for ever and ever amen. Those of us whose only role, and I'm facing up to this one, lad, oh yes I am, was to be a wife, and while that role lasted were happy to play it, but whose only role now is to be a wife no longer.

I keep thinking of that stack of letters in Pauline's underwear drawer, of course I do.

Three times I've been up into that room and opened that drawer and looked at them lying there wrapped round with their rubber band. And I've thought, Now shall I read just one? And I've thought, After all, June, you've read the postcards, why should the letters be any different, they'll just be merry, chatty letters telling him how she's getting on at school and what she wants from Santa Claus and all like that.

And then I've thought, Leave it, June. And I've left it. This evening I put the pile of letters under Pauline's knickers and bras and stuff, so I shouldn't be able to see them. Be gone from me temptation style of thing.

Damn it, Sam, I've absolutely no wish to read your daughter's letters, swear to God. No, not swear to God. But I don't want to know. Yes I do want to know but no I don't want to know. I'll tell you what I do want for certain, though, and that's to see that bastard Eric Grant in hell.

Because this is what he's putting me through, which is that there's only one way to get it settled, one way or the other, and that's by knowing what you yourself wanted me to do. And there's only one way of finding that out, and that's by going to young Sheila's Auntie Clare. And I don't want to go through that palaver, Sam, I couldn't do it. What would I be doing listening to the likes of Mao Tse Tung and Oscar Wilde? I shouldn't be able to keep a straight face. No, Sam, I won't go there. But thank you I don't think, Eric Grant, for making me even think about it.

And I've yet to throw her visiting card away.

While I was having a break from stuffing envelopes today, Helen asked me if I'd made any holiday plans at all. As you do.

I said, No, not really, I've picked up a few brochures from the travel agents but that's as far as I've got, I've barely flipped through them.

And the only reason I did that was so as to leave them lying around on the coffee table for when Pauline gets back from Spain, so she'll see she's not the only one around here who goes on holidays. Just because it never entered her little head to ask me if I'd like to go with her – not that I'd ever dream of so much as going on a day trip to Brighton with your Pauline – I don't want her running away with the idea that I'm incapable of organising a break for myself.

Not that I'd the remotest intention of doing any such thing. I've said I could do with a holiday, but who would I go with? I've asked you that before, and answer came there none. Maybe I should put the question to young Sheila's Auntie Clare. There are these group tours, of course, but the idea of for ever piling in and out of a coach with a lot of big-bummed women with bad feet doesn't appeal to me at all, quite frankly. I'm not all that mad keen about sightseeing as you know, for one thing, and for another, do you remember that coach party who were in that hotel we stayed at in Florence, ooh, must have been ten years ago? And they used to have sing-songs in the lounge every night? Can you see me belting out 'We'll Meet Again' with a crowd of complete strangers? I'd sooner get up at a karaoke evening in Camberwell.

I said as much to Helen.

She says, Yes, I know what you mean, June, I'm in the same boat, I did have it penned in to go to Corfu with Euan, but of course all that's gone by the wayside now.

Euan's the ex-steady boyfriend, the one who may or may not be the father of her unborn child.

She says, Then I was planning to go away with a girlfriend who's been having man trouble, same as me, but now she's made it up with her fellow so she's going off with him, self-catering flat in Devon. What they'll find to do in Devon besides the obvious who knows, but one thing's for sure, they don't want me with them and who can blame them, three's a crowd as they say.

I says, Looks like we're a couple of wallflowers, Helen, still, you must have plenty of friends, I'm sure you can find someone to go with.

I hoped that didn't sound as if I was feeling sorry for myself, or worse, that I wanted Helen to feel sorry for me.

She says, It's not a shortage of friends that's the problem, June, it's that this late in the season they've all made their arrangements, I suppose I could gatecrash my two oldest school-friends' holiday, they're going to Turkey some-where, I don't know where, but at this stage of the game it would mean paying a single occupant supplement and that's money just thrown away, always assuming they've still got a room going and there's seats on the flight, it's a problem, June.

Now you're probably ahead of me here. Yes, the notion did cross my mind of saying something on the lines of, Well, Helen, you want to get away and I want to get away but we've both been stood up after our different fashions, why don't we club together for a double room and go away together, the pair of us?

But before I'd a chance to open my big mouth I was telling myself, Don't do it, June, forget it, don't even mention it. Because what if I was rebuffed? What if she said something on the lines of, Oh, that's a very sweet thought, June, but now I've more or less promised to go down to my sister's in Hastings? I should have gone into the toilet and stuck my head down the loo. Besides, look at the age difference between us twenty years if a day. She wouldn't want to be traipsing about with an old biddy like me.

So I held my tongue. But then Helen goes, If you did take the plunge and decide on a holiday, June, where would you go?

I thought she was just making conversation while we had our coffee and digestives. I says, With me, Helen, it's not so much a question of where I'd go as where I wouldn't go, because I'm very picky, I don't like beaches, I don't like places that are boiling hot, I don't like secluded little islands, I suppose I'm a city person, either because I was raised in Manchester or maybe that I've been spoiled but I like New York, Rome, Paris, Copenhagen, places with a bit of life in them.

She says, Have you ever been to Dublin?

I says, I love Dublin.

Which I do. Not that I remember much about it, Sam, because when we went on that facility trip I don't think we drew a sober breath between us from the moment we landed to the moment we left. Do you remember going on that pub trail – Bloomsday, was it? Another twenty-four hours and I should have been carried home on a stretcher. What a trip that was.

I says, One of my favourite cities in all the world.

Helen says, quite shyly, How do you feel about making up a twosome?

I was amazed. And flattered.

—Are you sure, Helen?

—I'd like nothing better, June.

Then from feeling flattered I went over to feeling anxious. Insecure. Was she patronising me? Feeling sorry for me? Helen's heart's in the right place, otherwise she wouldn't be working for peanuts at the Animal Trust, so was going with June to Dublin going to be her autumn good deed?

I said, Well, it would be very nice, Helen, but I warn you I'm beyond the age when I want to stop up all night, I can handle a few glasses of the old Liffey water but I'm a bit out of your age group, have you taken that into consideration?

She laughs. Patting her belly she says, You forget who I've got in here, June, all I want to do is eat, I've only been once but I know there's some very nice restaurants, I just want to sit around in one or two of their folk music pubs, go to those fabulous Oriental Coffee Rooms that they've got, and generally just relax.

I says, You're on.

She says, Only one snag, June, I don't reckon we could both be off for longer than a week at the same time, with no other help down here.

I couldn't see why, since by now I must have stuffed enough envelopes to just about cover the entire country twice over. But a week in Dublin would be ample so far as I was concerned. As I recall, Sam, four days was three days too many the last time we were there.

So we leave it that Helen's going to go into it and we'll see if we can get away next month when the weather's cooling off a bit.

I left my envelope-stuffing duties for the day feeling highly chuffed and already looking forward to a break in Dublin. But on the way home misgivings began to set in again. After all, why should Helen want to go there with me of all people? She barely knows me. And there must be plenty of her own set who'd jump at a jaunt in Dublin, because from what I've read it's quite a swinging city these days. But then I thought, Are there, though? How many fancy-free young women want to share a double room with a pregnant friend, listening to her woes? – because I don't fool myself, Sam, I know that's what I'm in for. Is she battening on to me because she's got nobody else?

That's an unworthy thought, June, I told myself sternly. But then you see, I want it both ways, don't I? I want her not to be patronising me but I want her at the same time not to be just looking after Numero Uno. Whereas the truth of it is probably that she just wants a little holiday, she quite likes the middle-aged envelope-stuffer who's not going to give her any trouble, and in her condition she prefers the company of an older woman to a younger one.

Widows spend a lot of time looking gift horses in the mouth, as you will have gathered by now.

Do you want to hear about the most upsetting day I've had since all this started? Worse in a way than the day you died because at least I knew that was coming and I was prepared for it, whereas this just blew up in my face like a bloody landmine.

Day, I'm saying. Evening leading to the wee small hours is what I should have said.

I'll start at the beginning, which is bad enough. But then it gets worse. I don't think I've ever mentioned it, but there's a nice little restaurant I've been getting into the habit of going into for a bite of supper, perhaps once a fortnight. I don't think you'll have heard of it, pet, it's quite new – the College

Green it's called, up that alley that runs by the side of the old public library. Why the College Green I do not know since there's neither green nor college within throwing distance of a bread roll, but it's seemed a pleasant enough place up to now. Not up to *Good Food Guide* standards I dare say but quite acceptable. Very good for fish. Anyway, I've always enjoyed going there and if you want to know the truth I like to tell your Pauline I shall be eating out tonight then get myself dolled up a bit, so giving her the impression that I've got more of a social life than I have. Childish, really. Not that she was there tonight either to be impressed or not impressed. She gets back this weekend.

One reason I've taken the College Green up is that the staff have always been very nice to me. Young girls they are, ex-students looking for jobs I should say, and what they lack in expertise they make up for in friendliness. They make you feel welcome, unlike some places where the sight of a middle-aged woman on her own has them looking round for the table nearest the lavatories.

I've never booked because it's never been more than half full and so it hasn't crossed my mind, but tonight for some reason it was quite crowded. One of the girls, Patsy her name is, comes forward with a big smile and says, Hello, nice to see you again, we've got quite a rush on this evening, can you give me a little minute and we'll sort something out for you.

Fair enough, I thought. It would still have been fair enough if having gone up and talked to Peter, the maître d' or owner or manager or whatever he calls himself, she'd come back and said, I'm terribly sorry, you've caught us at such a busy time, you couldn't give us an hour, could you?

That would have been understandable. But it's not what happened.

What did happen was that Peter himself comes forward.

Now I've never taken to this Peter, Sam, not that I've had anything to do with him – only when he's brought the bill over from time to time, or opened half a bottle of wine for me because the girls always make a hash of it, and even then he's had little enough to say for himself. He's English and superior with it if you know what I mean, with the air of doing you a favour in letting you buy a meal instead of regarding himself as providing a service. And though the room is quite smart – in fact too smart for what it is, I'd say, candles on the tables, crisp white napkins, menus the size of bedsheets – he wears an ordinary lounge suit instead of a DJ, as if to make the point that he's a cut above being a common waiter.

Anyway, over he comes and I can only say, Sam, he looks down his nose at me. No sign that he's ever clapped eyes on me before. No Good evening, madam.

He says baldly, Do you have a reservation?

I says, I'm afraid I don't, I've never found it necessary before, I'm glad to see you so full.

He says, looking even more snooty if that's possible, It's always as well to book, were you expecting someone else or is it just for one?

I thought, You know very well I'm not expecting anyone, you supercilious devil, you've seen me here enough times. But I said, brightly, Just the one.

Just the one. There should be a widows' national anthem called 'Just the One'. We go through life being just the one. Just the one glass is it, madam? Just the one ticket, on the edge of the back stalls, behind a pillar?

He says, One moment.

Then he makes a great palaver of going over to this lectern thing where to be fair there does seem to be a list of reservations. He pores over it for what seems like half an hour then looks slowly round the room, frowning. Now there's four tables still vacant and either they're available or they're not available, so what does he think he's playing at?

At long last he comes back and says, This way please.

The first please I've had out of him, and the last. I follow him over to this little rickety table for two, wedged between the swinging doors of the kitchen, the in door and the out door. Charming, I thought, at least I'll get some ventilation. But why doesn't he go the whole hog and put a screen round the table?

He does at least hold a chair out for me, but I think that was more out of habit than inclination. And off he blows. No Enjoy your meal, madam, no Can I get you an aperitif, no I'll just get you a menu, no Your waitress will be over in a moment.

I wait and I wait. To do the place justice, the girls are rushed off their feet, but this Peter is doing what you would have termed absolutely sod all. After a few minutes two couples come into the restaurant together and he checks their names on his list and escorts them to a table with, I have to say, a bit more charm than he's displayed to me, although not all that much because I don't think charm's his strong suit. It turns out there's only three chairs at a table laid for four, something you'd think he would have noticed if he was doing his job properly. So he seats three of them and leaves one of the chaps standing there while he comes over to my table and without so much as an Excuse me or a Do you mind, takes the chair opposite me and carries it off, leaving me wedged at this little table between the swinging kitchen doors for all the world as if I'm the cloakroom lady. I tell you, with a saucer of change and a book of raffle tickets I could have cleaned up.

I mean to say, Sam, it's one thing being Just the One in a public place, but when your table announces for all the world as if it could speak that no, you're not waiting for a friend because besides there being just the one you there is also just the one chair, then I reckon it's a bit much.

It got the evening off on the wrong foot, as you can imagine.

Then things began to improve, as I thought. Patsy came over with a menu, apologised for keeping me waiting, got me the Campari and soda I'd asked her for, and had soon taken my order. I was about to choose what I nearly always have, the crab and prawn tartlet followed by a grilled lemon sole, because the menu's all very simple and very English which is what I like – I should say liked – about the place. But then I spotted another dish on the evening's specials and I said, No, Patsy, sorry to mess you about but I've changed my mind, I'll still have the tartlet but I'll follow it with the roast breast of duck with pear and madeira sauce. I says, With the usual half-bottle of Frascati, thank you, Patsy.

No, I know it doesn't quite go with duck, Sam, but I have what I please these days, rather than what pleases you. You see, there's an upside to being widowed. Joke.

But shall I tell you why I chose the duck with the pear and madeira sauce? Go on, think back. It was what we had for our anniversary dinner two years ago – we didn't have an anniversary dinner last year, because you had to be somewhere, where the thump was it, oh I know, circulation conference in Glasgow, but two years ago we did have what turned out to be our last anniversary dinner ever, at the Connaught, and I had the duck with the pear and madeira sauce. You of course had the steak. And the reason I chose it tonight was that that anniversary looms up again in another six weeks' time and when that evening comes I didn't want to be sitting here stuffing duck into my face with tears rolling down my cheeks, I thought I'll get it over with now while I'm in a foul temper with that Peter and in no mood for sentiment.

Now you'll remember that little stockpile of tattered old

green Penguin books I dug out, the crime ones – I've taken to reading them on the bus to and from the Animal Trust. And if it's a particularly juicy murder I might take it with me when I go for a bite to eat. So here I was with my crab and prawn tartlet, and my half-bottle of Frascati, and *The Four Just Men* by Edgar Wallace propped up against the pepper grinder, and I began to feel a little better. And with the first glass of wine down me I began to feel a lot better.

But then the duck arrived, and Sam, it was downhill all the way from there.

I cut into it and I kid you not, it's raw. And by raw I mean raw. It didn't look like a meal at all, it looked like what it was – a dead duck, as the chef would have known if he'd cut into it himself and arranged the slices in a fan like they do at the Connaught. I felt really queasy.

I put my knife and fork down again and waited for Patsy, passing through from the kitchen. Instead it's this Peter, doing some work for a change, passing through *into* the kitchen with some dirty dishes. I noticed him glance at my plate and I wondered, shall I make the complaint to him or shall I wait for Patsy? Then I thought that as Patsy was the one who was serving me, I'd best talk to her.

I catch her eye at last as she's coming out with a basket of bread, and I say, Excuse me, Patsy, when you've a minute.

She serves the bread and comes back to the table.

I said, I'm sorry, Patsy, I can't eat this duck, as you can see it's raw.

She takes one look at it and says, Ooh, blood! Then she says, Let me take it away, you should have stayed with the grilled lemon sole.

I says, Yes, and I think I'll switch back to it, if that's quite all right.

She's just about to pick up the plate when this snooty voice behind her says, Is something wrong here? And of course it's Peter.

I says, I was just sending this duck back, I'm sorry to say it's not been cooked properly.

Picking the plate up he sends Patsy on her way with a nod. He peers into the duck's innards as if searching for shotgun pellets. Then he has a sniff of it, evidently with the idea of impressing on me that he knows what he's doing. Then blow me if he doesn't plonk the plate down in front of me again.

—This is just as it should be, madam – crisp on the outside, the flesh moist and pink.

—Moist and pink? It's red raw!

—No, it's not raw, it's rare. This is how the duck with pear and madeira sauce should be served.

—Oh, yes, then how come that your own waitress, Patsy, wrinkled her nose in disgust and was about to take it back into the kitchen?

—She's not very experienced, she may not have seen this particular dish before.

—No? Well *I'm* quite experienced at eating out, and I definitely have seen this particular dish before, and if I may say so at an establishment that knows more about cooking duck than you seem to do, namely the Connaught, no less.

—I don't know how the Connaught serves its duck, it doesn't concern me, but this is how we serve it here.

—What, running in blood?

And do you know what he had the cheek to come out with then? He says, That's not blood, madam, it's the sauce, be assured by me, this is how the duck with pear and madeira sauce should be brought to the table, as you'd know if you had an escort to advise you.

I was astounded. I couldn't believe my ears. And this is how I made my mistake, Sam, and how the night could have turned out differently. I should have got up, slapped his chops for him, and marched out.

But no, being June, I had to sit there and wait for more insults and humiliation.

I says to him, I'm not even going to dignify that outrageous remark with an answer. But I says, You can take this away, because I couldn't eat it even if I were starving.

He shrugs, and as he picked up my plate again I distinctly saw him roll his eyeballs and blow up his nostrils at one of the nearby waitresses, as if to say, We've got a right one here.

He says, in a martyred way, I'll have a menu brought over

I says, No thank you, I've lost my appetite, I'll just have some coffee and the bill.

He says, There's no charge, if you've not been entirely satisfied with your meal. But he says, May I ask, shall you be coming to the College Green again?

I says, Well you haven't totally succeeded in putting me off, I expect I'll be here again, yes, although I shall stick to the fish in future, why do you ask?

He hesitates and twists his face into a grimace. He looked as if he'd had a sudden twinge of toothache.

He says, You see, it's very difficult, trying to cater for parties of only one person.

I knew what was coming. It's never happened to me before but I knew what was coming. I should have picked up my bag and gone.

Instead, I have to try to be witty. I says, Now I wonder why that should be, I would have thought it was half as difficult as catering for parties of two, and four times easier than catering for parties of four.

Another grimace, this one with bared teeth, to show that he appreciates my little joke. He says, contorting his shoulders as if the words are having to be dragged out of him with pliers, You see, on a busy evening like this for example, a single person on their own takes up the same amount of space and requires the same amount of service as two covers, but in return for only half the turnover.

I says, Quite frankly, I beg leave to doubt whether you could get another cover as you call it on this squashed-up little table, even if there was another chair which there isn't. I says, I've never seen anyone having to sit here before, anyway, and quite frankly, if I hadn't brought a book to read I should have felt downright embarrassed, stuck here between those two kitchen doors.

He clears his throat and looks quite embarrassed himself. Then he says, That's another thing, now how can I put this, please don't take it the wrong way but we don't encourage our patrons to read at the tables, we like to feel they'd prefer to give their full attention to the enjoyment of their meal.

If he hadn't been holding that plate of duck himself I might just have smashed it in his face.

I might mention, Sam, that with a stream of waitresses passing back and forth I was keeping myself quite calm, even though I didn't feel it. I says, So what are you telling me, then – that I'm not welcome here again?

He says, Anyone's welcome, provided they make a reservation and that they're prepared to give proper appreciation to what Chef has taken the trouble to cook for their enjoyment.

That was it. I could feel tears scalding my eyes.

I said, Forget the coffee, take that bloody duck back into the kitchen and stick it down Chef's throat.

He says, If you're going to be abusive, I must ask you to leave.

I says, I'm off, don't you worry.

I fumbled in my purse for a couple of pound coins to leave for Patsy. I hope they didn't turn out to be five pee pieces, because I couldn't see what I was doing. I blundered out of the restaurant with customers staring at me as I passed by. I just pray to God I didn't know any of them. Out in the alley I remembered I'd left my book on the table. Bugger it, I know how it ends anyway.

I badly needed a drink. I didn't care to go into the Duke of Clarence, because if The Suit chanced to be in there and he saw my puffed-up cheeks he'd want to know what had been going on and I didn't feel like telling it. Not that I was banishing it from my mind, far from it. As I stormed along I was composing a letter in my head to the local paper, giving that restaurant or rather the jumped-up little turd who runs it the slagging-off of a lifetime. Oh, don't worry, Sam, I shall never write it – I can see you slashing through it with your green ballpoint and snarling, Libel, libel, libel, did he really say this, girl, or are you gilding the lily, I tell you, if the local rag printed this and he had you and the editor prosecuted for criminal libel you'd get two years apiece.

I was still blinded by tears and I'd not the foggiest idea where my feet were taking me. I finished up by the station. There's a pub opposite if you recall, the Junction Inn. I'd never been in it but while it didn't look up to much it seemed respectable enough. I'd pulled myself together by now, so I fondly imagined. I went into the station ladies' and tarted myself up a bit, and then I went across to the Junction.

It was just one big room as most pubs tend to be these days, I could have done with one of those little snugs that they used to have. Very quiet, though, thank goodness – about a dozen men, all business types, having the one before they either wended their way home if they'd just got off a train, or back to Town if they were waiting for one to come in. No women of any description, which didn't make me feel too comfortable. I bought myself a large Remy Martin, neat, and took it over to a corner table.

I sat there sipping it. I wished now that I'd remembered to pick up my *Four Just Men*, because I'd nothing to do with myself except stare at a big framed photograph of the High Street as it was in the year dot.

There was a chap sitting three tables away who looked like what we would at one time have called the commercial traveller type, except I don't think they have them any more, do they? It's all done by computer these days. Seedy but respectable, looked as if he should have been wearing a hat. Pint-drinker, you know the kind I mean.

I catch him glancing in my direction once or twice and after about the third glance he gives me a brief nod and a smile, so I see no harm in giving him a half-smile back and then fixing my eyes on the sepia picture of the High Street, *circa* 1910. I never knew the trams used to come out as far as this, did you?

Presently he drains his glass and gets up, but instead of taking it straight over to the bar he ambles up to my table, all diffident. I thought, Oh, bloody hell, not now!

He says, Good evening.

I says, Good evening.

Well, I could hardly have said Piss off, now could I?

He says, I don't think we've seen you in here before?

I says, That's because I've not been here before.

If that sounds flirtatious, Sam, it wasn't – it was said in a mind-your-own-business sort of voice. But there was no putting him off.

He says, Could I freshen up your glass, as our Yankee cousins would say?

I says, No thank you, I'm very happy with this.

He says, Then when I've got myself a refill, would you object if I joined you?

No way. He was pleasant enough but I just didn't feel like company. Furthermore I don't intend to go through life getting picked up in public houses, you'll be relieved to hear.

I tried to be kind but firm. I said, Would you mind very

much if you didn't, I'm not being stand-offish but I've just come in here to be on my own for a few minutes.

He says, Oh, I do beg your pardon, I didn't mean to intrude.

I says, That's quite all right.

You'd think, seeing as he seemed a nice enough chap, that he would now take the hint. But no. He lingers on. He loiters.

Then he says, You'll excuse me, dear lady, and you can tell me it's none of my bloody business, but is something upsetting you?

I realised now he was half-cut. It was the bloody that did it. I thought, I've got to get rid of him. Either that or walk out leaving yet another drink unfinished. But Remy Martin doesn't grow on trees.

But why did I come out with what I did, Sam? You tell me.

I blurted out, If you must know, I've just lost my husband.

I do know why I came out with it, of course I do. There's no quicker way of clearing a room than to announce that you've just been bereaved. But what a thing for me to say! I felt ashamed of myself. Still do.

He says, I'm most terribly sorry, if I'd had any idea at all I wouldn't have dreamed of imposing upon you.

I said again, That's quite all right.

He says, My deepest sympathy.

I thought, through gritted teeth, Is this going to go on all flaming night?

He wasn't deliberately being a nuisance – having dug himself into a hole, as he thought, he'd simply no idea how to extricate himself. I decided to do it for him and with a murmured Excuse me bolted for the ladies'.

But when I came back there's another large brandy on my table. And when I say large, we're talking trebles here, Sam.

He's back at his own table with his pint. He raises his glass. I raise mine, and knock back the brandy I've already got.

The rest is a blur.

Did I finish or even start the one, or rather the three in one glass, that my new friend had bought me? I don't know. All I do know is that when I decided it was high time to get up and leave, I couldn't. Or rather I could and did start to do so, and that was the trouble. I rose to my feet, edged my way around the table as you do, and went crashing over a bar stool I didn't even know was there.

Now when I say it was all a blur I don't mean I was completely rat-arsed as you would put it – not yet, anyway. I knew what was happening, but in a far-off way style of thing, as if I was watching it happen to somebody else.

I must say it was a pub full of gentlemen. Three or four of them came rushing over to put me back on my feet and sit me down again.

One of them says, She must have fainted, should I get her a brandy?

Another says, I should think that's the last thing she needs.

Funny how in these circumstances they talk about you as if you're not there, isn't it? And in a sense I wasn't there, it was like a dream sequence.

Then I heard my would-be new friend, the triple brandy dispenser, saying soothingly, The thing is the lady's had some very bad news lately, that's why she's not herself, I should say the best thing for it is to get her into a taxi.

And then kneeling at my feet and putting his hand on my pulse for no known reason, he says to me, You're in good hands, dear lady, that was a nasty tumble, how are you feeling now?

First one of them to concern himself with such a question. But I shouldn't say that, Sam, they were all being very good to me. As was the landlord, who came over with a glass of water.

I sipped it while all but the commercial traveller type drifted back to their drinks. Although I ached all down my right side where I'd fallen and I knew I could resign myself to being a mass of bruises, I began to feel better in myself. Apart from the one who'd made that snide remark about brandy being the last thing I needed, I believed, or at any rate I hoped, that they'd been persuaded it was a fainting fit that had brought me tumbling down in such an undignified way. And Sam, and I'm not trying to fool either you or myself, it could well have been the case, for I was certainly light-headed. Bear in mind that apart from a crab and prawn tartlet the size of a cocktail canapé I'd had nothing but a bowl of muesli all day, because I hadn't bothered with lunch on account of going out in the evening. So although I'd only had a Campari and soda, a glass and a half of wine and whatever amount of brandy I'd taken, I'd been drinking on an empty stomach. Add to that all the stress of the upset I'd suffered in that restaurant and is it any wonder I keeled over? Or am I justifying myself?

I said in reply to the query as to how I was feeling, A wee bit shaken but I shall be all right, thank you, I must have had a blackout, it's happened before.

He says, You should see your doctor, now do you live locally or—?

I says, Yes, not far away but too far to walk after that tumble, that's for sure, would you mind calling me a taxi?

He says, There's a cab rank over by the station, now you stay there, don't move, while I go and get one.

And two or three minutes later he's steering me across the room, with me doing my level best to look sober, and helping me into a taxi. He wanted to see me home to make sure I was all right but I wouldn't hear of it.

And I was just thanking him kindly, because he had been

kind, when the cab driver has to say, She's not going to be sick, is she?

Not my day, wouldn't you say? Stick around, pet, there's more.

I get home, and with the driver's last words ringing in my ears, which were Are you sure you can make it up the path, I got the front door unlocked with difficulty. I was in a terrible state again. After all I'd been through I felt degraded, there's no other word for it.

I knew what I needed, and that was another brandy. There wasn't any, so I had to settle for vodka. Nothing to eat – I'm on self-destruct by now. I'll say this for myself: at least I was drinking out of a glass. But no ice, because I didn't think I could make it to the kitchen. No tonic either. I detest neat vodka but I swallowed it down. And I sat there brooding and brooding to the point where I'd caned a good half-bottle without even noticing.

So then of course I felt sick, didn't I? Surprise surprise. I stagger upstairs to the loo, and we'll draw a veil over the next ten minutes if you don't mind, thank you very much. I totter out with sweating forehead and go to clean my teeth. The floor's swaying so much I have to sit on the edge of the bath and in so doing I topple back and fall into it. More bruises for tomorrow.

I'm not proud of telling you any of this, Sam, falling into the bath may sound funny but it wasn't, not a bit of it, it was more degradation. And I couldn't lever myself up again. I had to swing my legs over so my whole person was in the bath if you see what I mean, and then clamber out, in doing which I fell on the floor and cracked my head against the bathroom door.

I says to myself, Come on, June, pull yourself together before you do yourself some serious damage, there's only one place for you, my girl, and that's a hot bath followed by bed.

The best advice I'd given myself all day – or so I thought at the time. It would have been better advice if I'd skipped the bath and gone straight to bed.

I lurch into the bedroom while the bath's running and get myself undressed somehow, leaving my clothes strewn on the bed or on the floor where they fell. I grope my way back into the bathroom where I see that the towels too are all over the floor, where I must have grabbed them off the rail while trying to steady myself. And they're damp, being as how I'd only had a bath two or three hours earlier before taking myself off for that disastrous evening at the College Green restaurant.

Now if there's one thing I hate it's trying to dry myself on wet towels – a message I never succeeded in getting through to you in all our years of marriage. How many times did I tell you to regard the two big bath towels as His and Hers? But no, you persisted in using both, and then leaving them all of a crumple in the bath before it's even drained off properly.

There should have been some clean ones in the linen cupboard but there weren't. I'm not as meticulous as I was over that sort of thing nowadays, and I remembered that I'd only got them off to the laundry that very morning, being too idle to do it last week. But then I remembered something else as well: that your Pauline always keeps her own bath towel draped over the rail at the foot of her bed. In that respect she doesn't take after her father, she's like me, finicky: she doesn't like anyone else using her bath towel. Nothing wrong with that.

But not tonight, Pauline. My need is greater. So I crash into her bedroom and yank the towel off the bed-rail and throw it round my neck, and I'm just turning round to go back into the bathroom when I have another of my turns. The room's going round.

I'm telling you, it was one of those nights when you look up to heaven, that's if you're capable of looking up, and you say, Almighty God, don't make me well, I know that's asking too much and I deserve all I'm getting, but just stop me feeling dizzy and I'll swear on your Holy Book that I'll never drink again.

I had to sit on Pauline's bed. Then I had to lie back on Pauline's bed. And it's going round and round and round – it was exactly like being on a carousel. It's not a completely unfamiliar experience – I used to get it back in our really hard-drinking days when I was still trying to keep up with you. So I knew what to do. You don't close both eyes, that makes it worse, you close one eye and focus on some article of furniture – wardrobe, chair, dressing table, anything – until the roundabout slows down. And so I did, and that's what happened. And I found that the article of furniture I was focusing on was the chest of drawers, and in particular the underwear drawer where I'd placed Pauline's letters.

I only read the one and then I had to go and throw up again.

I hadn't taken in the postmarks the other times I'd taken the bundle out of the drawer and riffled through it, but I noticed now that apart from the seaside postcards they were all written within a few months of each other, just after you and I had set up home together. So she must have been – what? Seven?

You can't tell me she wrote that letter all by herself. Apart from the bits that are obviously her own work, Tricia must have either dictated it to her, or else written it out for her to copy. No child of that age could have composed it although I can well believe it expressed what that child wanted to say. And that was why I had to go and be sick. Not that I'd anything left to be sick with, except thin green bile.

Dearest Daddy, How are you, we are well. Bobby send you all his love and kisses . . .

Who Bobby? Dog? Teddy bear? Rocking horse? Kid next door? You never mentioned a Bobby. But then you never mentioned very much at all about your home life. With good reason, as I now see.

> . . . I like the new cartoon strip in the paper, The Muddles. I think you should make Mr Muddle go to the office without his trousers, he has forgotten to put them on. Then he fall in a puddle and have mud on his knees. You could call it Mr Muddle fall in a puddle.
>
> I love you, Daddy. Daddy, when you coming home? You said you would but you have not. It not good for you to sleep at the office because you so busy, you will get a sore back sleeping on the sofa. Couldn't you make one of the others be the night editor when it is long past bedtime? Mummy say you could if you wanted. Perhaps Mr Muddle could be the night editor. He would mix all the pages up so that the crosswords and The Muddles were on page one, whilst page 26 was on page 2. That would also be funny.
>
> We both miss you so much. Mummy cries every night and this makes me cry. I sleep in Mummy's bed now because you are not there, to keep your place warm, and she wake me up with her crying. She think you do not love us but this cannot be true, I know that you love us and that you will come home as soon as ever you can.
>
> Uncle Derek came over on Sunday and took me to the Waxworks, but he would not let me see the Murderers. I wish you had come with us, you would have let me see the Murderers because I know you like Murders, whenever there is one you are always kept late at the office. Perhaps that is why you do not come home, there a lot of Murders. But I do not understand why you do not come on Saturday any more, the paper does not come out

on Sunday except for the Sunday one and you are not the night editor of that.

Please come home, Daddy. Have we done anything wrong? If I have been making too much noise I will not, I will be quiet as mouse if only you will come back to us.

Love and kisses. (some of these kisses are from Mummy) . . .

Sam, Sam, Sam.

You lied to me.

You said Tricia was glad to see the back of you. In fact you didn't even pack your own bags, according to you she packed them for you and threw them down the stairs. And told you never to darken her doorstep again style of thing. What was it you say she called you? Useless Eustace? I must say I had to have a secret smile at that one, because I knew what she meant. In fact how you managed to produce a daughter at all has always been something of a surprise. She must have been a lucky shot.

But none of this squares with that letter, does it?

And then what's all this about you said you would come home but you have not? Am I to understand that you didn't have the courage to tell the child you were off for good, that you deliberately encouraged her to believe you'd be coming back to her? And then there's that stuff about missing you and crying every night. You told me, over and over again, because I was most anxious about it as you very well know, that Pauline wasn't over-bothered about your absence, that she'd hardly ever seen you during the working week anyway and that so long as you turned up of a Saturday with a prezzie and a treat in store she was happy enough. But here she is saying she can't understand why you don't come on Saturdays any more.

It's easy to see why, though, isn't it? It's all in that one letter. Because you were too much of a coward, that's why,

Sam Pepper. You couldn't face a wife and little daughter begging you to come back to them – or rather the little daughter doing her mum's begging for her, because from what little I know of Tricia she would have primed your Pauline to turn on the waterworks once a week.

In one way I can't bring myself to blame you, because you've always been one to avoid trouble or unpleasant scenes, you always swung it on to someone else to do the dirty work. Delegation, it's called, isn't it? But why couldn't you have come clean with me?

And another thing. That's always the trouble with opening this kind of Pandora's box or can of worms – there's always another thing and then another. Where did you go to, my lovely, all those Saturday mornings, when you drove off with a story book or a box of colouring sticks under your arm that you'd got me to go out and buy, and which I'd chosen with care? What a fool you've made me look, Sam. Did you take them down to the Oxfam shop, where I took your suit? What a farce. And then what? How did you spend the day? Down in Fleet Street with your cronies I shouldn't wonder. What a shitty thing to do. I often wondered why you came home half cut but I never said anything, always concluding that you'd been in need of a few swifties after the ordeal of having to face up to your ex-wife, as she was in the course of becoming.

It all leads me to wonder why we never quite got round to living together while we were still up and going and having it off in Manchester. Why you shipped Tricia and Pauline two hundred miles south to London as you did, knowing that you were going to dump the pair of them. It was because you didn't dare tell Pauline, wasn't it, couldn't look your only child in the eye, couldn't say, Look, poppet, Daddy's got to live somewhere else, with another lady in point of fact, I hope you'll meet her in due course, but that doesn't mean to say Daddy doesn't still love you, I shall be here often and often, see if I'm not. But it was a career move, wasn't it, chum? You didn't want to rock any boats by walking out on Tricia and getting yourself into *Private Eye* while you were up for the night editorship in London. Good decision. Who knows that otherwise we might still be all stuck in Manchester. And I might be stuck with you still being alive, if what they say about the pressures of the job is true.

It's not opening old wounds that we're talking about here, it's ripping in with the knife and starting new ones, do you understand that? You've deceived me, Sam. You let me down badly.

Why couldn't you have levelled with me? I'll tell you why, shall I? Because if I'd known the truth of it, how Tricia and Pauline were crying themselves to sleep every night, I should have ended it there and then and made you go back to them. Even if it had proved, as it could well have done if you'd ever been man enough to discuss it with me, that it was all manipulation on Tricia's part and that she was just using Pauline to get you back, I would have been out of your life. Because it was on the clear understanding that she didn't want you back, not at any price, that I took you on. And you know it.

What a thing to do to me. If Tricia had had any sense, she would have posted her little daughter's letters to that pokey little flat we first lived in, when there would have been a good chance of my seeing them and reading them. In which case it would be Tricia who was the grieving widow out of the two of us. And at this moment, I can tell you exactly who I should prefer in that particular role.

As I say, I only read the one letter out of the fifteen or so. There was no way I wanted to know any more – it could only get worse. Well, it wasn't going to get better, was it? I left the bundle strewn on Pauline's bed, to be tidied up and put away in the morning. I went and threw up in the loo as

I've said, not because of what I'd had to drink which had all been flushed away long ago, but out of disgust with myself and yes, out of disgust with you, Sam, I'm very sorry but there it is.

I stumbled into my own bedroom, our bedroom as was and as I'm now inclined to think should never have been, and flopped down on the duvet, stark bollock naked as you would say, and passed out at once.

I woke up at five in the morning. Blundered across the landing with the memory that there had been a bath somewhere on the agenda but of course it was stone cold. I went into Pauline's room and straightened her bed, bearing in mind that she'll be back on Sunday, which by this time is tomorrow. I stacked her letters together again with their rubber band and put them away in her underwear drawer. Too late I remembered I'd never got round to cleaning my teeth last night. Why the hell should that matter? But it does. Just one tiny flake of a crumbling life.

I dozed off again, as you do in that condition, only to be awakened at around ten by the phone ringing. It's Marion. Sister-in-law. Well, she's your sister-in-law, it was your brother she was married to. But is she mine as well? I've never been able to work these things out.

Anyway, that's who it is. She says, Hullo, June, oh, I do hope I haven't woken you up?

Now at ten in the morning, how would she know that? Because I'm still a bit fuddled, I expect. I'll be getting a reputation if I'm not more careful.

I says, Bit of a late night last night, Marion, I'm up, but not yet entirely in the land of the living.

She says, I'm glad you're enjoying a social life.

I says, I'm not sure enjoying is the right word, how are things with you, Marion?

She says, Oh, coping, you know, coping, I've got myself

on one of these correspondence courses, freelance journalism, you've probably seen it advertised, not that I've sold
anything so far but it's early days yet, I'm still feeling my
way, but they do guarantee if you don't make a sale in the
first year you get a certain proportion of your fees back.

I says, Sounds interesting, Marion.

Whereas I thought, With the market swarming with
wannabe journalists, you've got about as much chance of
breaking into it as I have of becoming a freelance vivisec-
tionist.

But good luck to her. Has she got any talent in that
direction? I beg leave to doubt it, and I shouldn't think
you'd know one way or the other. She would only have
had to mention the subject of journalism, on one of the rare
occasions that we ever socialised, for you to start talking
about the price of fish or any other topic to hand. Not that
she would have done so, because so far as I'm aware she
had no interest whatsoever in freelance journalism until
Derek went, and then she presumably picked it out of a
list of courses as an alternative to book-keeping or learning
Spanish or whatever.

Just wants something to do, I suppose. And a bit more
constructive than my envelope-stuffing, even if she never
does succeed in selling an article to the *People's Friend* or
Our Dogs. But why? Why should losing a husband be the
signal for taking on a hobby? It's a bit demeaning when
you think about it – I mean from the point of view of the
dear departed. You lose the love of your life and you take
up stamp-collecting. Not much of a trade-in, is it?

Anyway, it's none of my business. I did wonder what
Marion wanted but I supposed it would all come out in
God's good time. I did wish, though, that I'd taken the call
down in the kitchen where I could have made myself some
coffee while she was rabbiting on.

She says, But I'll tell you why I'm ringing, June, otherwise than to ask how you've been keeping, and it's this, now you'll remember Mrs Clapper?

In my condition, it was too early in the day for memory.

I says, Mrs Clapper, Mrs Clapper, no, I don't think I do, Marion, remind me.

She says, She was at the funeral, I thought you knew her, she told me she got you your voluntary work at that animal charity you mentioned, I'll tell you who she is, June, her niece is one of the secretaries at Sam's old paper and she introduced you I believe.

I says, Oh, you mean young Sheila's Auntie Clare.

And I thought, Oh, my God, another bad penny turning up.

She says, Anyway, I'm sure you're aware she's psychic.

I says, Or so she claims.

—There's opinions and opinions about that, June. I had a long talk with her when she came round to the house after the funeral, although what she was doing there I've never got to the bottom of, because I don't think you brought her there, did you?

—I most certainly did not, Marion, I wouldn't do such a thing.

—She earned her cup of tea and vanilla slice, anyway, June, whoever introduced her into the house. But like yourself, because she told me she'd left her card with you the same as she did with me, I didn't think to follow it up at first.

—The sales pitch, do you mean?

—If that's what you want to call it, June, though some might say that's not a very helpful way of putting it. But you see then I started on this journalism course, and one of the exercises was to do an interview, if possible with a famous personality. Now I don't know any famous personalities, but then I had what for me was a brilliant idea.

—Don't tell me, Marion – you fixed up an interview with George Bernard Shaw.

—Now how on earth did you know that, June?

—By having been married to a newspaperman for the best part of twenty-five years.

—In point of actual fact it wasn't GBS, June, because her Red Indian spirit guide couldn't get through to him, so we had to settle for H. G. Wells.

—Even better. He was interested in women.

I could sense Marion getting chilly. She says, Something tells me you're not taking this altogether seriously, June.

She could say that again. And I was gagging for a cup of black coffee.

But I says, Oh, I am, I am, Marion, don't mind me, it's just my way of talking.

She says, But listen to what I'm coming to, June, because after I'd got the interview, which I might tell you was nothing to do with women, it was all to do with the state of the world and the way we're heading if we don't cherish the environment, it was highly fascinating, but then Clare tells me she's got another message waiting. She says, And who do you think it's from?

I says, Derek.

She says, Now who could have told you that, you haven't been speaking to Clare, have you?

I thought, Oh, do come off it, you silly cat. But all I said was, It just came to me, Marion, I sometimes think I could be psychic myself.

She says, You may laugh and you may scoff, June, but it was definitely Derek, because shall I tell you how I know? She says, Because his very first reference, through the spirit guide, Hawkeye, was to a certain blemish on his body that nobody else except his doctor and I could possibly know about, which is to say a mole in a certain intimate place. She says, So of course that established his credentials.

I thought, Well, I've got to play along with her, even if her case does rest on your brother having a mole on his willy. So I said, And how is Derek?

She says, How do you mean, how is he, he's dead, June, you came to the funeral.

I felt such a fool.

I says, I was meaning how is he in himself, I mean how does he pass the time, does he say what it's like up there or what?

She says, Oh, they don't go into anything like that, June, no, everything they transmit through the medium, who gets it from the Red Indian spirit guide, is limited to what's happening or what they know's about to happen on this side. She says, And they advise you, as to what to do for the best.

I says, Such as?

—Well, financial matters, for one. He told me to hang on to my gas shares but sell British Steel. So I did, and gas has gone up ten points while British Steel has dropped fifteen.

—And I suppose Sheila's Auntie Clare couldn't have seen the way share prices were going by keeping an eye on the business pages?

—Ooh, you are a cynic, June, she didn't even know I had those shares. And here's something else she couldn't have known about – her spirit guide's advising me to put the house on the market and buy a maisonette that I've looked over.

If they want to believe, there's no telling them. But I did try. I said, But Marion, I could have given you that advice myself, knowing as I do that you've been thinking of selling the house.

She says, Ah, but you couldn't have known I had my eye on a maisonette, and neither could Clare.

I says, Are you sure you didn't mention this in conversation with her?

She says, Oh, I can see you're determined to set your face against all the evidence, June, although I have to say I can't imagine why, I would have thought the knowledge that the dead live on would be a comfort to you, the same as it is to me.

Not necessarily, Marion. Not now. Not after reading that letter.

I says, I'm not setting my face against it, Marion, let's just say I've yet to be convinced.

She says, That day may come sooner than you think, June. She says, Sam wants to speak to you.

—What did you say?

—That Sam wants to speak to you. He's reunited with Derek and Derek has passed on the message. He wants to speak to you urgently

Is this true, Sam?

If so, you're a bit late with your barrow.

Did you mean to warn me against reading Pauline's letters, stirring the viper's nest so to speak – or is it that knowing I was bound to read them whatever you said, you reckoned you would have some explaining to do? Either way, Sam, it's too late now. However you try to wriggle out of it you can't get out of what you were putting your Pauline and her mother through while telling me the exact opposite.

So now you want to speak to me, do you? Urgent. But who says I want to be spoken to?

I says, Tell me all about this maisonette, Marion.

She says, Won't you even consider getting in touch with him, June, it could be important?

I says, Maybe at one time, Marion, but not now. I says, There is one thing I'd like to know, though, and that's did Sheila's Auntie Clare use Sam's full name, Samuel Herbert?

She says, The spirit guide did, Hawkeye did.

I says, And where did he get it from?

I could hear her sighing with exasperation.

—That's what I'm telling you, June. From Sam! How else would Clare know his full name?

—By having a good memory for death announcements.

—Oh, you're impossible, June!

—Tell me about the maisonette.

Which, giving me up as a bad job, she did, at length. I couldn't get her off the phone. But at least I'd got her off the subject of life after death, or so I thought. Yet once she's described every inch of the place plus the nice street it's in and how convenient it is for the shops and the good bus service, she says, Getting back to that H. G. Wells interview, June, do you think Sam's old paper would be interested?

I says, I shouldn't think so, Marion, but you could always ask him, otherwise try the *Spiritualist News*, now I must ring off, the kettle's boiling itself to steam.

No sooner have I hung up on Marion and put the coffee on than Helen rings. She says, My, you've got some chatty friends, haven't you, I've been trying to get through for the best part of an hour.

I felt quite pleased at that, don't know why. Yes I do. Because it gives me a little kick having Helen think I'm in demand socially, if the truth be told. How pathetic can you get?

She's got us a five-day City Break in Dublin, very reasonable package, three-star hotel, leave on the 26th, Aer Lingus, or Air Cunnilingus as you insisted on calling it when we went there. And I had to pretend to be amused. You could be quite crude when you wanted to be, do you know that?

It can't come soon enough for me. I shall be ready for that holiday. What with one thing and another, I'm just about at the end of my flipping tether.

I felt better as the day went on so I took myself down to the Duke of Clarence. Hair of the dog. Besides, your Pauline comes home tomorrow and I'm dreading having to look her in the face, so I needed something to steady my nerves.

I was surprised to see The Suit sitting in his usual place, because it was well after four and he's usually only in there at lunchtimes.

I says, Oh, hello, Duggie, I didn't expect to see you here.

He says, I can see you didn't, June, having a crafty afternoon snort, eh, same as me, we've caught one another out this time.

I knew he was only being flippant but I wasn't in the mood for it, and in any case, flippant or not he was verging on the impertinent in my opinion.

I says starchily, Caught one another out, how do you mean, caught one another out?

At least he could see he'd flicked a raw nerve because he comes back quickly with, Just my little joke, June, I expect you'll have had a busy day, I'm sure no one deserves a drink more, I'll get you one in.

He gets me a half of Guinness and I simmer down. I says, mollified, Actually you have caught me out in point of fact, I'm not in the habit of coming into public houses at this hour.

He says, There's no law against it, June, there was once but there isn't now.

I says, picking up my glass, But for once I really need this, it's been one of those weeks.

He says, Oh dear me, we all get those, they're sent to try us, what's the problem, then?

I says, Oh, something and nothing.

I didn't realise I must still be looking uptight, because he was quite persistent. He says, Come on, June, you can tell me, you know what they say, a trouble shared.

I says, after he's gone on in this strain for a minute or so,

No, I know you mean well, Douglas, but I've come in here to forget my little troubles, not to talk about them.

I couldn't have told him even if I'd wanted to, which I most definitely did not. What should I have said? I've had the shock of reading a letter Pauline wrote to her father when she was a little girl, and it's making me look at my marriage in a whole new light? Oh yes, and I've had it from my sister-in-law who's had it from a clairvoyant who got it from a Red Indian chief who heard it from her late husband that said father is trying to get in touch with me to explain the whole thing, or do I mean explain it away?

Should I have ever read that letter? What good has it done me? It's going to haunt me, I know it is. And I look back on these past twenty-five years, and I think, it's all been a sham.

Or am I being too hasty? We did have happy times, not wildly happy perhaps, we weren't that sort of couple, but you weren't play-acting, so no one could call it a sham in that regard. But we weren't entitled to those happy times, they were stolen from someone else, and you know it and I know it, Sam Pepper.

I didn't want to talk about it and I didn't want to think about it. I says brightly, We haven't heard your side of the story yet, what brings you into the Duke of Clarence at four in the afternoon, are there no fridge doors that need mending?

This has become a standing joke between us. Or I hope it has. He gives me a rueful grin and says, There's no shortage of fridge doors metaphorically speaking, June, the bluebottle in the ointment is they're all out in Bexley and Bromley and suchlike inaccessible places, no-go areas so far as I'm concerned. You see, June, one thing I've learned very quickly is you've got to price your time, if a job's an hour's bus ride away and an hour back, and the job itself is an hour, you've put in three hours for a one-hour invoice, even with a call-out charge it doesn't make sense, do you see what I mean?

I says, Still, all that'll change when you get this transport you've been talking about, won't it?

He gives a big sigh. He says, When, though, that's the question?

I says, Why, what did the bank say?

—They didn't want to know, June, I might as well have saved my breath to cool my porridge with. In fact they were quite contemptuous. Do you know what this business loans berk had the cheek to come out with? Oh, he says, I'm afraid odd jobs don't qualify as a business, otherwise we'd be opening the door to window cleaners and any manner of people. He meant any manner of riff-raff. I said, Well I'm certainly not too proud to clean windows but if that's your attitude I'll wish you a very good day. I'd switch to another bank if I could be bothered. But then they're all tarred with the same brush, aren't they?

I felt that sorry for him and I said so.

He shrugs and says, Can't be helped, June, I don't suppose you've got an old jalopy lying about that you want taken off your hands, by any chance?

I says, Jalopy, no, Sam had a company BMW for his own private use, and they were round for that before the ink was dry on the death certificate.

He says, What about Pauline, does she run a car?

I says, No, she can't even drive so far as I know.

I didn't like the way this conversation was going. If it had turned out that Pauline did run a car, what then? Would he have tried to get me to ask her for a lend of it? The Suit was suddenly getting too pushy for my liking.

And yet this is the odd thing. Even while I could feel resentment swelling up in me at the turn all this was taking, I knew that I was going to offer to lend The Suit the money he needs for his transport.

I've known it all along, if the truth be told. I've just been holding it back from myself.

Why should I want to lend him money? Not as an investment, that's for sure. I don't believe that little business of his will ever do more than tick over, especially if he's to be found sitting in pubs at four in the afternoon, and whatever sum I do pump in I can quite see I'll be waving it goodbye. The sympathy vote? He does have that vulnerability that makes you want to help him, and seeing him for ever in your suit always brings on a pang of pity. But in the end I was going to lend him that money for no other reason than it would give me pleasure to do something for him. Call it an act of friendship. Or call it what you want.

Call it, if you like, reaching out for another's hand. And forget the embarrassing fact that the hand doing the reaching has a big fat cheque in it. Widows can't be choosers – not if they're looking for company.

I says, It means a lot to you, getting hold of transport of some kind, doesn't it?

He says, Put it this way, June, with wheels I can operate, I can expand, you'd be amazed at the amount of work there is out there just begging to be done. But he says, Without wheels, I might just as well have a lie-in every morning and live on social security, it's as clear-cut as that.

I says, And have you worked out how much you'd need to get these wheels?

He says, without a blink, and leaning forward in his eagerness, I could show you very precise figures, June.

I thought, Hang on, chum, not so fast, I haven't even offered you the money yet. But even though the warning bells were ringing, there was no going back now. Wanting to please somebody – what's at the back of it? Needing to be popular? It's never bothered me overmuch before, whether I've been well-liked or not, so why start now? Boosting my self-esteem after the blow of that letter? Who's to say? I'm not about to start delving into psychology at my time of life.

I said, Would you let me see them?

He says, Any time you like, June, I worked it all out for the bank – capital cost, running costs, taxation et cetera et cetera, then on the other side of the ledger my potential turnover, increased business, I've done all the projections, touch wood I could have the loan repaid with interest within eighteen months to two years.

I thought, We're talking here about mending lavatory cisterns, replacing broken windows, putting shelves up, and he's banging on about all the projections he's done as if he were running a chain of DIY shops, this man is a fantasist. But aloud I said, So what sums are we talking about?

He says, It depends on the type of vehicle, how old she is, what state she's in, you can get a second-hand Austin Maestro 500 van, one owner, for ooh, two and a half thou trade price, or you can get a clapped-out one, F registration, for less than a thousand, what you buy is what you get, but you see the lower the asking price the more you've got to bear in mind your escalating repair bills.

I says, Yes, I can see all that, but for a half-decent van in reasonable nick, what are we talking about in round figures?

I don't know why I was coming on like a second-hand car salesman in a soap opera – perhaps because I wanted to sound as if I knew what I was talking about. Which I didn't.

He says, In round figures, June, all in and covering all my overheads for the first year, four grand would see me up and running.

It was a lot more than I was expecting. I'd been thinking around the two thousand mark for some reason. And then he was so glib. He was playing a very different tune from when we'd last talked about the subject, when he'd ruled out the very idea of borrowing from me as if shocked by the mention of it. Why wouldn't I let myself have second thoughts?

I says, Look, Duggie, I'm taking myself off on holiday in a few days' time, get me some figures for when I come back, and then we'll go into the whole thing. But I says, It's got to be done properly, agreement drawn up, sign on the dotted line and all that.

He says, Oh, most definitely, I wouldn't have it any other way.

I says, Right, we'll talk about it when I get back on the thirty-first.

He says, You won't regret this, June.

I will, I know I will, and I knew I would even as he grabbed my hand and shook it like a village pump. Because only then did it occur to me that I'd never actually offered to lend him the money in so many words, and in his eagerness he hadn't even gone through the motions of pretending that he couldn't dream of borrowing it. Talk about jumping the gun – he was halfway round the track before I'd even got the safety catch off. He might have waited for a formal invitation.

Yes, and I know what you're thinking, lad – that I'm a mug. And maybe I am. But who cares?

He got me another drink in, the least he could do, and starts going on about the prospects in store for him and the snips he could have picked up at this or that used vehicle sale if only he'd dared take his cheque book, and the advantages of the Bedford Rascal van over the Bedford Astra or it might have been the other way round.

Then he gets out his diary and says, And you're back on the thirty-first, you say? And he jots my name down, June. I couldn't help noticing as he flipped through the pages that they were totally blank. I only hope for my sake his diary doesn't double as an order book.

He says, And you're off when?

I says, Twenty-sixth. And he puts that in his diary too.

Then at long last it occurs to him to say, So where are you going on holiday?

Thank you, The Suit. Thought you'd never ask.

Pauline's flight was late, so it was getting on for half past ten when she finally rolls up. Although I could have done with an early night, I waited up for her in case she wanted a bite of supper – you don't feel like cooking when you've spent half the day hanging around airports. My mistake.

The evening started well, because to my surprise she brought me back a carrier bag of duty-free goodies – drink and cigarettes. She has a nice tan, and we spent a few minutes chit-chatting over a glass of wine about her holiday. It seems to have gone down well so no doubt she and her pal met a couple of chaps. She doesn't want anything to eat and soon she declares herself dead beat and goes upstairs.

It's funny what you can forget. It had gone clean out of my mind to tell her about the bundle of letters that Eric Grant had fetched round. Not that it made any difference, because I'm just locking up when she comes downstairs again. And she's clutching the letters.

She says baldly, You've been reading these, haven't you?

Now was that a shot in the dark, or had those letters been arranged in a certain order so she'd know if they'd been tampered with? I wouldn't put it past your Pauline and Eric Grant between them to lay a trap like that. I'm very sorry, but even though I've every sympathy with her for what I now know she had to go through as a child, I still can't bring myself to like her. She's cold. Maybe the one fact's connected with the other, I don't know. Or maybe she just takes after her mother.

There was no use blustering. I says, I read one of them, Pauline, and one only.

She says, One's enough, they all say the same thing.

Her voice was dead. She seemed so forlorn.

I said, Would you like a drink, Pauline?

She nodded. I poured us both a large Spanish brandy, the size you used to drink.

She has a gulp of hers and then takes a deep breath and says, So now you know, June.

I says, Yes, now I know.

She says, Or did you know all along?

I says, No, I hadn't the faintest glimmering, I'd been led to believe it was all amicable and that you'd taken it in your stride style of thing. I says, Maybe that's what I wanted to believe, but had you written to him at home instead of to the office I might have learned otherwise.

She stared at me.

—I didn't know where he was living, did I? I thought he was staying at the executive flat at the office while he worked on something to do with the paper. That's what he told me, anyway, and my mother never told me any different. And I certainly didn't know anything about you. Not till after the divorce, a good year later.

I'd always suspected as much, you were always so evasive when I wanted to know if your daughter ever asked about me. And as for waiting over a year for the divorce, we now know why, don't we? Not because the solicitors were messing you about as you said, but because Tricia was hoping to get you back, which was why she wouldn't have told Pauline of my existence. It was all piecing together.

I says, Who broke the news to you in the end, your father or your mother?

—A girl at school told me, as a matter of fact. She'd heard her parents discussing the divorce – it had been in the *Evening Standard*. She came up to me in the playground and sneered, you know how horrid kids can be, Your mother and father are divorced, that makes you illegitimate nyah

nyah nyah. Luckily for me I didn't know what the word meant but I knew what divorce was. So then it all came out. My mother explained it to me when she found me in my bedroom, crying.

Poor child. The hoops we put them through, and then we wonder they don't grow up model citizens.

I said, What can I say, Pauline?

She says, Not a lot.

I says, I'll ask you to believe one thing, and that's that if I'd known the effect it was having on you, I'd have ended it there and then.

Like a shot I would. After all, what difference would it have made to me? I'd have got over you. I was young, someone else would have come along. And I wouldn't have had that bloody funeral to go through. But then who knows, I might have had someone else's bloody funeral to go through. There's no telling, is there?

Pauline says, It's all water under the bridge now.

I says, I'm afraid your father made a complete hash of it, Pauline, he should have told me about you and he should have told you about me.

She says, It wasn't his way.

No, we know it wasn't. I poured us both another stiff brandy. We were both drinking far too quickly but it was excusable in the circumstances.

I says, Once you'd heard about me, didn't you ever want to meet me?

She says, No, of course I didn't.

I says, Oh, I see, didn't want anything to do with Daddy's fancy woman.

She says, Something like that.

Well, I asked for that. I walked into it.

She says, Come to that, didn't you ever want to meet me?

I said, Yes, I did, very much, but he always said he didn't want to mix his two lives.

—Yes, he would do.

—So when you did finally come to meet me, when you were already quite the young lady, what persuaded you to change your mind?

—I didn't. If you remember, we met for the first time in that restaurant up in Soho. So far as I was aware he was just taking me out to lunch during the school holidays. We're taken to the table and you're sitting there and he introduces us. Short of throwing a tantrum or walking out and having to find my own way back home, there wasn't a lot I could do about it.

Quite. Typical Sam strategy.

I said, But even if you'd no curiosity about meeting me, weren't you curious during all these years to know where he was living?

She astounded me then. She says, Oh, I'd known where he lived since soon after the divorce, he took me there several times, but always when you were away somewhere.

Something else we didn't know. More things in heaven and earth, eh?

—So going back to when you did get to meet me, Pauline, after that you must have decided to accept me?

She shrugged her mouth.

—To tell you the truth, June, by that time I didn't care about you one way or the other, if you happened to be in when I came round to see Dad then you happened to be in, but I certainly wasn't coming round to see you. If you want me to be brutally frank.

I was still asking for it and I was getting it.

—It's quite understandable, Pauline, you'd been through a lot by then.

—I know I had. Did he tell you about my anorexia?

—No, he didn't. Never a word. When was this?

—When I was fourteen. In that case I don't suppose he

told you about my pregnancy. That was when I was fifteen.
It was terminated.

Oh, my God.

You see what you get for dying? It all comes out.

I says, Pauline, if only we could turn back the clock.

She says, But we can't, can we?

If there were any more revelations she was keeping them
to herself. Because I didn't change the subject, she did.

She says abruptly, June, you don't like my living here,
do you?

Now I'm a good liar, I've had to be, living with a newspaperman, but I could never have bluffed my way through
that one. I says, frankly enough, It's not a question of liking
or not liking, Pauline, I didn't expect to be sharing the house
with another woman after your father died, but of course
you're just as entitled to be here as I am. I says, and this one
was a lie, and well she knew it, So you're most welcome to
stay as long as you like.

She says, Be that as it may, you'll be relieved to hear I'm
looking for a flat.

I didn't let on I already knew.

I says perkily, Oh, really, and have you got any particular
place in mind?

She says, Not yet, I shall have to wait for the divorce
settlement coming through first.

And on the spur of the moment I made a decision.

I said, Well, Pauline, I may be able to help you there,
because as you know if I sell this place and buy somewhere
smaller, whatever money's left over falls to you.

She says, Why, you're not thinking about moving, are
you?

I says, Not just thinking about it, Pauline.

She says, Tell me more!

As I'd only just that minute finally made my mind up
there wasn't much to tell, but on that note we had another

drink. Chatting away, we even got dangerously near to becoming friendly, but that was probably just the brandy talking. Despite the battering I'd just taken, I felt elated. I did. Why I hadn't decided to sell the house months and months ago, instead of sitting here day after day and night after night rabbiting to you, I shall never know. Marion made the right move: she was round to the estate agent's almost before your Derek was cold in his grave. Mark you, she did have the benefit of his advice from beyond that grave.

Your paper once printed a table to show that moving house is the most traumatic experience you can have next to a bereavement, according to some so-called authority. A likely story, but I don't care – I can handle traumas by now, I've had the practice. It'll give me something to occupy my mind, and I know I shall be doing the right thing, putting this house behind me. It's got too many memories, now. And I don't mean old memories, I mean new memories.

You won't be surprised not to have heard from me of late. Even if the diary was written down it would still be a blank just now. I'm sorry, Sam, but I've had nothing to say to you. What's been done has been done, and there's no discussing it. And certainly not through some bloody Red Indian chief.

Besides, I've been busy. I had to put in three extra mornings' envelope-stuffing to keep Helen's Animal Trust appeals quota on target as she puts it, while we toddle off to Ireland. And then there's been clothes to buy, shoes to buy, new suitcase to buy – the ones we've taken on our various jaunts are all too big for someone on their own, while the zip-up job you've always used when you've had to go away on your Jack Jones is too small, and as you always complained without ever doing anything about it, it crushes clothes to buggery. Currency to get, that's something else, the banks round here never seem to have heard of Irish punts, I had to go traipsing from one to another. First time I've had to get my own currency in twenty-five years, you always used to wave a magic wand and lo and behold, your secretary would come back with the foreign readies after her lunch break.

And now I'm packing, in readiness for an early start tomorrow. I've just got the bulk of it done apart from a silk dress that goes in at the last minute, otherwise it'll crease, and I've got my passport, currency, traveller's cheques, ticket and Dublin guide all laid out on your desk, and I'm wondering whether to knock myself up an omelette or just open a carton of chicken and leek soup, when your Pauline trolls in.

I says, Hello, stranger, to what do we owe this honour? Because ever since she came back from her own holiday and we had that long talk about you know what, I've hardly set eyes on her. When she's gone in the morning she's been gone for the day and half the night. Sometimes she'll dash in straight from work but only to tart herself up, and then she's off again – with which particular person I can but conjecture – only to roll home at well after midnight. It's all right by me: it's open house, this. But tonight when she comes in it's around eight thirtyish, so it's difficult to work out whether on this occasion she's coming or going.

She says to me, There's no need to be sarky, I do still live here you know, June, with your gracious permission naturally.

Despite that little truce the other night there's still no love lost between us. But I'm in no mood for resentment – I'm off on my little holiday, and the day I get back I shall start doing the rounds of the estate agents and get your darling daughter off my back for all time. Because I can't imagine she'll be a frequent social caller.

So I said, quite invitingly for me so far as Pauline's concerned, I was just about to make a start on an omelette, or there's some smoked salmon needs using up before it reaches its best-before date, I could always do smoked salmon and scrambled eggs.

She says, I'm not here, June, I'm late for a date, I've only dropped in on my way past with a message. That Douglas fellow that you go about with has been looking for you, he wants you to ring him.

I didn't ask her where she was on her way to on this date as she calls it, I didn't know they still used the expression – there's only one person around here it can be to my knowledge, and anyway, she wouldn't have told me even if I had asked. And anyway again, I was too curious about this message from The Suit.

I says, I don't go about with him as you put it, but how do you mean looking for me, looking for me where, in the Duke of Clarence I suppose, is that where you've seen him?

She says, I never go in the Duke of Clarence except for that one time on Dad's birthday when you asked me to, no, it was in Looney O'Mooney's, that fake Irish pub nearly opposite the Nail Boutique, actually it's quite nice, only one of the girls, Steph, she was celebrating her twenty-first today so we all trooped over to toast the birthday girl and there he was with some mate of his as I imagine he was. And he said he was fed up of hanging around in the Duke of Clarence lunchtime after lunchtime waiting for you to drop in, and would you please get in touch.

I said, I've had more to do with my time these past few days than sit about in pubs, in any case, I'm under no obligation whatsoever to keep calling in at the Duke of Clarence, what does he want, anyway?

She says, He didn't say, don't you know?

I'd a good idea, but I didn't crack on.

I says, And you say ring him, ring him where, I don't think I've still got his number, I did have but it was on a scrap of paper and I've no idea where it can be.

She says, Don't ask me, June, I assumed you would have his number, I only spoke to him in passing otherwise I'd have asked for it to be doubly sure.

I says, Don't worry about it, I'm sure it can wait till I get back from Dublin.

She says, I'm not worrying, June, I've given you the message, now I must fly, if I miss you in the morning which I probably will if you say you've got a seven o'clock start, enjoy Dublin.

And she was off. I went into the kitchen, poured myself a glass of wine, and cracked two eggs into a bowl. Going to the cutlery drawer for a whisk I remembered slipping into it the trade card that The Suit had scrawled his number on that time when he came round to look at the fridge and we were interrupted by Pauline. I say I slipped it into the drawer – tucked it under the lining paper, more like, where your Pauline wouldn't see it. Though what reason I had for not wanting her to see it I'm sure I couldn't explain. BETTER LUCK NEXT TIME. RING ME, the message went. Well yes, maybe I do know why I didn't want her to see it.

I didn't ring him, anyhow. He would only be fussing me to get something down on paper about that money I've agreed to loan him, although agreed isn't the right word, volunteered more like, and I thought it'd do him no harm to stew on it while I went off and enjoyed myself. So I made the omelette I'd been promising myself and a bit of salad, and just as I'm sitting down to my little supper at the kitchen table, the phone rings, and it's him.

Now how did he get hold of my number? Because I never gave it to him, I've had no reason to, and I've kept the phone ex-directory as it always has been with a newspaperman in the house, you had a morbid fear of nutters getting through to you. I can only conclude that Pauline gave it to him when she just spoke to him in passing as she puts it. She'd no right to. Although to be fair, she

couldn't very well refuse, if he asked her for it, it's hardly
a state secret.

I says, Oh, hello, Duggie, Pauline said you wanted a word,
look, I'm in the middle of my supper, could I possibly ring
you back?

He says, Ah, now that would be rather difficult, I'm in
a call-box, it does happen to be rather urgent, June, you
couldn't put your supper under a low light for a couple of
minutes, could you?

Blooming cheek. I says with some feeling, because the
smell of that nice fluffy omelette was wafting across the
kitchen, Surely it can't be so urgent it won't wait half
an hour, Douglas, if I can't ring you back why can't you
ring me?

He says, Ah, well that's just it, June, I've got someone
waiting for me across the road in the pub, their pay phone's
out of order so I had to come outside, but he's got to leave in
fifteen minutes maximum and he wants an answer one way
or another, in fact I'm crossing my fingers he hasn't gone by
the time I get back over there, he's in a big hurry.

I could see this coming as clearly as a twenty-ton truck
down the motorway. But I says, obediently, An answer to
what question?

He says, I've seen this immaculate red Ford Transit van,
June, F-registered dropside, one owner, only 43,000 on the
clock, excellent nick, I've test-driven it, only it belongs to
someone I've been laying a stair carpet for, and there it was
in front of his garage, not a scratch on it, with a cardboard
for sale sign on the windscreen, it's a steal, June.

I says, How much?

—Just a minute, June, let me tell this in my own way. I
said, I see you want to sell that Ford Transit out there, what's
the asking price? He said, A lot less than you'd imagine, my
friend, in that condition and with that low mileage. But he
said, I've got my eye on a Dodge four-berth motor home

that's even more of a bargain, belongs to a friend of a friend, but there's no way I can clinch the deal without selling this, which I must do in the next twenty-four hours, otherwise you've heard of gazumping?

I could see my omelette sinking like a soufflé. I says, I thought you were in a hurry to get back?

—All in God's good time, June, this won't take long. I said to him, Yes, I can see you've looked after her but how does she drive? He said, Where are you going after this? I said, Round the High Street direction. He said, That's just where I'm going, I've got to go to the bank in the wall, I'll let you drive her. But he said, It's only fair to tell you, I've already had an offer.

—They always say that, Douglas.

—Of course they do, June, of course they do. But in this case it happens to be true. Because as he dropped me off he said, I'll tell you what I'll do, I'm not going to set one prospective buyer against another, whoever's first to put a cheque in my hands gets the van. Now, he said, I'm really worried about that caravanette slipping through my fingers, do you think you could raise the money by tomorrow? I said, I'll have a damn good try. He said, Right, I've got some business to do while I'm up here, see what you can do and meet me in Looney O'Mooney's around eight.

—How much does he want?

—Two four nine five, June, and she drives like a dream. I came looking for you in the Duke of Clarence but you weren't there, so then I went up to the house but as luck would have it you were out.

I didn't like that at all, The Suit ringing on my doorbell out of the blue. I said tartly, Yes, I do go out sometimes, Douglas, I've had some shopping to do.

He says, So it's a good thing I bumped into Pauline.

Who as I say must have given him my number. So why does she come to me asking me to ring him? In the hope that I'd get hold of him first, I expect, and then I wouldn't know she'd given him the number. She can't have known she was dealing with a bit of a hustler as The Suit's turning out to be.

I said, So why are you in such a hurry to tell me all this, I thought we were going to work it all out when I get back from my holiday?

He says, It won't wait for that, June, he's got to have the cash by tomorrow morning or it goes to this other bloke, all he's got to do is drive the van out to New Cross and there's a cheque waiting for him on the other bloke's mantelpiece.

I said, Two four nine five, you say, I seem to remember you telling me you could get an F-registration van for around a thousand.

He says, Not in this class, June, it's cheap at the price, I could resell it tomorrow for three grand and we'd be five hundred pounds in profit before we've even started. And he says, Look, June, I know it's a lot to ask, but could I come and see you for a few minutes?

I says, You most certainly can not, I'm just about to have my supper then I'm going to have a hot bath and off to bed, I've got to be up at crack of dawn.

Also I know just what would happen if he did come to the house. I'd write him a cheque and he'd want to express his gratitude. And at that price I'd very likely let him.

He says, And you don't fancy a nightcap down at the Clarence?

I says, No thank you, I've got too much to do. I said, But I'll tell you what I'll do, as I say I've got to be off first thing in the morning but I'll leave a cheque with Pauline, she doesn't work on Saturdays so you should find her up and about around tennish. But I said, Two four nine five, are you sure he won't take less?

—I'll try and beat him down, June, but I highly doubt it. I'll tell you what, make out the cheque for a round two and a half thou, and then you'll owe me the other one and a half when you get back and we've got that agreement drawn up.

I liked that, I must say. I'll owe *him*. I hesitated.

—June, my last fifty pee's running out and I've no more change.

—I'll leave a cheque with Pauline in an envelope, then. And there's no need to tell her what it's all about, in fact I'd rather you didn't.

—Trust me, June. And I'm very grateful. Tell you what, soon as you get back I'll take you for a spin down to Brighton.

—In a van? No thank you.

And we hang up. It occurs to me that he hasn't wished me a happy holiday. I make out a cheque and kiss it a fond farewell, and seal it in an envelope. I scribble a note for Pauline, then I go back to my cold omelette.

A fool to myself. Yes, I know all about that.

Dublin. And it's raining. And it rains, and it rains, and it rains, the same as it did when we were there all that time ago. I began to wonder if it's ever stopped since.

The hotel's very nice, big double room overlooking one of those streets leading into St Stephen's Green. Not in the same class as the Shelbourne, of course, but it'll do me quite nicely for the short time we're here, and anyway I've got to get used to the fact that my four-star days are over. Nice big bathroom with all the little goodies, bath gel, shampoo, mouthwash, sewing kit, which Helen immediately commandeers. I don't think she's seen the inside of many hotels. Or if she has I don't know what she's so excited about, she's like a dog with two tails.

I asked her where she stayed the last time she was here, and she says, with a friend, actually.

I says, Oh yes, and is she still here?

She says with an arch smile, Who says it's a she, I don't know for certain, I'll have to make some enquiries.

We got our umbrellas out and I wheeled her off for lunch at that very good Italian place off Grafton Street, where those nice people from the *Irish Independent* took us for supper and we got through bottle after bottle until you were finally asked to leave for trying to sing 'Kevin Barry'. It's all come flooding back to me, what a grand time we had and what a nice man you could be; and how I wish I didn't know what I do now know. It's a constant ache, that, and I shall have to do something about it, it's like having a permanent stitch in the side. But do what, I haven't the first idea.

So we have a very nice meal there, just a bowl of pasta apiece because we shall be eating again tonight, and then we go across to Bewley's Oriental Café for delicious freshly roasted coffee and a sticky bun. Start as you mean to go on. Wonder of wonders, it's stopped raining by now, so then we go for an amble. No museums or anything, we'll save those for another rainy day of which there's bound to be several – no, we just wandered around, O'Connell Street, Trinity College, the Liffey, Halfpenny Bridge, seeing sights I never saw with you, because even on pub crawls any journey of more than ten yards had to be done by the limo you'd had laid on.

By the time we got back to St Stephen's Green my feet were playing up and I was beginning to feel a bit bleary-eyed, after all I'd been up since half past five for a seven o'clock start. You would have thought Helen would be tired too in her condition but no, she was keen to go and see some friends of hers who run a record shop just across the Green. So we agreed that I'd get my head down for an hour and then we'd meet up in the Horseshoe Bar at the Shelbourne at six thirty.

Which we did. Feeling refreshed, and in goodish spirits

with the rain keeping off and it promising to be a fine evening, I treated us to a split champagne each.

We raised our glasses. I says, This beats stuffing envelopes, Helen.

She says, It beats typing out address labels, cheers, June, and thanks for keeping me company, it's much appreciated.

I says, And did you find your friends?

She says, Oh yes, we had quite a chat, you must come and meet them, Judy and Terry they're called, they're English, they're ever so nice, maybe we could all have a drink.

I says, That'll be nice, unless you want to go off on your own, I mean you young people . . .

I'm calling her young but of course she must be Pauline's age. She's no teenager. But I should definitely be the odd one out among her friends so I thought I wouldn't push it.

Now it had occurred to me while I was dozing off earlier that for someone who'd only ever been to Dublin once before, not only did she seem to know her way around, not that it's such a big place, but also that she seemed to know quite a few people. Trying not to sound nosey, I said as much.

Helen laughs. She says, Ah, but you don't know how long I was here for.

I says, So how long were you here?

She says, Three months.

I says, You didn't tell me that bit.

She says, You never asked, anyway it might have put you off if you thought I knew Dublin better than you do, which in fact I don't, I didn't even know of the existence of that smashing Italian place we went to, and as for the Shelbourne, I've never set foot in it before this evening.

I says, So what brought you here, Helen?

She says, I was doing a summer job for the Irish Guide Dogs Association, nothing special, just clerical, that's what put me in touch with the Animal Trust when I landed back home.

I says, giving her a twinkle, And all that time you were staying with this friend of yours, who might be a she and might not?

She says, looking very demure, Now, now, June.

So I dropped it.

We had a nice evening lined up. I'd booked a table at that very Irish restaurant we went to with your Dublin correspondent, Jimmy O'Something, so we could look forward to pigging it on Irish stew and dumplings, starting with a platter of Dublin prawns. Then Helen has got the name of a folk music pub from her friends who run the record shop – although it's off the beaten track it's supposed to be currently the best folk music pub in Dublin, it's called Michael Dillon's. I love Irish trad folk as you know, so that's the cabaret fixed up.

We stuff ourselves silly at Mahoney's Irish Experience, as you may or may not remember it's called. No room for puds, so we're sitting in the window knocking back a Gaelic coffee and calling for the bill when it starts pouring again. It is raining stair rods. Taxi? Saturday night? In this weather? No chance. Forty-five minutes wait at least.

Luckily we've both brought our umbrellas so there's nothing for it but Shanks's pony. Helen's friends have sketched a little map for her, so guided by this we set off.

The place is in a maze of little streets in the Temple Bar area and finding it isn't made any easier by the fact that after squelching along for twenty minutes we discover the sodden map's upside down. And if you think I said sodding map, I nearly did. My new shoes are pinching my feet and the rain's dripping off my umbrella and down my sleeve.

There's no shortage of pubs in Dublin as you know, and filtering out from one that we passed was the jolly sound of fiddling. I says to Helen, Look, Helen, this seems a nice enough bar and the music's exactly what we're looking for, why don't we forget this Michael Dillon's for tonight and go in here?

She doesn't even pause in her tracks. She says, No, it really is special, this place I'm taking you to, well worth the walk I've been told and anyway, we're nearly there now.

We weren't. And the rain's streaming down and there's puddles ahead of every footstep. We pass another folk music place, ever such a cosy old-fashioned pub it looked, but she wouldn't go in there either. She says, We've come all this way, June, we may as well press on now.

So we did press on, splash on more like, and at long last we see it, Michael Dillon's. We traipse in, looking like a pair of rag dolls that have just been fished out of the Liffey and all right, it's a nice enough pub, all mahogany booths and green plush, but I couldn't see what was so special about it in a town teeming with decent pubs. And there was no music, folk or otherwise. Not that I cared one way or the other by now. All I wanted was to get my wet coat off and pour myself round a Guinness.

I says to Helen, all sarcastic, Very good class of folk music, Helen, worth coming all this way for.

She looks embarrassed and says, They must be taking their break, at least they'd better be.

Looking around me I saw that luckily for her she was right, because at one end of the room there's a little platform with microphones, plus a collection of fiddles and pipes and flutes and penny whistles strewn across a couple of pub tables.

I must be very dense because although I could see that Helen had become all tensed up I still didn't have the first idea what she was getting in such a state about. The penny didn't begin to drop until she cried out breathlessly, They're here! And four young chaps clutching pint glasses trooped up to the platform out of the back bar.

I says with a knowing sigh, All right, Helen, which one is it?

But she took no notice whatsoever of me, she was busy waving frantically at the tallest of the four, handsome lad he was if he'd shave his beard off and give his long black hair a wash.

Not surprisingly, seeing as she's all but dancing on the table, she catches his attention. He looks boggle-eyed for a moment, then after standing stock-still with shock he puts down the fiddle he's picked up and comes over.

He says, doing a bad imitation of Humphrey Bogart, Helen, of all the gin joints in all the world!

She says shyly, Hello, Euan. Then remembering her manners she says, June, this is Euan, Euan, this is June.

Euan. Her ex-steady. The one that made her pregnant. Or the one that made her pregnant if it wasn't the other one.

He seemed a nice enough lad. Bit younger than Helen I should say, but there's a lot of that about these days. He says, Good to meet you, June, so what bring you to this neck of the woods?

The question was put to me but it was easy to see it was meant for Helen, I'm not as thick as all that.

She says, June works with me, Euan, she fancied a little break in Dublin so I said I'd show her some of the sights.

Not quite the truth and nothing but the truth, Helen, but it'll do. So this whole trip was her little plot to track down her flipping boyfriend. She looked that relieved at finding him I couldn't feel annoyed at her, although I could easily have worked my way into a state if I'd felt there was any point in it.

Neither of them seemed to know what to say next, so I said idly, Euan, I always thought that was a Scottish name.

He says, It is, June, my mother's Scottish, I don't come

from Dublin, this is just where the work is, I was born in Stevenage. Listen Helen, we've got to get cracking on the next set, you'll be sticking around for a bit?

She says, gazing up at him, Make it a short one, we've got a lot to talk about.

And I thought, as he threaded his way back to the platform, My God, he doesn't know about the baby, well that certainly is going to make his evening.

I says to Helen, So that's the famous Euan, is it, you've never told me anything about him, did you meet him in Dublin?

She says, Followed him here, he used to play at a folk music club in Purley that I sometimes went to, then he came here to try his luck, wasn't getting all that much work so we went back, he finished up getting a lot of gigs in London where he was doing very well. But then we had to go and have a big stupid bust-up and we lost touch, the last I heard was that he'd come over here again.

I says, And so here we are.

The music had started up and Euan was jigging away on his fiddle. He was very good, in fact very good indeed, and I said as much to Helen.

She says, Oh, he is good, and he's getting established, if only he could stop himself going off the rails from time to time, which he does when he's had a few, that's what we used to row about. Look, June, I don't want you to run away with the idea that I dragged you over to Dublin just to hold my hand while I looked for Euan.

I says with mock innocence, Goodness gracious me, Helen, the thought hasn't even crossed my mind!

Privately I wondered whether they could make a go of it now, if he has this drink problem. But even if they don't, so what, in this day and age? At least she won't have to bury him.

I went on, But seriously, you two have got a good deal

to talk about, I think before he comes over again I'm going to call it a night and toddle along.

She says, Oh, June, you can't, the night is young yet, besides, you'll never find your way back.

I says, The pub's not been built that I can't find my way home from, and anyway you don't want me playing gooseberry while you tell him what he's got to be told.

She says doubtfully, I don't have to tell him straight away.

I says, Get him told and get it over with, Helen, then you'll know how the land lies.

And after a few more weak protests I finished my Guinness, put my coat on and left her to get on with it, giving Euan a wave as I passed him by. He looked quite chirpy at seeing me go, so evidently he was happy enough to have Helen back. I hoped so, anyway.

The rain had eased off for a while and I found my way back to the hotel without too much hassle. I got out of my wet things and put my feet up with one of my detective novels. It's been a long day and I think to myself, I'll just close my eyes for five minutes and then I'll get ready for bed. The next thing I know the phone's ringing. I look at my watch and it's ten past one.

Of course it's Helen. She says, Oh, June, did I wake you, I just thought I'd better ring in case you were worried, I've not thrown myself in the Liffey but I don't think I'm going to get back tonight.

I says, I guessed as much, is everything all right?

She says, Couldn't be better, June, and thank you for being so understanding, but we're right out the other side of Phoenix Park and honestly I'm that dog tired I don't feel up to coming back at this hour, even if there were any cabs on a rainy Saturday night, are you sure you don't mind?

I couldn't recall saying I didn't mind but I didn't anyway.

I said I was glad it was all working out and I'd see her tomorrow.

Comes the morning and I'm up with the lark, as always when I stay in hotels. Except there was no lark, a bloody seagull more like, because it's raining harder than ever. What you would have elegantly described as pissing down.

I went down and had a leisurely cooked breakfast, excellent Irish bacon, then leafed through the Sunday papers in the lounge for a while. I was beginning to feel at a bit of a loose end. I'd no idea when Helen would be back and of course being half asleep when she called it had never occurred to me to get a number from her. I bought a couple of postcards and addressed one to Pauline, seeing as she'd sent me one from Spain. I was about to write one to The Suit when I realised I don't have his full address. And I've just lent him two and a half thousand pounds. I want putting away.

To give myself something to do I decided to brave the weather and get round to Bewley's for a cup of coffee. I take my time over this and then while away another half an hour looking round the museum of old coffee-grinding machines and what not that they've got upstairs, it's quite interesting. I've got a list of likely restaurants for Sunday lunch that I've copied out of the guide book, so as the rain's knocked off for a while, although I could see from the clouds that we'd not heard the last of it by a long chalk, I have a saunter around to sus out menus.

It was near enough to eleven by the time I got back to the hotel. No Helen. No message. I was beginning to get quite cross with her. She might at least have rung – she only had to pick up a phone after all. I sat in the lounge and leafed through a magazine – the morning was really dragging by. I thought, I'll give her till noon and then bubbles to her, I'm off round to the Shelbourne for a Bloody Mary, I'll leave her a note saying where I've gone. And in fact I was just going up to the room to put my coat on again when there's a message on the tannoy, Mrs Pepper, wanted on the telephone.

She says, I'm ever so sorry, June, after last night's excitements we slept in.

I says, keeping my feelings to myself, It doesn't matter, Helen, there's nowhere to go in this weather and nothing opens till two on a Sunday, have you had any thoughts about lunch?

She says, Ah, now that's what I want to talk to you about, June, we've arranged to have lunch out at Howth, you know, the seaside place, with those friends of ours I told you about, Judy and Terry, it's a lovely seafood restaurant run by another friend of ours, you'd be most welcome to come along, we could pick you up about half past one if you like, they don't really get going till mid-afternoon.

I thought, For welcome to come along, read all right to tag along. And I thought, No thank you, Helen. I could just picture that lunch, starting around three o'clock with the four of them half-cut by then plus whatever other friends they might have picked up on the way. I've nothing against pissy lunches as you well know, but with my own kind. And besides, why should I twiddle my thumbs until half past one, waiting for the young woman I'm supposed to be on holiday with to roll up?

I was that annoyed I could barely keep from snapping at her. But I did. I says, Oh, it's very kind of you, Helen, but I've half-promised to have brunch at the Shelbourne with the Dublin correspondent of Sam's old paper, I thought you might care to join us, but you go along with your friends and enjoy yourself.

She says, with obvious relief, So long as you've got company, June, are you sure?

I says, Don't worry about me, Helen, I'll see you when I see you.

And I did have that brunch at the Shelbourne, albeit

alone, preceded by two stiff Bloody Marys in the Horseshoe Bar. After which I felt better, although still most resentful at Helen who I thought had treated me very shabbily. Not thought, knew. All right, she's over the moon at getting her chap back but she really should give some consideration to who she came here with. I suppose she'd say in her own defence that she did at least go through the motions of inviting me out to lunch. But that's what it was: going through the motions.

After treating myself at the Shelbourne I traipsed round the National Gallery for a while. I'm not much of a one for museums as you know but it passed the time. After that the pubs were open again so I went and sat in a bar nursing a Guinness and fuming quietly to myself. It wasn't yet five and I knew Helen wouldn't be, couldn't be back yet on the timetable she'd given me – that's if she'd any intention of coming back at all, now I'd served my purpose. I could visualise another phone call saying meet her at that Michael Dillon's pub later on.

The rain had given way to a thin, mean drizzle. It was still no weather for wandering about and I didn't want to spend the next couple of hours sitting in bars getting slowly paralytic, while waiting for her ladyship to show up.

I made my mind up. I thought, Blow this for a game of soldiers, I'm not hanging about here like a spare part. I went back to the hotel and packed. I wrote a note to Helen – quite a nice one, considering the way she was treating me – saying in effect three's a crowd. Less than an hour later, still quietly seething and feeling sorry for myself, I'm on a flight to Heathrow.

It never crossed my mind to try calling Pauline and tell her I was coming home, so she was in for a surprise. We both were.

It being still earlyish on Sunday night as I got out of the

cab I didn't expect her to be in, but there was a light in her bedroom. I let myself in and there's a note on the pad, Call Marion. In a pig's ear I'll call Marion – that's you and your blessed message again, isn't it? That young Sheila's Auntie Clare is nothing if not persistent. But I don't want to know. Be told.

Pauline's bedroom door is ajar so she's evidently still up. I'm just about to call up the stairs when she comes out on the landing. And with one glance I knew. Or I thought I did. For one thing, instead of the towelling robe she usually slummocks around in, she's wearing a Chinese silk kimono style of thing that I've never seen before. And obviously nothing else. And she reeks of duty-free scent.

She looks agitated, as well she might. She says, Oh, it is you then, June, what brings you back, you weren't expected.

I says, No, I can see that, you've got someone up there with you, haven't you? I says, Now if it's that Eric Grant—

—No, it's not Eric Grant, June. I'm sorry.

You know how your mind sometimes takes a photograph but doesn't develop it till later. I'd seen, but I hadn't registered, a red van parked outside the house. Just as it flashed into my consciousness there's the sound of the toilet flushing and along the landing pads The Suit in his bare feet. Wearing your tartan dressing gown, the one I bought back from the Oxfam shop.

I went berserk.

I screamed at him, You pig, get out of that dressing gown and out of my house!

He dives into Pauline's bedroom like a rabbit down a burrow. Then I start on her.

—And you! You can get out too! Pack your bags and go!

—June, if you'd just calm down for a second and let me—

—Explain? What is there to explain? I've got eyes to see

with, haven't I? You'd screw anything in trousers that comes through that front door! God almighty, aren't you ashamed of yourself? Sleeping with your father's suit! It's practically bloody incest!

Oh, yes, har har, very comical. I can just hear you saying, Hee hee, she does come out with them, our June.

But I mean it. I'm sobbing now. I'm done. I'm finished. And I'm going to tell you something now, Sam Pepper. I blame you for all this. I blame you for the state I'm in.

What a bloody brilliant idea it was, I don't think. Keep a diary, let it all pour out, what you're thinking, how you're coping. And that's what I've been doing – pouring it out and coping, month after flaming month. It's been like treading water at the top of Niagara Falls. And for what? 'I Did It My Way' we had at your memorial service. Why couldn't you have let me do it my way? How could I get on with my life when I was so busy getting on with yours? Because that's what I've been doing, Samuel Herbert Pepper – getting on with your life, keeping you alive, stoking up the flaming fires of remembrance. Well, you've had your last shovelful of coke from me. It's done. It's over.

They're going now. They pause to stare at this weeping, ranting woman and they change their minds about saying anything. There's the door slamming. Sound of a red van starting up, a snip at two four nine five.

I shan't hold it against Pauline for long, not with the screwed-up life she's been made to lead. I shan't even hold it against The Suit – if I'd bedded him when I had the chance instead of reporting back to you all the time, this probably wouldn't have happened. But I do hold it against you, Sam – trying to be immortal, that's what you've been doing. No more. From now on, you'll have to do the same as what I mean to do. Get a life – you know how the saying goes.

A message for me you've got? You see this visiting card of

young Sheila's Auntie Clare? I'm tearing it to shreds. Keep your message, because I've got one for you. Get a life, did I say? You've had your life, now let me get on with mine. Get a death! Do you hear me? Get a death!